THAT GREEN
ITALIAN WAGON

LM SELBY

THAT GREEN ITALIAN WAGON

FROM HUG & FUG BOOKS

www.hugnfugbooks.com

ISBN: 978-0-9924334-0-6

Dedicated to John Selby (Uncle Joe), who passed away before he had a chance to read this book.

TO LEARN MORE ABOUT THE AUTHOR, GO TO

http://lmselby.webs.com

• CHAPTER ONE •

'KRIS. HI. YES, WE have arrived in Rome.'

Wanda did not take more than an hour or two of being in Italy, to realise it had been a stupid idea to order that brand new car. Yes. She would love to get her hands on the latest Italy had to offer. She loved cars. But ..... her 17yr old son Jay just got his driver's license before they left Sydney and he was champing at the bit to hit the roads of Europe.

What had she been thinking?

Wanda excelled in her love of places, people and life in general. She had spent quite some time in Italy before so why had she not remembered just how crazy they were on the roads?

Not just the driving. Try to park if you dare. Bumper to bumper. Door to door. They squeeze in regardless.

A change of plan was called for.

Tracking down a more suitable second hand car, would now become a top priority for the Italian segment of this new adventure Wanda was taking with her two children.

Her friend Kris had been a new car dealer in Sydney and still had connections. Managed to get her a good deal on a very sporty Italian job ex-factory, because she could pick it up in Italy herself. Now she was asking him if she could cancel the order.

'If you are absolutely sure it won't cause any problems? That would be fantastic. Thanks ever so much. I owe you one.'

A sad thing for logic to take over but Kris agreed, it was probably for the best. He reassured her it would be no problem. There was a waiting list and someone would be very happy to hear they had stepped up on their delivery date.

Wanda, daughter Lou and son Jay, headed for their rental apartment just off Piazza Navona. Having spent a relaxing week in the Greek islands on their way over from Sydney, the excitement of Rome being right there on the doorstep for two weeks, gave the trio a real buzz.

Smells of amazing food. Busking musicians and artists everywhere. History all around. They were staying in the heart of Rome and would even be disguising as residents very soon.

The September weather was perfect. Sun sun and more sun. The scorching heat of Rome's summer now gone. Vatican City, Spanish Steps, Trevi Fountain, Colosseum, unique piazzas, parks and just sitting in cafes watching the world pass by. This would be a great way to kick off their road trip, as they made their way to Holland to set up a new home.

The Colosseum visit would turn out to be more memorable than for just the architecture but overall, they knew they would fall for Rome in a big way. The courtyard to their little apartment was a hive of activity and clearly a meeting place for residents. They loved it.

Everyone seemed to be local. Ciao was the order of the day, for the Australians with very limited Italian. Fellow resident Antonio introduced himself. His brother lived in Sydney and the frequent visits down under had given him an ozzie accent, when he spoke English.

'G'day,' was forthcoming, as soon as he knew they were from Sydney. The full story of the brother followed and next thing anyone knew, in true Italian style, the wine was flowing.

Jay had gone straight up to their apartment. Not happy that mum had decided to cancel the new car. Wanda had no luck convincing him, it would be much easier for him with an older car.

After all, this was when he would really learn to drive. The real deal when you hit the streets of Rome or Naples and face oncoming traffic around the Amalfi coast.

'Your son do not like the wine then? Daughter is OK for a little glass?' Antonio was a delightful old man and clearly wanted to make friends with his new neighbours.

Lou and Wanda took wine and they all chatted for quite some time, making excuses for Jay that he had not slept well the night before.

Wanda quizzed Antonio on how to buy a second hand car in Rome. Where did people advertise? Did they have car sales yards in certain locations? Lou took down all the information on where to go and how to get there. She was only 14 but a very efficient little organiser.

There would be no more talk of cars today. Tomorrow Wanda and Lou would head out to see what they could find. Jay had already made plans to meet an online friend, at a nearby record shop.

'Mum. I am sure this is the bus he told us to take. Just 4 stops and then we need to change. The first car yard should be on the right side of the 2nd junction, next to the last stop with that bus.'

Lou and Wanda were arm in arm as they went about their adventure. This was just the sort of challenge they liked to take on. A new place and new things to be discovered.

Antonio had given them loads of information but they were still not quite sure how they would communicate, once they got there.

When it came to mother/daughter relationships, they did not come any closer than Wanda and Lou. Wanda would often tell people how 'umbilical' they still were. Clearly very proud of her beautiful daughter. Lou was a lot like her mother and there was no-one else in the world she admired more, than her mum.

It had been tough for Wanda growing up as the 8th child and not even knowing who her father was, let alone having one around to support the family. Her mother had done her best but was a simple woman who just loved to have babies and did not think much about how she would manage to feed and clothe them. Most of Wanda's older siblings had left home at an early age. She had really only grown up with three of them.

Despite being very bright, Wanda had left school at 15, to earn money to help her mum. Whatever she did in her work, she did well. She had taken on more and more responsibilities and eventually ended up running a London advertising agency, at 27 years of age.

No training. Just a positive can-do attitude and the energy of a charging bull.

That said, in later years, when she led global communications for a multi-national gaming company, she had achieved a Master's Degree in International Business. Accepted for the studies, purely on the back of her successful track record in business.

The bus took them exactly where Antonio had promised and they were feeling totally on track. It was a great area. Car sales as far as the eye could see. As they looked around the third location, Wanda became much clearer on exactly what they needed. Jay had obtained his license driving an automatic so that was a prerequisite. With all the travel they planned to do, and way too much luggage, a station wagon would make life a whole lot easier.

Did not take long to realise, that a station wagon with automatic transmission was going to be a tall order.

Both Wanda and Lou were stunned by the salesperson they found in the next yard. Tall dark and handsome was putting it mildly. The smile! The slick tailored dark blue suit he was wearing. Masses of hair, all perfectly groomed. Totally jaw dropping. When they gained their composure, they also discovered he could speak really good English.

'So .... you come to live in Rome heh? But I hear so much that Australia is amazing. Why you choose a Roma?'

After he was enlightened on the actual plans, he put an immediate proverbial spanner into the works.

'It is not possible I'm afraid. To buy a second hand car in Rome, you must to be resident.'

Aghast, Wanda and Lou bid him ciao and went on their way. Lunch and a quiet rethink were next on their agenda. A great little pizza place just across the street.

As they sat there with the locals, Wanda felt every bit the resident. She decided they should return and ask this handsome man exactly what demonstrated residency. It turned out that all you really needed was to have a proper address in Rome.

They were renting an apartment so ..... no problem at all!

She did not tell him that of course. He already knew the bigger picture plan and that they were only going to be in Rome 2 weeks. In any case, all his cars were too expensive and there was not an automatic or a station wagon in sight.

Another four car yards and they were beginning to get tired.

'Maybe we should come back again tomorrow mum? At least we know the key words in Italian now and have an idea of the sort of prices being charged. There has to be at least another eight car yards here. We could come back in the morning and make a fresh start. Getting a bit late now.'

On the way back to the bus stop, on the opposite side of the street, there was just one yard they would pass that they had not already been to.

'Wow. Lou. Look at that green Italian wagon over there at the back. I love the colour and it's just the right size for all our things.'

They could not believe their luck. It was also automatic. And the asking price was around the budget. As they went over the vehicle and took it for a test drive, it was clear this was going to be it. Having five brothers that were keen on cars, Wanda knew what to look out for. Now she just needed to do her thing with the bargaining.

'Jay. We found a car. It's perfect. In great condition. Mum negotiated for them to put new tyres on and still got the price down heaps. Has to be in cash of course so mum gave them a couple of hundred as deposit and arranged for us to go back in two days with the rest. She also asked them to keep the car until the day we leave Rome so we don't have to worry about parking. Gives them plenty of time to sort out the tyres and paperwork too. We have to arrange insurance ourselves. That'll be fun. You have to come back out and see it when we take the money. You will love it. That green Italian wagon is just the job for our big trip.'

Took a couple of hours to get back to Piazza Navona. Wrong first bus led them on a merry chase but they were fine with the adventure. Mixing it with the locals and seeing the suburbs of Rome.

When they finally made it, Jay was waiting for them at a café in the square. Starving, as always. Been sitting there for over an hour but quite happy to watch the world go by.

Jay had not spent long at the record shop with the young lad. Always weird when you build up these online relationships and then meet someone in the flesh. It had all been a bit awkward. They checked out some vinyl together and said they would stay in touch. He then spent most of the afternoon in an internet café and was now deep in thought, about some news he had heard from a mate.

Jay had several mates he had grown up with in Sydney. Many of them had been at school with him since kindergarten. His love of music was there right from day one so, as he got older, he found the mates he most preferred to spend time with, were also into music.

There were always different types of music playing at home and in the car and the whole family would jump at any opportunity to see people performing. Dad still played trumpet professionally and mum had been a singer in a band..... 'a hundred years ago BC' (before children), she would often say.

Having really broad taste in music led to Jay having his own community radio show, when he was a mere 12 years old. He had a great speaking voice. Some people thought it quite posh. Being born in London and having a Scottish dad must have had an impact.

This mate Jay was thinking about used to do the radio show with him sometimes.

Now he was at University and had a great gig with their student radio network but his parents were putting the screws in for him to get more serious about life. To them, that meant no playing around with music. They really just did not get it.

Jay felt sorry for his mate and at the same time realised how lucky he was, to be so in sync with his parents. Did not seem to matter that they had split up when he was just four years old. They always got along really well. Dad had remarried and provided a close brother and two extra sisters. The step family got on really well with mum and her side of their big family too. Jay knew how unusual that was and it made him feel good to sit and reflect. He was excited about living back in Holland and having this big European adventure. Yet at the same time, he could not help but think how much he would miss everyone in Sydney.

'Just as well they eat really late here heh my lovely son. Sorry about that. Would not even be here now if Lou hadn't convinced the last bus driver to let us off, where there wasn't even a stop. If he hadn't, we might have ended up in Firenze I reckon.'

Lou had taken pictures of the car with her phone and Jay became excited about driving that green Italian wagon, as they flicked through the pics. Mum was right (oh no…not again). This would be better than driving a brand new car. He would have been paranoid about hitting kerbs and heaven only knows how he would have gone parking. With an older car, everyone would be a little less precious.

Jay had not driven that much in the lead up to getting his licence. Actually, he could not believe it when he passed first time. Uncle Joe had let him drive his automatic car loads of times but just around the neighbourhood. Driving schools were really expensive so most people started with a booking for ten lessons and complimented that with driving family cars whenever they could. Jay had not liked the thought of having to learn the gear shift so it was really only Uncle Joe that could take him out. Mum had a manual car and so did his dad.

Once they knew when they would fly out of Sydney, Jay's driving instructor went gung ho to see if he could get him through. The test was scheduled for the day immediately prior to their departure.

Et voila. Jay passed!

Up up and away and here he was in the driving chaos of Italia. He would really learn to drive now.

That night they focussed on eating, watching the sights in the piazza and later wandering around some of the nearby squares. Amazing weather meant people were happy and smiling.

Lou was a budding artist so she was particularly interested to watch the creative brushstrokes of the street artists. She had already decided she would take Art, as a main subject for her International Baccalaureate in Holland.

Wanda had taken a one year contract in Amsterdam, when Lou was 6 and Jay was 9 so they had lived in Holland before. She had put them both into the local Dutch school then and they had no alternative but to learn to speak the language. Immersion.

Always the best way to learn.

Lou had been so funny. For the first three months, she had walked around with her fingers in her ears most of the time.

'Mummy. They're all speaking Dutch', she would exclaim.

When she finally took her fingers out of her ears, she was fluent. All the guttural sounds and looking every bit the part, with her white blonde hair. Wanda had gone to classes to learn the language but working for a Japanese communications company on multi-national clients, she did not really get to speak it that much. Lou and Jay had loved to correct her bad Dutch.

Not quite the same this time. They planned to live outside of Amsterdam. Wanda chose the location because of the great international school for Lou and the multitude of radio stations for Jay. He had decided he was over school and had no interest in University.

Wanda was relieved. Getting Jay through to the end of high school had been a challenge so work it would now be.

Jay was born at a top London hospital, facing the biggest clock in the world. Big Ben! When Wanda had seen him having little twitches soon after the long delivery, they were well equipped to test him for everything. Wanda and Larry's worst nightmare. Their first child being moved to intensive care and put through brain scanners. It was two weeks of hell before they were finally allowed to go home. Wanda's world had stopped, seeing her first born connected to endless tubes and machinery. Tears sent her to sleep briefly each night.

One of the world's leading paediatricians was in charge of Jay's case. His diagnosis was a bleed in the frontal right lobe, prior to birth and for no particular reason. It was now scar tissue. Jay should develop normally but they would monitor him for a couple of years. Medication would need to be taken for three months, to stop any chance of further fitting.

The impact this bleed had on Jay as he grew up, was highly advanced auditory signalling mixed with diminished visual signal uptake. He was exceptionally bright when it came to everything to do with music but found it extremely difficult, taking in the less interesting subjects high school presented.

They woke to yet another beautiful day. Wheels had to be put in motion for finding suitable car insurance. Wanda was up early and into the internet café to do her research. When she returned to the apartment, Lou and Jay were getting breakfast.

'I have emailed the top three companies here in Rome and forwarded that copy of my no claims bonus so hopefully they will get back with a quote over the next day or so. They did not seem to have the same loading as we do in oz, for drivers under 25.

Fingers crossed on that. Told them your age Jay so let's just see what they come back with. I expect it will be pretty steep but what the heck.'

Wanda had grabbed some fresh bread from the local baker. Cheese, bread and juice in hand, she ventured to the courtyard to eat her breakfast and see if anyone was about to chat with.

Antonio saw her out of his window and was down there like a shot. He could not help but think he would love to be 20years younger and trying his luck with this charming and pretty lady from down under.

'Bon giorno senora. Are you enjoying your stay in my lovely city?'

He was disappointed she had not seen very much and at the same time, impressed she had managed to secure the car they wanted.

'Please. Today it would be my great pleasure to take you all on a special walk around my city. If you will please permit me.'

Jay and Lou were up for it. Antonio was a funny chap and they knew he would put a different spin on things. Wanda also enjoyed the admiring glances and special attention Antonio paid her.

As the day progressed, they were more and more amazed at the number of people that seemed to be part of Antonio's extensive family. They stopped at several people's houses and the food and wine was out before they knew it. Jay didn't care much for wine and Lou was still a little young but a glass every now and then was OK. Wanda loved trying the different wines and was always wanting to be polite. Quite clever at not taking refills though. Each stop felt very special to them all. Such lovely welcoming people.

That was, at least, until the incident at the Colosseum.

'Please lady. Money for my baby?' A beggar woman, holding what seemed to be a very young baby, was hustling Wanda towards a group of cohorts.

Wanda had left Antonio, Lou and Jay briefly to pop to the toilet. The crowds around the Colosseum were enormous.

Antonio was reliving tales of the incredible things that had taken place in this amazing arena. Jay and Lou reflected on films like the Gladiator and were feeling very much a part of that history, listening to Antonio. He spoke loudly to be heard over the noise of Rome and they were busy taking photos. They had not realised they moved so far away from the public toilet entrance, where they were supposed to wait for Wanda.

Before Wanda knew it, she was surrounded by four or five more beggar women carrying babies. It was clear they were trying to take her handbag. Shit! Wanda knew nobody could really hear her but she stood firm, hugging her bag close to her body and screaming POLICE!

Antonio, Jay and Lou were nowhere to be seen.

"Don't panic," she told herself as the adrenalin pumped through her veins. Wanda had always been one to stand her ground. There had been many times during her life she'd been exposed to bullying. Always one to avoid a fight but, at the same time, ready to stand up to people who thought they could push others around.

Having grown up in some pretty rough areas of Sydney, Wanda could look after herself. As the youngest of eight, she had also reached a point at around 12 where she decided she wouldn't be bossed about by her elder brothers anymore.

Antonio saw what was happening and ran to Wanda's aid. His arms became very expressive, as he waved vigorously and shouted to the women to back off. All in Italian of course. He sounded quite magnificent and Wanda was elated to have him there. The women scattered.

What angered Wanda the most, was the fact little babies were used in these wicked deeds. She was shaken but keen to make a formal complaint at a nearby police point. The polizia listened intently but she could not help but think, they had heard this story a million times. Probably even arrested the women on a regular basis and they just ended up back on the street. It was upsetting but Wanda did not want to let it spoil the wonderful day they had. Neither did Lou.

'So glad you are OK Mum. Let's just go back to our apartment now. Jay and I can cook dinner. Antonio. Will you join us for something to eat? Jay makes a mean spaghetti and I put together the best salad you will ever taste.'

Lou shuddered at the thought of her mum being hustled by those women. What if they had a knife or hurt her mum in some way.

She knew her mum had a tough upbringing and could look after herself but it did not stop her feeling upset. Jay and Antonio were pretty shaken too.

Wanda had been dragged from place to place growing up and often shared a bed with her sister and mother. Driving around Sydney, she would see streets that she recollected living in for a short while.

A garage, a caravan, bedsits and whatever her mum had been able to afford. Wanda's mum had worked as a cook or did ironing for a living. Most of their clothes came from various charities. When her mum was finally allocated a council house, they had only stayed in it for two years. That was the longest Wanda had lived in any one place growing up.

Lou often thought about her mum's rough upbringing and her Nan's nomadic way of life. Nevertheless, she really loved her Nan. They would sit together drawing for hours on end. Nan also had an ear for music and could pluck out a tune on their keyboard, with no trouble at all. She always had plenty of time for Lou and Jay. Lou had been sad when they said goodbye to their Nan before leaving Sydney. She was almost 89 and they all knew it could be the last time they saw her.

Lou pushed all unpleasant thoughts to the back of her head. She would make every effort to ensure this evening ahead was a happy one for all.

The supermarket near their apartment had everything they needed to put together a nice meal and for sure, she could rely on Antonio to keep them amused.

'Si. Gracie.' Wanda thanked the lad running the internet café, as he pointed her in the right direction and asked if she had understood where the insurance broker was.

She had woken really early that morning, still reeling from the shock of those women with babies trying to take her bag. It gave her goose bumps as she remembered. Feeling really lucky that it did not end badly but nevertheless, still a little upset by it all.

Not disturbing the children, she had set out on her mission to get the car insurance sorted.

Only one reply from the emails and she was not clear on how to complete this mission. As luck would have it, the lad in the internet café had known just the place for her to go. It was close by and the people in the broker's office spoke good English.

'Done. Car all insured and good to go. Bit tricky filling out forms but have required insurance certificate. Yeah! They will post policy. Might be something to do with making sure we are residents! Back in 20 minutes xx'

Lou laughed as she read the text from her mum.

Better wake Jay up so they could be ready with breakfast for mum.

That afternoon they all ventured out, on the magical mystery bus tour of many connections, to pay the final monies for the car. The salesman was delighted to see them and happy to let Jay take his first short drive, to try it out...... once he had seen the insurance cover note of course.

Wanda took the back seat and let Lou ride shotgun. The road at the back of the car yard, was wide and without traffic.

A perfect place for Jay to get to know that green Italian wagon. A little nervous of course but only to be expected. Jay adjusted the seat and made sure all the mirrors were right. Familiarised himself with all the knobs and dials. Spent ages tuning the radio and speaker controls. Most important part of a car for him was naturally the sound centre. He pumped up the volume and could not have been more impressed. A great sound. He was sold. And they had not even left the yard yet.

Lou wondered if maybe Jay was just a little too cautious. He drove onto the street at a snail's pace, looking in all directions for what seemed to be way too long. He was, after all, on the wrong side of the car and on the wrong side of the street. A double whammy. After 10 minutes driving up and down the long wide street, he finally seemed at ease. Lou had to admit, it felt pretty strange to her sitting on the other side of the car too. She decided her brother was doing well and was happy to tell him so.

Celebrations were in order. The trio knew that green Italian wagon was going to make a big difference to their trip being a success.

For now, it was back on the bus and 'home' to the Piazza Navona. This time Lou knew exactly which buses would give them the best connections. Feeling right at home and very much the local, she took total control and got them to the square in record time.

Light opera was being performed by a young new talent. They had booked a table in a restaurant right in front of the stage. Magnificent! Incredible food and an up and coming young Pavarotti. They felt very privileged.

'Jay. You really should try something other than pasta tonight. I think I'll go for the veal parmigiana. That guy looks like he has it. Lots of vegetables being served with it too. Yum. Or should I say 'lekker'. We should be using our favourite Dutch word again don't you think? No other country really has such a word. Love that.'

Lou was getting a lot more adventurous with her food choices but Jay had a fixation for pasta. Did not matter what country he was in. He could eat pasta for breakfast, lunch and dinner if he had his way.

The ten days that followed were bliss. So much to see and do.

Coins tossed into the Trevi Fountain. Actually, Lou almost fell in herself. Some young lad had taken a fancy to her and got way too close for her comfort. She was backing up to avoid him and slipped. He reached out and grabbed her just before she went over. How gallant. Maybe he was not so bad after all. Wanda managed to capture it on film. A great shot.

Cycling around the main park and finishing a beautiful day sitting on the Spanish Steps watching the hubble, was a favourite.

Another day they were leaving the Vatican City and noticed staging, lights and masses of security. The Pope was actually going to speak to the people the following morning.

That afternoon Wanda, Lou and Jay had covered most there was to be seen in the Vatican but they would come back the next morning to hear the pontiff.

Wanda believed in believing but was not quite sure about the control of the church. She had always encouraged her children to be open to people's different beliefs. Most of all, they should believe in themselves.

Jay had been in a Christian group during high school and they met frequently to study the bible. These days he was heading much more towards Hindu or Buddhist type of worship.

Lou had also been in a local church group. Their gathering place was more of a community centre. Always lots of singing and very sociable. Wanda had been along a few times. The girls had formed a dance troupe and often performed at local events.

No matter what your religion or beliefs, it was impossible to not be impressed by the scale of the next morning's gathering in the large Vatican City square. Thousands of people, quiet and focussed on one man's words. A moving experience.

Time had flown past and the day to collect that green Italian wagon and head out of Rome had arrived. The car yard was in the direction of their next destination. Pompeii. Jay's excitement at finally taking charge of a car in real life, was clearly evident. Little did he really know of the challenges the road would bring.

Look out Italy and arrivederci Roma!

• CHAPTER TWO •

POMPEII WAS AWE INSPIRING. Sad to think of the great many people buried alive in hot ash from Mount Vesuvius so many years ago. Incredible to realise that millions of people living in the immediate vicinity still, today, risked a similar fate. Vesuvius being reputed as one of the world's most likely to erupt volcanoes.

Wanda had not driven very far at all after picking the car up in Rome. Once they hit the motorway, she headed into the first service stop.

'No point letting you get comfortable in the passenger seat Jay. Let's grab a quick coffee here and then you can take over.'

Jay did really well. Wanda had jumped in the back and Lou moved up front, with map in hand, to be chief navigator. Lou was not so good with her general sense of direction but was dynamite at reading maps and working out signs. Only a couple of turns they did not need to take and before they knew it, they had reached Pompeii. Wanda was amazed at how calm Jay had been. Even the odd wrong direction from Lou did not phase him. He loved it. Probably helped that Jay and Lou had always been close.

Lou looked up to her big brother and, as they grew older, she had also looked out for him. They were good chums. Occasional brother/sister disagreements but never any major arguing.

As little tikes, it was Lou who was the fearless one. No roller coaster ride too big and no ghost train too scary. Jay was often hesitant. He would tell her she was too little and would be afraid. She would convince him it would be fun and they should take the ride. Ever so funny.

When they lived in Holland the first time, they had been on a mission to visit as many theme parks as possible. As 6 and 9 year olds, Lou and Jay had visited Legoland and Tivoli Gardens in Denmark; Disney in Paris, Los Angeles and Florida; plus a host of other fun parks in Holland, Germany, the UK, Singapore and Australia.

Heading out of Pompeii, had proven to be just as difficult as the way in. Wanda had booked a hotel in Salerno for the next few days and they were looking forward to being by the sea but Lou had trouble working out how best to get them there.

'Wow mum. What a great room. Sun chairs on our very own big balcony overlooking the Mediterranean Sea. Can we afford this?'

Lou always looked out for her mum's best interest. She knew she had no guarantee of work, once they got to Holland. Not that she thought for one minute, her mum would not have people jumping at the chance to hire her. Lou was ever so proud of her very talented mum.

'It was a fantastic last minute web deal. I found it online when we were in Greece. Did not think it would be so flash though. Excellent! We have three nights here so let's enjoy it. I'm up for a chill day by the pool tomorrow. What do you think?'

When they finally left Salerno, they were indeed chilled. That first day by the pool had been perfect but then the weather had taken a turn for the worse. Extremely cold and wet. This was the day that Jay would really get his driving skills tested. Combine bad weather with the winding cliff side road along the Amalfi Coast and it could mean trouble.

Jay had braced himself for the challenge. Being an avid computer gamer, he liked to think he could take on pretty much anything. He had played those wild car racing games and always scored high points. How different could this be?

That green Italian wagon was suddenly much wider than Jay had thought. There he was, perched high above the Mediterranean. A small stone wall to his left. Not much room between him and the mountain rock face to his right. Certainly not enough room for the large tourist bus coming the other way, to get past.

The bus driver was determined Jay should go backwards, until he could find a spot in the road that allowed them to clear one another. Visibility was not good. As calm as Jay had been right up until then, he suddenly froze.

Lou was too scared to say a word. Wanda saw sweat on Jay's brow and she knew she needed to get him out of the driver's seat quickly, without causing him further concern.

'OK Jay. You've been doing great but we should maybe swap over now. Let me take on this crazy bus driver. What the heck does he think he's doing? Make sure the handbrake is on and the car is in park. Take a deep breath and just get out of the car slowly, while I get into the front. All in your own good time. He can just wait.'

Jay focussed on his mum's voice and things went into super slow motion for him. Even though his mum told him specifically not to, he looked over the edge. Low visibility but still he could tell it was a long way down to killer rocks and rough seas.

Wanda ushered Jay into the back and took the driver's seat. After reversing to a wider point in the road, the bus went through.

She then decided to change plans and see if they could get a room in nearby Amalfi for the night. Positano would be too far in this horrendous weather.

Resting in the back of the car, Jay was calming down. Disappointed he had not coped with the challenge but pleased they planned to stop the night. He would get another crack at this road in the morning. Weather forecast was much better for tomorrow and Wanda reminded them the views would be spectacular.

As they came into the tiny town of Amalfi, Lou went on a mission to check out the different little pensiones and see if they had a room for the night. She had practiced how she would ask.

'Per favore senior. Possibile per una stanza per tre persone per la notte?' Difficult when they replied to her in Italian but she got there.

'Well done my clever little girl. This will do nicely. Parking is a big plus and the price is right. Don't suppose they would have many people knocking on their door tonight.' Wanda was impressed with Lou's ability to get around the task at hand and not get flustered at the high speed Italian responses and hand waving.

When the sun came up the next morning, all the horrors and grey of the day prior were forgotten. They had indeed woken up to majestic views. Just stunning! Lady luck was with them yet again. Incredible! The sea was sparkling and the sound of water crashing on rocks was music to their ears. The uniqueness of the Amalfi Coast, on show in all its glory. Clusters of quaint white buildings, crowded onto cliff faces around tiny coves. Beautiful!

Vivid memories came rushing into Wanda's head of the time she had spent there with Larry, when he proposed. Jay and Lou had gone off for a look around. She could let her mind run free.

Larry and Wanda had been so very much in love. As a professional musician, he was away touring for weeks on end in the early days of their relationship but that did not bother her.

She recalled the first night they met, in a London nightclub. He was seven years her junior but had been on the road for a few years already and quite the man for someone not yet 20. Wanda had sung in a band herself a few years earlier but had moved on to the high flying world of advertising. Already very successful at just 27.

Larry could not help but be swept off his feet. The new sports car she was driving. The apartment she owned. He had never met anyone quite like Wanda.

It was electric from the very first moment their eyes met. Larry was a tall handsome Scotsman, with a soft confident accent that sounded a little like Sean Connery. A top trumpet player with a good singing voice, he had all the moves and a fantastic stage presence.

Wanda was also a good mover and wasn't afraid to go after what she wanted. Friends that knew some of the band members, had invited her to the club and she had been formally introduced to Larry. As she danced with her friends, right in front of the stage, she knew Larry was watching. Her moves were seductive and she could feel him checking out her great legs and fit body.

Cheeky glances were exchanged and her big rolling blue eyes were clearly letting him know she was keen. The band was staying at a nearby hotel but Wanda moved straight in, as everyone prepared to leave, and took Larry to one side.

'My apartment isn't so far from here and I could show you a few of the London sights on the way there if you like. The car is outside.' Wanda always did have a knack for finding good parking spots.

She now recalled the intense passion exploding, as they finally reached her top floor apartment that very first night. That passion that had taken on greater depth over the years that followed. Learning about each other's bodies and discovering endless ways to share the pleasures of a deeply sexual and affectionate relationship. Hugging and kissing was always something of a high priority in the early days and, in the end, this would be where they failed.

When Larry had taken Wanda to Amalfi to propose, they had been as in love as any couple could possibly be. She had tried to convince him she was too old for him but the numbers meant nothing to either of them in reality.

They married eighteen months after their first encounter and led the high life. Great holidays skiing and visiting exotic locations around the world. A life filled with music and love. Their sex life could not have been better. A beautiful couple.

Three years into the marriage they conceived their first child and the world was perfect…. even with the challenges Jay had at birth. A second beautiful child and ten years on, the marriage was over.

It often made Wanda sad to reflect on this but she would snap right out of it and re-confirm that she had made the right decision to split.

The state of numb acceptance that their partnership had become far less than she wanted it to be, had been sapping her life force. She had a clear view that the best time to do something about it, was when the children were very young.

The break-up had been heart wrenching but civil and they had never fought or been horrible to one another. Parenting is for life and they knew how important it would be to remain on good terms.

Larry had re-married several years later and had three more wonderful children. Jay and Lou had siblings and they had all scored a warm and loving extended family. Larry and his second wife Dee had their moments but, all in all, they seemed content.

Wanda had a few long term and incredibly passionate relationships but had never come close to ever wanting to marry again.

'Mum. You asleep?' Wanda confirmed to Lou that she had drifted off slightly. She had not reminded Jay and Lou, that this was where their dad had proposed. It was all so very long ago.

'Time for us to hit the road.'

Jay got back into the driver's seat with no hesitation. Narrow roads along cliff edges. Total traffic chaos around the streets of Napoli. Trying to take in the sights, as he carefully manoeuvred that green Italian wagon across the cobblestones of Florence.

He felt comfortable and loved the entire experience. Even the adrenalin of near misses. He was living the computer game experience.

Pisa, Venice .....Verona and the magic that was Shakespeare. Milan and the bustling port of Genoa. Italy in all its splendour.

Now they were crossing into France. After Rome, the longest they had stayed in one place was just three days. It would be fun to again take up residence for a while.

One week in the stunning apartments of the exclusive Baie des Anges on the Cote d'Azur would be lovely. They had several close friends that lived in the area but decided it would be too frantic trying to stay with them all. Short visits would be much more enjoyable. The first night they had invited all of them to a little gathering, at a bar in the marina.

Three different groups of friends came along that night. They were almost as excited to see each other as they were Wanda, Lou and Jay.

For some strange reason, they only seemed to get together when Wanda was in town. Weird really. They got along so well and the distance between their homes in Antibes, Cagnes sur Mer and Monaco was really insignificant.

'Remember that time you were working in Monaco on that big photo industry event Wanda? Staying at the Hermitage and shooting with all those top models and photographers.

That winning shot of Naomi was one of my most favourite ever. You called the event Monaco Moments I think.' Janet was recollecting.

She was a yacht broker and had lived in the South of France for almost twenty years. English but totally fluent with her French so Wanda had roped her in for support on a couple of occasions, when she had work in the area.

Overall, Wanda did a pretty good job with French and could generally manage to get herself understood. It was a language she had often taken an evening class in and had studied during her last year at high school, when she was just 15.

Monaco Moments was indeed the name of the end product from that incredible six day shoot Janet was referring to. The Japanese communications company Wanda worked for in Amsterdam, had been commissioned to create an event that encouraged professional fashion photographers to move across to digital. A new top of the range colour photocopier on site and photographers asked to manipulate images they had taken on new digital cameras. Those images then exhibited by the next morning, in the Hermitage lobby. Brilliant! A revolutionary move to digital photography. Diehard photographers had been astounded by what they could now do, to extend their creativity.

'I reckon the time you were here with the Formula 1 Grand Prix and all those camera shop owners, was the best.' Dan piped in.

He was a fellow ozzie. Always good for the best barbeque on the Cote d'Azur and a good old laugh. Dan had lived in the area for as long as Janet and captained some enormous private yachts. More like mini ocean liners actually. Total opulence and mostly owned by rich Arabs. He and Janet met working for the same sheik. Janet had been one of the sheik's many housekeepers. Wanda had met Janet and Dan through Blossom, her next door neighbour in London.

Blossom worked at a famous London hotel, when the sheik bought it for cash. She had become his personal florist and been flown all over the world doing flower arrangements at his various properties, on his boats and for functions.

Dan really did not like the French people all that much but he and Janet had eventually married and made their home there. He even learned the language….as reluctant as he was to have to speak it.

'Wasn't that Grand Prix trip an amazing time?' Wanda replied. 'Not sure if my favourite bit was the practice day lunch on the Hermitage balcony or the boules competition up the mountain with the locals. Nigel was a hoot when he gave his little speech at the lunch. Cool that he had let some of the chaps jump into that Williams car for a spin too.'

Wanda was also thinking to herself, about the very lovely camera shop owner she had met during that incentive program she organised. She had known most of the guys for several years but there was a new face on that trip. The lovely and talented Kane.

He had been split with his wife for a couple of years and they took an immediate liking to one another. What a pity that had all come to nothing. They had been out on a few occasions, after that first meeting in France. It did not gel for them as a couple but they became excellent buddies. Also very valuable.

Jay was not as keen to lay by the pool, as Wanda and Lou. If he had his way, he would have just kept driving. The weather was great and they did loads of exploring around the area but he was happy when it came to their last day at the apartment and he could get back on the road again.

But first ….. a farewell barbeque at Janet and Dan's. Sure to be a good feast. Lou and Jay loved their pool. Loads of fun floating things to mess about on. As the gates opened to their amazing property, Dan was there to meet them. He stared in awe.

'I thought you were picking up a new car in Rome?'

Wanda told him all about their car purchasing adventures and how much they all now loved that green Italian wagon.

When Dan stopped laughing his head off, and re-counting all the fabulous cars Wanda had driven over the years, he finally conceded it had been a good move.

The Cote d'Azur was a long way behind them, as they wound their way up through the Alps. Reaching Munich in time for Oktoberfest had been a target but that was now out the window. Who would have thought it would actually take place in September? They were already a few days into October. Just a week or so more and it would be Lou's birthday.

Loads of people skiing on the glaciers, even at this time of year. As much as the trio all loved to hit the slopes, the limited facilities and high prices for the glaciers, had been enough to keep them happy just to be spectators this time.

Swiss chalets made from the oldest black woods they had ever seen. Rolling valleys and extraordinary peaks. Simply spectacular! They would definitely return for some serious skiing, at some point in the near future.

The youth hostel stopover in the centre of Bern, was in a prime location. Great facilities, easy access and plenty of parking. A giant chess game at the front to amuse guests and provide a general meeting spot. Lou and Jay loved to play chess. They had commandeered the board for over an hour, whilst Wanda had checked out where they could go for a special birthday celebration dinner.

'Swiss fondue! Thanks mum. Truly memorable. And I love the boots. Thank you. Loved that cap too thanks Jay. Woo hoo. Happy birthday to me!' They all sang and the waiters joined in.

The cap Jay had bought for Lou had a bear on it. The symbol of Bern. In fact, Bern meant bear.

The next day they visited the bear pit in the main park. Sad to see animals in captivity but they had not known anything else and the historic links were well explained in all the material at the site.

Lou needed to start her new school in just one week now.

Favourite things during that last leg of their travels, included knodels in meat stew from Bavaria; the glockenspiel in Munich; driving right alongside the Rhine River for hours and stopping to watch the huge barges and visit castles. Cologne's cathedral was also a gem and best of all …the incredible windmills, as they reached Holland.

'The meeting with the head is for 10am so we need to stay somewhere close to the school.' Wanda had not booked anything yet. They would be staying on a friend's boat in Amsterdam until they found somewhere to live but she had not been sure when they would arrive. Could not reach the friends on the phone earlier so just planned on finding somewhere for the night, once they were in Holland.

'What about that little place there?' Lou was pointing at this quaint property. Then Wanda read the sign…Honden Hotel. She laughed.

'You really have forgotten your Dutch hey Lou. Think hard. What does Honden mean?' They all chuckled as they realised, this was a dog boarding kennel. Easy mistake to make. 'Hotel' being very misleading to the average tourist.

A little further down the road was another quaint property. The whole area was quaint really. This time it was a pub and they had a few rooms for accommodation. Excellent!

Weird how they all felt so at home, being back in Holland after nine years. Jay even managed to order most of his dinner in Dutch.

He went to great pains to make sure it included patats met (and knew that meant chips with mayonnaise).

They were up early, fussing over what Lou would wear for her meeting at the school. Wanda had phoned the school several times from Australia. She wanted to make sure it would work well for Lou. With the different start time to the school year, they had all decided it would be better for Lou to take a step back, rather than forward.

Before the school would finally confirm details, and indeed even confirm taking Lou on board at all, she would need to do an entrance test when they arrived.

What they had liked best about this International School, was that it was very 'Dutch'. There were several options in Holland for international schools but Wanda felt the others were either too American or too British. Did not even have a requirement for students to learn Dutch.

The International Baccalaureate curriculum was so much more worldly than standard high school studies. Wanda knew this would make a big difference for Lou. A pity Jay had not had the same opportunity perhaps. Nothing to be done about that now.

In the past year, of what was Jay's final year at high school, the teachers had all but given up on him. Wanda had been at her wits end. Jay loved all the social elements of going to school but the bleed in the frontal right lobe at birth, was having a major impact on his ability to take in what he needed to for exams.

Wanda had met with teachers on a regular basis. She had a tutor for Jay and supported all the work he had to do herself as well. Jay had been tested by an educational psychologist and given a report for teachers so they would help him more with notes and not tag him as just being lazy. Nothing had helped.

'My sister's son was in almost the same boat as Jay.' A well-meaning friend had said to Wanda. 'She sent him to this private school in Bathurst and they turned it all around. He did brilliantly in his final exams.'

Wanda would do anything to help Jay.

They had all gone to Bathurst and met with the headmaster. A nice man and he really did convince them, it would be a good move for Jay. Cost a fortune but Wanda did not care. She would find the money, if it would make a difference.

Jay was supposed to have study support every evening. Turned out teachers just walked the corridors and made sure students were in their room. After a few months, the final straw that broke the camel's back, was a call from Jay's head teacher.

'We really think Jay might need to take anti-depressants ……'

Wanda had stopped listening at that point. This was not the place for Jay. How could they even think of drugs, as an answer to his challenges? She had been horrified.

The very next day she collected Jay from that private school and the following week, he had returned to his old high school.

The teachers were very kind and gave him as much help as they could. He was popular and they liked his zany nature and musical talents. Jay scraped through that final certification by the skin of his teeth. Wanda breathed a sigh of relief and they had all been on their way to Europe, before you could say Robinson Crusoe.

Now they were in Holland, where they would make a new home and yet at the same time, feel like they had come home.

Jay would look for work over the next couple of days and now have real driving experience to add to his CV. Never one to shy away from working, he had always been keen to earn his own money. Right through school, Jay had part time jobs that all added to his skill set. He was very personable and great with anything IT or music based. Just had to find the career path that was right for him.

Wanda also had to find work. She was still in touch with several people, from the year she had worked there for the big Japanese communications company, nine years earlier. When she was in advertising in London, she also had several clients in Holland. All in all, a good network of contacts to get the ball rolling.

The friend's canal boat was available for a couple of months, which would give Wanda some space to think about a permanent place to live. How cool to be staying on a big old houseboat, on the main canals at the back of Amsterdam's Centraal Station.

That green Italian wagon would make the 20km drive from the boat to Lou's school each day or Lou could take the train, if that worked better. Provided Lou was actually accepted at the school of course.

Lou was going over her maths. She knew this was one of the things they wanted to test her on the next morning. Butterflies were getting to her a little. What if they did not accept her? Mum would be devastated. She knew that a large part of making this move, had been her mother's desire to open up a bigger world of opportunities for her and Jay.

She could not let them down.

• CHAPTER THREE •

'YES! I'M IN. CAN'T BELIEVE HOW WELL I did on those tests. Thought my brain would have ceased up, not being at school these past couple of months. That's a relief. How nice were they all? So cool to meet that family from Israel, with the daughter my age just starting as well. Leanne seems really lovely. Very chatty.' Lou could hardly contain herself, she was so excited.

Wanda was also very happy…..and relieved. This had been an important first step in making their new home. Jay was pleased for Lou too and thought the school looked like a cool place to hang.

When they had woken at the quaint pub that morning, they were surprised and delighted to see they were surrounded by beautiful lakes. It had been dark when they arrived and the lakes were behind properties on both sides of the road. A real find. They would be back to explore for sure.

Now school was sorted, they would check out the town. One way traffic system around the centre. Pedestrianised in the middle. Jay was coping well, being totally lost and going around in circles, but that green Italian wagon was running low on fuel.

'OK. Let's just head into that parking area. We can walk around the centre and then ask someone where the nearest garage is, on our way back to the car.' Wanda was hungry by then anyway.

What a great little town. Loads of cool cafes and people sitting out under the trees. A big shopping mall hidden away, with every sort of shop and service you could ever want. Boutiques and record shops.

Bars with signs displayed about their upcoming live music nights. An arty film theatre and two multi-screen cinemas. Another huge live music and comedy hall. Wow! They were in heaven. Nice looking people cycling everywhere and a totally laid back sense of calm.

Having most of the Dutch radio and TV stations; and heaps of record companies; the town was known as Media Stad and often referred to as Hillywood.

On later cycling adventures, they would also discover it was completely surrounded by the most amazing forests. Those lakes they had seen earlier, were just a 25 minute cycle through the forests passing tiny canals. All on dedicated cycle paths, through totally flat terrain. The fields they would pass, having wild bison, deer, sheep and cows peacefully grazing, who were not at all bothered by the constant stream of cyclists passing. How very special.

'Good grief. It's now 2.30. I told Al we would be at the boat by 4 and I'm a bit fuzzy on how to get there. Need that petrol too. Might be best if I drive now Jay. Al gave me really detailed directions and I think it might require some last minute moves, as I actually realise where we are. That Amsterdam Ring can get a little crazy too.'

Fine by Jay. Still feeling very mellow, after the new food discovery. He had been brave and ordered an uitsmijter ham kaas. A huge plate of food had arrived. Three slices of bread covered with cheese and ham, then a fried egg on top of each one. He had never eaten three fried eggs in one go before. The pickle and cold tomato on the side, was a perfect compliment. Lekker!

'That was close. The red light has been on for ages. Imagine if we broke down on that Hillywood Ring. So much traffic. Only down side to this lovely town so far.'

They worked out the self-serve petrol machine and were soon on their way.

Wanda had a great feeling about this town. She would be driving Lou to school, from the canal boat in Amsterdam, then spending her days checking out properties for rent, until it was time to pick Lou up.

First they would have the weekend exploring Amsterdam. Finding all the old places they used to frequent and doing the obligatory boat trip around the incredible canals of this totally unique city.

'Your boat is so cool Al. Did it ever actually sail down the big canals or has it always been a houseboat?' Lou the budding artist just wanted to get painting it straight away.

What an incredible old craft. Al told her, with most of the large canal boats, the motors had been taken out and they were never to move from the moorings that cost them so dearly. Sewerage, water, electricity and gas were all connected, just like any other home.

Needed to mind your head on the low beams and, when smaller boats passed by, you would get the rocking movement. All very cool she thought. Al was a designer so this houseboat was especially cool. Pity about the noise from the pump, when you were trying to sleep at night though.

The next day they had wandered all over Amsterdam. Rented bikes and cycled through the Vondel Park. A safe choice. Cycling outside the park, meant avoiding trams and all their various tracks. Taxis, cars, bikes, buses and dazed tourists were everywhere. In the Vondel Park they visited the Film Museum. Later stopping by the house where they had lived nearby, nine years earlier. They had the top two floors of a beautiful turn-of-the-century home, with its own front door to the garden and street. An old lady lived there before them and she had installed an electric chair, to get her up the unbelievably steep and seemingly never-ending staircase.

Happy and sad reflections came to them, about their beloved Cocker Spaniel, who lived there as well. Frimley had come from a good dog breeder in Wales. He had been Larry and Wanda's first child.

When Jay had come into the world, they had to retrain Frimley so he would not jump on the bed. Larry had the dog sleeping under the duvet, on his feet. They had moved him to Sydney and then Wanda had moved him to Holland for that one year stint, when Jay and Lou were 6 and 9. Wanda had hoped the one year would turn out to be longer but that was not to be.

Frimley had been too old to do another long journey and they had good friends who wanted to keep him so they had left him in Amsterdam, when they returned to Sydney.

Frimley had loved it with his new family, those last couple of years he lived. The trio had been back to visit him after one year and saw clearly, just how happy he was. They had taken him to his favourite beach café but he was keen to get back to his new Dutch home. He lived to a ripe old age of 16 and had been loved by all.

'Mum. This is the swing park Jay and I used to play in. They still have that same seesaw thing. How cool!' Jay and Lou played on everything like they were 6 and 9 again. A happy sight.

Wanda grabbed herself a koffie verkeerd (literally translated as wrong coffee ....they really did not think it should have all that milk!) and watched them through the adjoining café's window. It was getting a little cold. Hardly anyone in the café. Her mind drifted.

Tim the fireman had come all the way from Sydney to Amsterdam, expecting Wanda would marry him. Those eight weeks they had known each other, before she had left Sydney for that one year stint nine years earlier, had been truly unbelievable. Instant attraction.

A great live band at the Woolloomooloo pub and fate had her pushed right up against Tim in the busy crowd. The place was jumping. He was cheeky. So was she. The mates they had been with, seemed quite keen on each other too. Perfect.

After the gig, it had been pies from Harry's. Walking around the piers singing and laughing, until way past 3am. Eventually ending up at Tim's. They had cuddled and talked, deciding they would hold back on the intense feelings for the moment. This was special. They did not want it to be a one night stand.

Wanda had gone home to get some sleep. Tim would cook her a fantastic meal that night and she would return. The intensity of feelings, hovered over the delicious meal. He was on his four days off and felt well rested. Not too much red wine. Neither of them wanted to feel alcohol had any role to play. It was a fine feast and they talked non-stop, wanting to know every detail about each other.

Tim had gone to the bathroom. He was taking a while. Suddenly he was standing before Wanda totally naked. What an incredible body. Being a fireman, he had a lot of time to himself. His body was his temple. She had noticed the body building magazines in the living room. Wanda had never seen anything quite so perfect. Tall, muscular and yet with this softness. His lips were hot and caressing. Lifting her with total ease, he could place her body wherever the next moments of passion would move. She had not known such intense pleasure.

Over those eight weeks prior to Wanda's departure, they had not spent one night apart. During the entire three years they went back and forth in their relationship, they had never slept in the same bed without making love. It had been impossible. They could not be in the same room, without the heat of passion overcoming them.

Tim could not believe Wanda was leaving the country.

Once she was in Amsterdam, the phone conversations were non-stop and the next thing Wanda knew, Tim had said he was taking leave and flying over to see her.

Wanda told Tim not to come with big expectations. If he wanted to see Europe, that was fine. She would show him around and make sure he had a good time. He had a brother in the UK. He could visit him as well.

Tim was 13 years her junior and Wanda knew he wanted to marry and have children. As much as she loved him, she knew it would not work. That said, she had been overwhelmed when she saw him coming through arrivals at Amsterdam Schiphol airport.

So handsome. Beaming with happiness and hugging her until she thought she might actually stop breathing.

Wanda had an au pair living in. Her work had often meant being away overnight. The au pair also helped the children with their Dutch. Particularly Jay, with the never ending words he had to learn. She was born in England but grew up in Holland so was totally bi-lingual. Having the au pair, meant Wanda could take Tim off on a couple of special trips, without the children.

Paris had been magical but by the time they got to Bruges, Tim was ready for a showdown. Every time he had tried to get deep and meaningful on the 'where is this going' conversation, Wanda had changed the subject. He was not having any of it.

Tim had fallen deeply and madly in love with Wanda. He also loved Jay and Lou. They had all had a magical week skiing in Austria over Christmas and worked well together as a family unit, he thought.

Sitting in the café, waiting for Lou and Jay to finish playing, Wanda now recalled just what a special week that had been in Austria. For much of Tim's stay, she had been tense about letting him down but that week skiing, they had cleared their heads and had a great time.

Maybe she should have married Tim. When he had finally left Amsterdam, they were both as distraught as one another. 'The Bodyguard' movie had just hit cinemas and they had been to see it. 'I will always love you' would be their song forever.

They had stayed in close contact and ended up back together, once the trio returned to Sydney. As the time passed, it became even clearer to Wanda that marriage would not work. Finally, after three years, Tim had accepted that fact. They had one last night of extreme passion and unbelievable sex on Wanda's birthday in May. By the time Tim reached his 30th birthday in November, he had a new girlfriend and she was pregnant with twins. They had married a few months later.

Driving along the A1 on that first day of school was so memorable. Wanda and Lou had left early. Not quite sure which exit would be best, coming in the other direction.

Jay went job hunting in Amsterdam.

As they passed the great lake waters of the Ijsselmeer, the sun had begun to rise in all its glory. Not just an incredible site but clearly a sign that this would be an amazing new piece of their life journey puzzle.

Wanda spent the day getting to know the town. Visited four gyms and looked in all the makelaar (real estate agent) windows. One seemed to have most of the rental properties. They had a few they could show her that afternoon. Not impressed. And the costs were ridiculous.

'What do you need to buy property here?' Wanda had asked the makelaar. She had a British passport as well as her Australian, having been married to a Brit. Jay and Lou had both as well. Now the European Union was well in place, one could generally work and buy property in any of the member state countries.

Wanda had a house in Sydney, she bought when she split with Larry. She had managed to get a line of credit against that. This was going to provide the stopgap for funds, until she started to earn money in Holland. The house was rented out so the mortgage was covered and she might even have a little over.

As she explored further about buying a house in Hillywood, she discovered the interest rates were unbelievably low and she could borrow up to 120%. Wow! That could cover legal costs and renovations.

Monthly repayments would actually be less than it would cost to rent. Done. Just one slight problem. She had to have a declaration from her employer, to confirm she was in work.

'Al. Can I explore a little possibility with you please?' He had his own small business now and Wanda had already discussed work she thought she could bring in for him. Having already had work from Wanda, when she lived there the first time, Al knew she would be true to her word. Now Wanda needed him to actually take her onto his books as an employee. He did not hesitate. The mortgage broker got his required declaration and the loan had been approved.

'Guys. You are going to love it. Loads of scope to improve with renovations. I have already scribbled a little plan for what I'd like to do. It's empty so we can move in as soon as the legals are done.'

Jay and Lou were amazed yet again by their mum. For two weeks, she had dropped Lou at school and then spent the rest of her day seeing properties for sale. Just two weeks and it was all sorted.

Their new home was a three minute cycle from the centre. Lou's school was then three minutes to the other side of town. It was not one of the huge posh houses, and could possibly be on the wrong side of the track, but they loved it. It had been nice of Al to say they could stay two months on the boat but none of them had slept well and they were pleased they could get into their own place sooner.

Jay would take the fast train to Amsterdam each day. He had already started at a call centre and that seemed to be going well. Once they were settled into their new home, he would hit the radio stations to see if he could get more of a career pathway happening.

'The roof space is enormous. With those ceilings out, you'll see the potential.

It will have a big main bedroom. Walk-in dressing room and wardrobe. Dual access bathroom with a proper bathtub. And there will still be masses of space for a utility area. Velux windows for loads of natural light. Exposed beams. This will be mother's space.' Wanda grinned and felt very pleased with herself. She had done her rough sketches and had a clear view on how it would all come together.

When Wanda and Larry had been together, he had become a carpenter and builder, to bump up his earnings as a musician. He and Wanda had done alright with property renovations and she knew her way around what was involved.

Jay and Lou were impressed. Then the fun and games began.

Why had Wanda expected building trades people to have good English? She soon discovered she needed a better command of Dutch, if she was going to brief the guys lined up to quote and have any idea of what they were saying back to her.

Loads of work to be done. She wanted a wall knocked out downstairs, to open up the living area and tiny kitchen space. That would need a new supporting beam. The loft space was a full rebuild and she also wanted the current bathroom to have a toilet added and new washbasin.

Old style woodchip needed to be scraped off the walls. Wanda could not believe it when they found carpet on the walls, under that woodchip.

The house also needed central heating, painting, kitchen units and new carpet. Front and back gardens were a nightmare. Loads of prickly bushes to come out and she would make a whole new area for that green Italian wagon to park. It was a nightmare trying to park in the street.

The bibliotheek (library) became Wanda's day home during school hours. Loads of books and audio tools to get her Dutch improved in a hurry. Free internet access.

Before she knew it, she was having detailed discussions for building quotes in Dutch and by the time they were able to move in, she had commissioned a carpenter/builder for all the work.

Wanda knew exactly what would happen and when. The house purchase price had been well negotiated and renovations might actually come in a little under budget. Excellent!

They had been living in their building site for three weeks and were now looking forward to the planned road trip, to spend Christmas and New Year in the UK. While they were away, the builder would get as near as damn it to finished. Or so they hoped.

A non-stop schedule was planned for the UK trip. Moving from friend to friend, trying to get quality time with everyone. No accommodation required. They would sleep at friends' houses.

Big challenge to put a schedule together, which kept them heading in one direction. So many friends to catch up with.

They would also spend time in Scotland with Larry's family. Had not seen Grandma and Grandad for a long time and Larry's brother, was in a different city.

Jay was looking forward to getting back out on the motorways again, for some serious driving. All well and good driving locally but nothing like knowing you have some distance to cover. More often than not, they had taken bikes everywhere and that green Italian wagon would just sit in the car parking space created at the front of the house. Should be cool driving onto one of those big car ferries too. They would take the Calais to Dover crossing. Jay could not wait.

It was an historic time in Europe. Most countries in the EU would switch to a single currency in the New Year. The Euro would be born. When they came back to Holland, everything would have converted. No more guilders.

Quite an historic evening was also unfolding in Hillywood.

Lou had made loads of friends and was full of the joys of being able to go out at night, even though official drinking age was 16. Lou would cycle into the centre to meet all her school chums Friday and Saturday nights. They had a few favourite bars. Mostly just spent their time playing pool or darts. Lou did not even like alcohol.

They would bop about wherever and just gossip. Most of the bars were really small. Very cosy.

This particular night, Jay had gone out with some workmates after they finished their shift. The Dutch call it a borrel. Drinks and nibblies to us. Wanda had been home alone.

Wanda had always trusted Lou to think wisely but she knew this new life would throw some temptations Lou's way that might be challenging. Something told her she should go see what Lou was up to that evening.

Larry had become a smoker, a few years after splitting with Wanda. Lou and Jay hated everything smelling of smoke, when they visited his house. They had vowed they would never take up this disgusting habit. Wanda had never smoked. Never done drugs. People had often accused her of being stoned, because she was always smiling and happy, but she had not touched a thing. Had the occasional drink but could easily do without that as well. Lou and Jay had felt the same.

Wanda just stood there staring. She had cycled into town and cruised around the bars she knew Lou frequented. There Lou was. Sitting outside one of the more seedy places, with Elaine and some guy twice their age. Beer in hand. She had not seen Wanda. Elaine handed Lou the cigarette she was smoking. Lou took it and puffed away.

'Not a good look.' Wanda had called out as she cycled up right in front of Lou. 'I'll see you at home!'

Lou turned bright red. She jumped up and headed for her bike. Elaine was supposed to sleep over but they had a quick change of plans.

By the time Lou had put her bike away at home, Wanda was already in her bed with the light off. Lou knew this meant her mum did not want to talk that night.

The silent treatment had always been the most cutting of all.

Lou had risen early the next day, offering to fix her mum breakfast. Wanda gave just a nod to say no. It wrenched at Lou's gut, to have her mum so mad at her.

'Mum. I wasn't smoking. I just took it for a minute off Elaine and had a drag. She kept pestering me so I figured that would shut her up.'

Wanda knew her daughter only too well. She knew that Lou was a great story teller. Jay on the other hand, could never tell a lie.

Jay would look you straight in the face and try but just take on this strange expression and you knew it was not the truth. You had only to raise your eyebrows at him and he would relent.

Wanda had always told them, the worse thing of all was lying.

Lou took a different tack. 'Alright. So I have had a couple of cigarettes. Most kids at school have. I don't even like it. Mum, I hate it when you're mad at me. I really don't want to smoke. Can you help me stop please?'

Once there was honesty on the table, Wanda had always approachable. She talked to Lou at length about smoking and how people start, just to be in, and then end up hooked.

'Mum. I think I do need help. Those one or two a week now seem to be something I crave for.'

Wanda had been relieved that was the extent of it. She would get Lou patches and that should stop any of those cravings she felt she was having. Lou wore the patches and was extremely pleased with herself to kick the habit quickly. She never smoked again.

'How great is it going to be, not having thick dust on everything we pick up mum?' Jay was grabbing the car keys. Everything loaded into that green Italian wagon. It was back on the road for the trio.

Jay had taken the car to get everything checked and fill the petrol tank. Wanda had made sure he knew how to do tyres, oil and all the basic car care things, when he had first set foot in a car. He was definitely the captain of this four wheel ship.

They had only driven 100km when a dense fog set in. Visibility was terrible. Jay put on the fog lights and continued carefully. He had a good sense of risks associated with driving in bad conditions. The motorway was packed with lorries. As the fog cleared, the rain started. Again, visibility incredibly poor. They stopped for a coffee.

Already late for their car ferry booking, they felt they should carry on. Wanda had offered to take the wheel but Jay had wanted to complete his mission.

Mum could take over when they got to the UK. He was not quite sure how he would go, being on the other side of the road, anyway.

'You idiot! That was close guys. Did you see him? Cut straight in front of us. Can you believe these people? Can't see more than a vehicle ahead and he has to be driving well over the speed limit.'

Wanda congratulated Jay on how well he handled himself. He had mastered the art of driving and knew the most important thing of all, was to make sure your passengers were safe.

Jay thought back to when he first got behind the wheel of that green Italian wagon in Rome. This car had somehow made all the difference. Seemed to be the magic ingredient needed, to help him become a really good driver.

The idiot that had sped past them had not been so lucky. He had clipped a lorry and sent himself and the lorry into a spin. They had both gone off the road.

'Jay. Look out!' Wanda and Lou screamed simultaneously.

• CHAPTER FOUR •

ONE LANE WAS NOW CLOSED and Jay needed to pass very slowly. How sad. Just like that. In a moment of stupidity those poor people's lives would be changed forever. It did not look good.

Jay had responded well but it had been close. A momentary lag in concentration and it could have ended very differently. He now made his way past the crash site carefully. The sound of sirens approaching sent a quick shudder through his entire body. That crazy driver could just have easily clipped them. Jay's mum had always impressed upon him, how important it was to be able to respond to other people's bad driving. This brought it all home in full living colour.

'There's the ferry port sign now.' Jay sighed, as he welcomed the couple of hours they would spend relaxing on the boat.

Wanda was also rather shaken by the near miss but soon they would be back in England. So many places to go and so many people to see. She was excited. She was also reflecting on the state they had left their new home in. Fingers crossed the work would get finished while they were away.

'Mum. Where are we staying tonight?' enquired Lou. She had not seen the near miss. Busy flicking through her music choices and thinking about a boy she had met at school.

Danny was in the same year as Lou but a little younger. His mum from Indonesia and his father Dutch. Gangster rap was high on his list of musical preferences too.

Wanda reminded Jay and Lou of the schedule for this UK trip.

Most days they would have breakfast, lunch and dinner at a different friend's house. Overnight accommodation generally provided at the dinner stops.

"Tonight we stay with Aaron, Sarah and the kids. Did I tell you he had been promoted? Heading up that big travel business now. They have a new dog too. Hope we can find their house. That one time I went there a couple of years back, Aaron was driving. Might need you to get him on the phone when we get close Lou. He can talk us in through his village maze.'

Wanda and Larry had taken a cheap ski package to Austria twenty years earlier and Aaron was the rep on the bus, organising lift passes and generally making everyone feel welcome. They all got along really well and skied together a few times. When Aaron returned to the UK end of season, he would visit Wanda and Larry in London. Lots of coincidences with this friendship. Jay's birthday fell on the same day as Aaron's. The day of Aaron and Sarah's wedding was the same as Wanda and Larry's – albeit a different year. Lou was just three days old when she attended that wedding. Aaron had raised a toast to her and to his grandmother ….. the youngest and oldest guests at the reception.

For six days they enjoyed the company of friend after friend. How lucky were they to have so many? These were true friendships that had stood the test of time, travels and life's many changes. It did n0t matter how many years passed between get-togethers. They were always very special times. The only thing that really changed was how different the children became as they grew up. Fascinating to see.

Wanda had done much of the UK driving initially. Jay was really put off by being on the 'wrong' side of the road when you're driving from the opposite side of the car. Now it was time to head to Scotland, he felt ready to take the wheel again. Keen to be the one in charge, when they arrived at Grandma and Grandad's house.

Grandad was such an incredible man. Still playing sax and now well into his 70s. Up on stage gigging with funk bands and big jazz outfits, often with people a third his age. The biggest chuckle of a laugh you could ever imagine. Maths teacher and a very clever man. He would fuss over Jay and Lou and make all their favourite food. Grandma had, however, been a little harder to take.

Wanda thought back to the first time she had met them.

Larry had a gig in his hometown. He had travelled up with the band and she had flown up from London on the day of the gig. Larry had his dad's car for the night and they would drive straight from the airport to the gig, then stay at his parents afterwards …. in separate rooms. They had been living together in London for six months so Wanda was already thinking things might be a little strained.

'Guid eenin ta ya. An affa fine eenin at uz'. This kind gentleman Larry had stopped to ask directions, proceeded to speak in the most unusual form of Scottish Wanda had ever heard. She understood nothing. Even Larry had struggled but they did eventually find the venue.

Larry was one of four children. The eldest had flown the nest in his early teens. Also a sax player, he had set up home in Edinburgh. Then there was his sister. Still living at home but feeling the strain of a very dominant mother. Ditto for the youngest son, who was often known to cause havoc. Stole his dad's car one night. No driver's license and no ability to even drive. Bit of a scallywag. Larry would share his room, these two nights of our first ever visit. Wanda got the sister's room. She had gone to sleep over at a friend's.

All the usual pleasantries, when they finally arrived at Larry's parents' home after the gig. His parents were night owls so still wide awake. Wanda felt odd going to sleep alone but the extra special hug from Larry had helped somewhat.

In the morning, Wanda had been amazed to find that Larry's mum held court in her bedroom and her children were expected to go in and sit on the edge of her bed, recounting their evening outings. Grandad would have been out to get fresh rowies (a sort of flat croissant) and taken a breakfast tray to Grandma. Quite the ritual.

Wanda did not join in. Instead she ventured downstairs to chat with Grandad.

He had brochures of Australia and the glint in his eye was amazing, as he talked about going to visit sometime. Two brothers had emigrated down under and he dreamed of going to see where they had gone. Could not believe his son was now attached to an ozzie. Fantastic. Wanda and Grandad got along brilliantly.

Months later, when Larry's parents realised his relationship with Wanda was serious, they had taken regular visits to London. Wanda would always arrange theatre and concert tickets. They got to know each other better and it seemed Wanda was in their good books. She worked in advertising and Larry's mum had been a model; knew loads of media folk and they had both sung in bands. Lots of common ground. A fun time was being had by all.

Until Larry proposed marriage.

'If she was a Scottish lass, we could better understand it. No-one from up here will be able to come down to London for the wedding. Why don't you just continue living together,' was all that Larry's mother could say. The chummy relationship had come to an abrupt end, as she reverted to the Scottish mother stance.

'Maybe we should go up to see them and get them involved with wedding arrangements,' Wanda had said to Larry in an effort to re-connect.

The couple of nights that had followed, at Larry's parents' small house in Scotland, proved to be a nightmare for all. You could have cut the atmosphere with a knife.

As soon as Grandma had Wanda on her own, she had started with 'of course if he was marrying a local girl ……..' Wanda eventually lost her calm and it all came out. The words that had gone unsaid. The tears that had been building up for months. Wanda was a quivering wreck and Grandad, for the very first time ever, was telling Grandma off.

'Now look what you have done', Grandma was bellowing to Wanda. 'He has never spoken to me like that before!'

Larry and Wanda headed back to London earlier than expected. Wanda in fits of tearful shaking and vowing never to step foot in that house ever again. Larry in full agreement.

Larry's brothers and sister came to the wedding. His parents did not. For the three years that followed that last visit, Larry's mother had written him letters with absolutely no mention of his new wife's name.

Wanda would encourage Larry to visit his family, whenever she had to be away on business. It was important he at least maintained some sort of relationship. She was sad not to see his dad but did not want a bar of his mother.

When Wanda and Larry announced their first pregnancy, the letters suddenly arrived addressed to them both. A first grandchild was too much for Grandma to miss out on.

Never one to stay angry, Wanda relented. She wanted Grandparents for her children. Larry's father would be their only

Grandad and an amazing one at that. Wanda had no clue as to her own father's identity so no Grandad coming from her side. Her mum was also in Sydney so the children were unlikely to see much of her.

At six months pregnant, Wanda had agreed to go back to Larry's parents for the first time since the pre-wedding nightmare. Grandma was on her best behaviour. Grandad as delightful as always and Larry, a very happy chappy about the reconciliation.

As the years passed, Grandma had done her best to be as good a grandma as she could be. Never forgetting a birthday or Christmas and always writing regularly. Even after Larry and Wanda divorced.

The second child being a little girl, had been the icing on Grandma's proverbial cake. A little model child for her to dress up and fuss over.

Staying at Grandma's house had, however, never ceased to be a challenge. Everything in its place and a place for everything.

Meals to be eaten at fixed times and generally only to be followed by being glued to the TV. Nobody ever to disagree with anything Grandma said and certainly no answering of the ringing home phone by anyone else.

Lou and Jay had happy memories of Grandad relaxing on the floor and playing with them when they were young though. Their happiest memories of all being when he played sax to them going to bed, after mum had read their bedtime story. Larry had stayed in Sydney after the marriage broke up but Wanda spent quite some time in Europe so Jay and Lou had continued seeing their Scottish Grandparents.

Now Jay was all grown up, his discussions with Grandad and Grandma were generally all about music.

Lou still scanned the fashion magazines with Grandma and tried on clothes. Grandma was ever the well dressed and sweeping figure of a woman on parade.

'This visit should prove to be interesting', thought Wanda. As luck would have it, Grandad had a gig on the 2nd day of their stay.

'Yer al lookin jest fane. Git yersels unside un tha warm. Ets affa frosty oot here.' Grandad's welcome made them all smile.

Lou had called when they were an hour's drive away and Grandad had dinner all prepared and waiting. Mince and tatties. Lekker. One of their favourites.

Grandma was on excellent form. She had loads of clothes she wanted Lou to try on. Their little modelling session lasted a couple of hours the next day. Records were taken down from the attic to share with Jay. Old jazzers. He was wrapped. A couple of classics he admired, were his to keep. Fantastic!

The pub was packed for Grandad's gig that evening.

'Can you believe Grandad Jay? How amazing is he?' Lou had been snuck in to the pub under Wanda's arm and took front row position with Jay, to boogie along to the big band sounds. Most of the band members had young followers so Jay and Lou slotted right in and she was hidden by the crowd. Christmas Eve gigs always proved to be a big bopping night. Grandad's endless energy came through in his soulful sax playing. Magical!

Exchanges of gifts preceded breakfast the following morning. Not the usual stockings out for Santa to fill regime this year. Another black t-shirt with loud messaging for Jay. Grandma loved to shop and bought things way before the big rush. The t-shirt for Lou had a cute little girl cycling on the front. Not something she would ever wear but it had always been the thought that counted.

Christmas lunch at Larry's sister's house. Cousin Blane getting Jay onto the video games, within ten minutes of the hellos. A nice sense of family. Radical younger brother to Larry a no-show yet again.

Jay was at the wheel, as they drove away from Grandma and Grandad's that affa frosty morning. Just a few days to go and it would be Hogmanay (New Years Eve). By then they would have arrived at Larry's elder brother's apartment in Edinburgh.

Bobby and his wife Carla had a special evening in store for them to see the New Year in. Jay had hoped Uncle Bobby might be playing but no luck this visit. Another excellent sax player.

'They have a great swimming pool complex here, with a cool café. Bring the kids over in the morning. I already spoke to the front desk and it is fine to have visitors.' Wanda convinced Bobby to bring Carla and the boys to the hotel they had booked into a few miles out of Edinburgh. Two nights there and then Hogmanay they would sleep over at Bobby and Carla's apartment, in the centre of town.

Although this visit to Grandma and Grandad's had been a pleasant one, Wanda was glad of a couple of days to just chill in a nice hotel. She had forgiven but never forgotten the pre-wedding traumas with Grandma.

It was now 2002. A tide change had happened across Europe. EU countries had ditched their national notes and coins, to switch over to one common Euro currency. Great Britain had not been one of those.

'Mum. Why does England think it's better off staying with the pound?' Lou was caught up by all the conversation around her, on the channel ferry crossing back to Calais.

As Wanda gave Lou her view on the economic policies of different European countries, Lou was beginning to wish she had never asked.

Jay was busy reading a new edition of the Broons he had been given by Uncle Bobby. Impossible to not laugh out loud at that.

Wanda was amazed at the speed of transition across to the Euro. They had driven into Antwerp to have a quick look around and dinner, before driving the final leg back to their new home in Holland. Parking meters only took euro coins. The restaurant menu quoted prices in euros (at least they still had the Belgian francs in brackets afterwards). Wow. Must have taken years of planning to prepare for this and within days, it had all been implemented. Even more so once they crossed the border back into Holland.

Hardly anywhere talked guilders. The basic number had halved so that made things easy for the Dutch. Travelling around the many different countries of Europe would now be much simpler for everyone, with just one common currency.

'Good grief. It looks fantastic!' As Jay opened the front door to their new home, a completely new downstairs area lay before them.

Better than Wanda had ever anticipated. Way beyond anything Jay and Lou could have imagined.

Wanda got straight on the phone to the builder. Dankjewel and a good few sentences in Dutch followed. He knew she was one happy customer. The top floor loft conversion had been even more incredible. Now all they needed was for their belongings to arrive from Australia.

Everything had been scheduled to be delivered the day after they arrived home from the UK trip. No call to say otherwise. No emails. Wanda had become more than a little concerned.

'Well. I'm sure you can also appreciate that we are sleeping on the floor. A little cold these wintery evenings. Just lucky that our friends were able to lend us some sleeping bags.' Wanda had been on the phone to the shipping agent daily and was now losing all patience.

It seemed the truck loaded with all their belongings, had been stolen from a car park. The driver had gone into a services restaurant to eat. Came back out and the truck was gone. All very strange.

Police had now recovered the vehicle, quite some distance away. It was believed the thief just wanted to get from A to B. Once there, the truck had been abandoned. Now it was a matter of the police doing what they needed to, with a view to potentially catching the thief. Then the shipping agent could get someone there to pick it up. More difficult than the making of Ben Hur it seemed.

Finally, when the goods had arrived, there had been quite some damage done. Much of the china was broken. A box or two completely missing. It took Wanda ages to go through the inventory bit by bit and make notes for the insurance claim. She expected it would take forever to actually be reimbursed.

Jay had been happy to take the smallest bedroom. It had no adjoining wall to neighbours so he wouldn't need to be thinking about noise so much. Lou had more clothes than he did anyway. She could take the larger room, with the small walk-in wardrobe. He also liked the way his room was on the corner and had two small windows facing in different directions. He would stare out those windows for ages, watching people cycle by and thinking how unbelievable some of the locals were to be letting their dogs just poop in the street …. not even attempting to pick it up. Gross!

None of Jay's things had been damaged in transit. Even his turntable was still intact. Not even one record bent or buckled. His bed was a king single. Loved that bed and it fitted perfectly in his new room. The speakers went nicely on top of the chest of drawers.

Computer table was a good size for all his gaming bits and pieces. He was all set.

Wanda had decided she would buy a new bed so Lou was now stepping up to her old double. Plenty of space for it in the new room. Not keen on the linen her mum had though. Something a little more abstract and colourful for Lou.

They had a list all prepared for things they wanted for the house. A shopping trip to their favourite furniture superstore, had been on the agenda for a few days.

Took a while to get used to the very steep and narrow stairs in their new home. Got even steeper going from the first floor up into Wanda's domain. Didn't the delivery men have fun getting Wanda's new bed up there. New washing machine provided even more entertainment. The utility area was also on that top floor.

No way you could walk those stairs unless you put your foot sideways. Something you got used to pretty quickly. Only took one good slide down a few stairs, to bring the point home.

'You OK mum?' Lou couldn't believe how many stairs her mum had missed, before coming in to land. Ouch!

The most important of acquisitions had of course been the fiets (bikes). A prerequisite for fitting in and getting about, in and around Hillywood. They had purchased those before they did the trip to the UK. Friends had warned them not to buy anything new or flash.

The older and more beat up, the better. Otherwise, they would just get stolen. Good locks were a must anyway. Big sitty-up bikes were the way to go. They had seen a small ad in the local supermarket for just the job. A retired gent who bought old bikes and did them up. Very reasonably priced. Wanda had fun conversing with him about the bike's features. Her Dutch was definitely improving.

Funnily enough, Lou and Jay's recall to what had been Dutch fluency, was slow in returning. As much as they loved languages, they had become a little arrogant about everyone speaking English.

'Yes Nan. We are in Holland. No. We won't be coming over this week. Have you been getting the postcards we sent you? One from London. One from Scotland. The one last week had tulips and windmills on it. Cool. I know. Windmills are so beautiful, aren't they Nan? Mum sent you a package for your birthday yesterday. You should get that next week. Yes. We'll be phoning you every few days. OK Nan. I'll hand you over to mum now. Love you.'

Jay had initiated the call to his Nan this time so he was all clear and already back up in his bedroom, on the computer.

Wanda told her mother yet again, that they were now living in Holland. It was her 89th birthday coming up and she was getting more and more selective with her memory. The most important topic was always food. Each meal would be relived and she would always want to know what you had planned to eat next.

Back in Sydney, they had lived just five minutes away from Nan. Wanda fought hard to get her mum a place in this wonderful assisted living complex, close to their home.

Most of the residents had needed to sell their houses to buy in but the government insisted a few places be made available for those of no means, other than their state pension. Wanda's mum had her own bedsit with kitchenette and bathroom. One of the nice units with sliding doors out to the gardens. From the rear of the complex, you could see down through the national park to the ocean, off in the distance. Meals were served in a central dining area and there were always outings and events.

When Wanda had returned to Sydney with Larry and the two small children years earlier, her mum was renting a cockroach infested room in a share house. They moved her straight in with them. The children loved having their Nan to play with. After the split, Nan also moved with them to their new home. She looked after them while Wanda did part time work. It was important for Wanda to spend more time at home with the children for a year or so at least so she had taken up extras acting work, to bring a little money in and keep herself sane.

She and Larry had split amicably with no lawyers involved. They sold their big home and could each buy a smaller property. Larry would have a small mortgage and Wanda had enough to buy her house cash. She preferred that to having maintenance.

It was often the cause of on-going pains, when people split up. Wanda knew she was more than capable of earning a living, for herself and the children.

Wanda's mother had always been one to expect that her own children and the system in general, should look after her. It was as though she felt she was owed a living. Giving birth to eight children without being able to support them, had never really crossed her mind. She would tell people how much she loved having babies and that it was the best years of her life.

Wanda had never even asked her mother who her father was. She knew her mum had fabricated a story in her own mind, which suited what she had wanted to believe. Growing up, Wanda had heard her mother tell other people that her first four children were born to one father and then the second four to another. That was clearly not true.

Her fifth child had memories of his father leaving and no-one ever filling that same spot again.

Other family members had told Wanda that her mother was dating two different men when she was conceived. One of those had apparently been a French naval officer. Perfect. Wanda had chosen him to be her father…..without any need to even know who he was.

After those couple of years living with her mother post the split with Larry, Wanda knew it was time to be finding a place for Nan to now live on her own. Lots of meetings and harassing the housing commission, soon led to a lovely new apartment being allocated. Nan was happy in that apartment for many years, until it all became too much. Wanda had then spent many months, securing her the spot at the exclusive retirement complex. She loved it there.

Wanda and the children had often just popped in or picked Nan up for shopping or to join them for a meal. Drives down to the beach for fish and chips by the sea, had always been a favourite. Most of the family were hesitant about going to see Nan. When they phoned, she would only complain that they never called.

Before Wanda left Sydney, she had prepared a roster with her brothers so they could take turns to visit Nan. Everyone would know who was scheduled to go when. That would be easier for them all. There were only six of the eight children left and Wanda's sister had been paralysed down one side since a car accident at 15yrs of age so it was almost impossible for her to make the journey over to visit Nan. The four boys had agreed they would maintain the regular visits and so far so good. It provided the perfect opportunity for them to bond more with their mother, before she passed. The plan was working well.

Wanda had spoken with Lou and Jay about the likelihood they might never actually see Nan in the flesh again. She was getting very old now and it could be that her time might come, while they were living in Holland. They had always been very spiritually aware so they understood people did not leave you just because their bodies gave out. Memories and magical moments stayed with you forever.

'OK Mum. Must dash now. Lou has a function on at school and we need to be getting over there. Yes. We'll call again Thursday. No. We won't be popping over tomorrow. We are in Holland, remember? Yes. I know. Windmills really are beautiful aren't they? OK bye now. Love you.' Wanda put down the receiver and gave a sad sigh.

• CHAPTER FIVE •

'RIGHT JAY. YOU HAVE THREE DAYS with no work next week so now is the time for us to hit the radio stations. Spend this weekend really getting your CV in good shape and then Monday we will start. I'll drive you around and you just take your CV into the reception and ask if you can see someone responsible for recruiting. Cold calling shows you are keen and it can sometimes make all the difference. Doesn't matter what the job is. Getting your foot in the door is the objective.' Wanda had already spoken to a few contacts in associated media businesses but there had been no doors opening for Jay.

'I'm up for it mum. Will be interesting to check them all out anyway. I've been on most of the websites but I reckon it's worth a shot to just front up.'

Wanda and Jay covered all the radio stations and not one nibble. Some really nice people though. They had suggested other avenues for Jay to try and a few emailed him with roles they had seen posted in other places. Jay got interviews for a couple of those but the lack of fluent written Dutch, was proving to be a stumbling block. He continued working at the market research call centre. They had given him more and more responsibility and taught him new software. He made some good friends and was generally enjoying life.

During their visits with friends around the UK, skiing had often come up as a topic of conversation.

So much so, that Wanda had said she would organise a ski trip, for any friends that were interested. Now she was contemplating where they might go.

'Lou. When is your next school holiday break? I'm thinking we three could maybe head off in that green Italian wagon and check out some ski resorts. If we are going to put together somewhere nice for our large group to go skiing, we really need to have seen the place first.'

Did not need to ask twice when it came to skiing. Jay and Lou had both been skiing since they could walk. This was the one sport that they both loved. Jay booked his time off work and it was only a few weeks until Lou would have holidays.

Wanda had already done one of her mass emails to friends interested in skiing and it looked like there could be forty or so people for the planned Christmas/New Year week in the snow. She would need to find somewhere high in the Alps, with a good record for decent snow falls at that time of year.

That green Italian wagon was cruising on the roads of Europe once more. Down along the beautiful Rhine River, stopping for a two hour lunch. They were captivated by the enormous barges travelling up and down the Rhine. Spent that first night in an excellent 'Jugendherberge' (youth hostel) just outside Munich in Germany.

A huge four bedded room, with its own bathroom. Excellent! Loads of interesting travellers to talk to.

Jay was back behind the wheel and Wanda gave a thought to the project she had just been commissioned to handle, for her big photo industry client in Holland. That would bring in a tidy sum of money to keep them going. The creative work would go through Al's company.

It felt great to be fulfilling her promise to Al. They would not be in their lovely new home, if it hadn't been for Al hiring Wanda so she could qualify for the Dutch mortgage.

Wanda had made contact with a few chalet companies that had different properties in Austria and Switzerland. The trio would inspect some of those chalets and travel across the two small countries, skiing wherever they felt the urge. This meant having their own skis and Wanda had already seen there was a big sale planned at their first ski resort stop…. Zell am See.

'How beautiful is this place mum! That lake is massive. Must be incredible when it's frozen and everyone skates on it. An amazing turquoise blue ….. and the mountains reflecting in the water …it is just spectacular.' Lou, yet again, would have been totally happy to get the canvas out and start painting. Umm. Difficult choice. Painting or skiing? Choice made. No painting gear to hand.

It's no secret that ski boots were never meant for comfort.

Not having skied for a couple of years, made it all that more difficult to try and work out how they each needed to feel in their new boots. Fortunately there were several shops running with the sale. Most of the first day in town was spent going back and forth between them all, trying to find ski boots they were happy with.

Then the skis. The shop attendant would make sure they were the right length and bindings suited the relevant skiing capability and weight. Ski poles at the correct height.

Colour always an important element for everything to do with skiing. That white backdrop lending itself so well to vivid colours. One of the joys of being in the mountains skiing, had always been the brightness of people all similarly dressed for the occasion. Fresh air and magical mountains. People gathering after an active day, to tell their tales and join in the fun of après ski. Truly wonderful!

Sitting in the shop watching Lou and Jay play around with ski gear, Wanda thought back to an old friend who had passed away some years earlier.

Mike had been instrumental in Wanda learning how to ski and her total enjoyment with just being in the mountains. They had worked together in Sydney and he had organised a long weekend to the Australian slopes, when she was in her early twenties. Mike was from the UK but had also lived in Switzerland for some years, working as a ski instructor. They had become great buddies and Wanda had taken him into her family, as another brother.

His infectious enthusiasm for skiing became the launching pad, for what would become a great love in Wanda's life. Of all the adventures Wanda would ever embark upon, skiing would remain at the pinnacle of her most favourite things to do.

Mike had managed to get Wanda skiing in no time at all. The gluhwein and Jagermeister might possibly have helped. Definitely a good thing to take ones mind off falling over so much. Icy VoVo biscuits in the car park, before hitting the slopes. The quick sugar hit often accompanied by a few verses of Rocky Mountain High. Singing and yodelling had of course continued throughout the day and night.

Mike was a brilliant skier. A marvellous character. Could be as silly as Wanda, with a totally infectious laugh. A great friend.

The day of Mike's death had been earmarked for a fun dinner on the balcony of Mike's rented room, sitting directly under the end of the

Sydney Harbour Bridge. They would all shout loudly, when the trains rattled noisily across the incredibly huge bridge overhead. Lou would show Mike her latest work of art. She had become his protégé and been to a couple of art classes he attended.

As a successful civil engineer for many years, Mike had enjoyed far too much red wine and cheese. He had decided a couple of years prior, to ease his pace of life and had made a move to Buddhism and meditation.

Setting off to Nepal, for a climb to his chosen monastery, only to be thwarted by a heart attack that saw him airlifted off the mountain.

He had spent several weeks in hospital in Nepal recovering. Returning to Sydney and taken a calmer stance, spending every moment he could painting. A brilliant artist was discovered. His 'Sunflowers' had continued to take prime position on the main wall of anywhere the trio had lived ever since.

There had been no answer from Mike's mobile phone, that fateful day. Wanda, Lou and Jay had been at the theatre seeing a matinee and were about to make their way to Mike's. Most odd. They had left a silly voicemail and told him they would go for a milkshake, whilst waiting to hear back from him. The call never came. They drove to his place. Rang his buzzer. Shouted up to the balcony.

'He complained of not feeling quite right, after we finished lunch. Didn't seem too bad though. His car was parked at the back of our house and by the time he had driven around to the front, making his way to the hospital just up the road, he felt he needed someone to go with him. Came back in the front door. Don jumped straight in to drive him up to emergency. Mike was dead by the time they got there!' The mutual friend calling Wanda had spat the words out, like you might expect of someone in total shock. They both then sobbed inconsolably.

Mike's body was at the coroners. Once they confirmed cause of death, it would be released to a funeral home.

Wanda and Mike had often spoken about the ridiculous costs associated with disposing of a body, once the person had passed and it was of no further use. They had both agreed it was not the person, merely a vehicle that person had moved about in. The person stayed with loved ones forever..... in their hearts.

'Bodies should of course be treated respectfully, in appreciation of having served that person well but the pomp and circumstance that wraps itself around funerals, is just a total waste of money.' Mike had often commented to Wanda.

They had talked about them both wanting to be cremated. If any of the bits could be useful to someone else prior to that, fantastic. Then they wanted to have their ashes symbolically scattered, somewhere nice their loved ones could go to. Certainly not hanging out with fields of dead folks in a graveyard. At any wake, songs should be sung and people should be focussed on the good things that came from that person's time on earth.

Wanda had asked for Mike's ashes to be split into two boxes. One would go back to his family in England. If at all possible, to be scattered on his favourite football team's grounds in Manchester. The second box of ashes would be used for a wake that Wanda would arrange for all Mike's friends.

'Larry, can you please tip the ashes into Mike's favourite teapot.' Wanda, Lou and Jay had placed all Mike's paintings around the quaint old sandstone hall.

His favourite music was playing and guests helped themselves to Icy Vo Vos, Jaegermeister, cracker barrel cheese and other favourite delicacies of Mike's. Friends had come from as far as Perth and Brisbane. Larry had also been close to Mike and played trumpet to see his old friend off. He was horrified at dropping some of the ash on the floor, as he tried to get it all into the teapot.

People had been invited to get up and say a few words if they wanted. Lou wrote a beautiful piece. Wanda followed but broke down half way. Recalling silly lunch breaks they took when they worked together, with Mike doing ski jumps all along the main street, Wanda's laughter had quickly turned to tears. Jay relieved her with a few of his own thoughts. A few Ashram friends led a chant. Loads of people spoke. It had been a beautiful send off for a beautiful man.

Wanda and Lou had chosen the same silver ski boots. Lou already wearing a larger size than her mum and she was only 15. Wanda went for a bright green pair of skis. Lou went for blue. For Jay, as usual, it was black on black. Mike would have been proud of them all, in their flash new gear.

After Zell am See, they had skied Kaprun …..a place Wanda and Larry had been to a few times, when their friend Aaron lived and worked there as resort manager. It was just up the road from Zell am See. Jay had been there before ….when he was two years old.

Wanda had then purchased all the lederhosen clothing for Jay to wear to a special New Years Eve party. Some memorable photos in the trunk from that night. He had looked so cute.

New ski gear in tow, the trio set about hitting the various slopes. They stayed close to Zell am See for a couple of days, just in case they needed to take anything back to the shop.

Skied to their hearts content and all was good so off they had driven, towards Innsbruck and then up into the Arlberg region.

St Anton had been amazing but no suitable chalet for a group of forty, in their price range. Wanda promised herself she would return to St Anton another time, without the children. So many tall handsome men. Amazing party atmosphere.

That green Italian wagon had gone like a dream. No puffing up the alpine hills. Always starting the very first time, no matter how cold it got. On they drove into Zurich and down through fabulous Swiss resorts. Day ski passes not as expensive as in Australia ....by a long shot. Generally half the price in most places. Having their own skis, meant they could just stop wherever they fancied. There always seemed to be a zimmer (room) available when they needed to sleep.

One overnight stay was perhaps a little more interesting than the rest, for just one reason. They had come out in the morning and not been able to see that green Italian wagon anywhere. It had been completely buried by a major snow storm during the night. Fun times digging it out.

Several chalets had been inspected and one had been OK but Wanda had a gut feeling the very last one on their two week long trip, was going to be the right one for their group. The chalet was run by a Dutch company. It was in Crans Montana. With skiing to an altitude of 3000 metres, the resort had an excellent track record for Christmas snow. It was perfect.

The people running the chalet were lovely. They could have two whole floors allocated to their group and it would all be catered.

They stayed in that chalet one night. Skied one and a half days. Checked out the ice skating, bowling alley, theatre and loads of wellness centres. With several people in the group not being full on every day skiers, this town would provide loads of alternative things for them to do. Excellent! Wanda started negotiations with the office in Holland, as soon as they returned home.

'Can't believe the deal they are doing for our group. Amazing!' Wanda had just hung the phone up from the chalet owners. The deal was done.

'Now….. Jay. I think these Dutch classes will be the best ones for us. You have loads more vocabulary then I do so I think you will need to be in a more advanced group but they seem to be on at the same times.' Wanda and Jay had spent quite some time exploring all the options for classes. Now it was decided. They would start at the evening college the following Monday.

After two weeks touring around ski resorts, having an unbelievable time, the trio had to really kick themselves back into gear. Wanda hoped improving Jay's Dutch would help get him into more of a career role. She was happy to also be learning. One of the best ways to become a part of a new country, was surely to master the language and local cultural differences. Lou had to take Dutch language at school so she was all sorted. She also did Spanish.

All IB students had to study two languages and, if they were not already Dutch, that home language was automatically one of the two scheduled.

Some wonderful new friends had been made in those Dutch classes Jay and Wanda attended. People from countries all over the world. Senegal, France, Ireland and Bulgaria to name a few.

With Jay's birthday approaching mid-March, they had planned a party at the house and invited all their new friends. Lou also invited a couple of the families from school. Jay had made friends with the brother of Lou's Israeli friend, Leanne. Dan was a lot younger than Jay but he had all the latest computer games and a wide taste in music. Wanda got along well with Leanne's mum and dad too. The dad ran a software company and had plans to give Wanda some work, in the very near future. A new product coming out and he would enlist her help for the launch.

Lou and Jay having their birthdays in March and October, had always provided for a perfect interval between big house parties.

Jay had finished at the call centre company by May. The project had come to a close. He immediately moved across to a large retail company, working in the IT department ...but that would only be a short term assignment. Still no bites from radio stations. Loads of production studios contacted too. Nothing.

Wanda's brother .... Uncle Joe to Lou and Jay .... had a dream to travel to Europe. He had lived with the trio in Sydney, for a few years prior to them leaving. When he split with his wife after twenty five years, he had nowhere to go and no money.

Wanda had looked up to Joe as a father figure growing up. He had been almost 19 years old when she was born and the eldest of the eight children. At the time he split with his wife, Wanda had a full on job back in advertising. She needed some help around the house. Uncle Jo went to live with them, to act as housekeeper and after school driver.

Lou and Jay had always been in different drama, dance and music classes outside of school and had very busy agendas.

Uncle Joe had always been into gambling. He had owned racing greyhounds and in his youth, run different pool halls. Big card games would take place in the back room. He had always seemed happy and obliging when Wanda had been to visit as a little girl, with their mother. Nan had often popped by Joe's pool hall to see if he could give her some money.

When Wanda left Sydney, she told Joe that, if he could save up enough money to buy himself an air ticket to Holland, she would cover his costs while he spent a couple of months with them and they did a bit of travelling. Uncle Joe had cracked it. The ticket was bought and he would arrive in Holland beginning July.

Meanwhile, the time had come when that green Italian wagon had to take up Dutch citizenship. In fact, it had been well past the time and there had been threats of legal action. The Italian license plates had to go. What a procedure. Paperwork and more paperwork. Test after test. Charges for the weirdest of things.

It was a strange feeling, when Wanda finally had the new plates fitted. That adventure in Rome would always be dear to her heart.

'Mum. It doesn't matter about the plates. He will always be that green Italian wagon to us.' Lou had reassured. She and Jay felt the same as Wanda, on this all important subject.

Spring had sprung. Weather was simply perfect. Just as they all liked it. As much as they all loved skiing, it was always nice when the days suddenly warmed and you could be out and about all the time. Mind you ....the Dutch cycled right through the year, come rain or shine. Obviously why they were all so healthy looking.

The amazing re-growth that took place, as trees came back to life and flowers started to blossom, had always been something to behold. Their own garden was a place of new discoveries.

Yellow roses bloomed right at their front door. Red azalea found to be hiding in their corner garden. The winter start to them having taken up residence, had held all of that back from them. Little pine trees along their front fence, also had a sudden burst of growth.

Cycling through the forests around Hillywood, there were wild bush shrubs growing everywhere. Bison were out in the fields and baby deer jumped about, as happy as they might ever be. Cafes down by the lakes all getting into full swing. One favourite had purchased new bean bags to go out on their 'beach' area. Very cool.

Wanda had just been asked out on her first Dutch date. Romance was in the air. He was a colleague of Leanne's dad. Wanda had been to their office for a few meetings. She had taken on the new software launch project and had it all under control. The poor chap had been smitten, the first time he set eyes on Wanda. For her, the keen interest was not really reciprocated ….. but why not at least go on a date and see how it went.

Disaster!

He clearly had the wrong end of the proverbial stick. A first date and he had talked about what he wanted from his next wife and asked Wanda if she had ever considered having more children. Mon dieu! He had seemed so easy going and pleasant in the office. For some reason, the pleasant exchanges Wanda had shared with him, had led him to believe she was his for the taking.

A first and last date with him. Wanda could not get home fast enough.

• CHAPTER SIX •

'THANK GOODNESS UNCLE JOE arrives in a few days. I could not bear it, if mum went out with that guy we met last night. She really does not seem to gel with these Dutch guys she's been meeting Jay. Why on earth she ever agrees to go out with them, is beyond me. I could tell you straight away that they were not her type. Not quite sure what that is but I just know they are not it.'

Lou knew that their friends had only acted out of the best intentions but she had really wished they would all stop trying to pair her mum off, with anyone that came along.

Wanda had always been polite and accepted the invitations. Now that Uncle Joe was arriving and they would soon be off on their trip around Europe, she had the perfect excuse to decline.

Lou had just started her summer holidays and Wanda had arranged everything with her various projects so that she and Lou could travel with Uncle Joe for six weeks.

Jay had a couple of good interviews lined up and was now working at the local video shop. He would not be joining them on this trip. That green Italian wagon had been serviced and Wanda and Lou had prepared a really organised itinerary. Being summer school holidays in Europe, they knew they needed to have bookings in place. Jay would have some company though. Leanne's family were going back to Israel for their holidays and they had asked Jay if he would look after their dog PJ. Her family had planned to be away just 3 weeks so they would drop their dog around to Jay before they left.

Uncle Joe had stopped over in Vietnam, on the way across to Holland. He drove a taxi sometimes in Sydney and it belonged to a nice Vietnamese man, who had arranged for a family member to show him around. Joe loved his time in Vietnam and his private tour guide had taken him well off the beaten track. Wanda could not help think how racist her big brother had been on different occasions but now there he was, mixing it with those very people he had been negative about in the past. It had warmed her heart to see him become so worldly. This was the first time he had ever been out of Australia.

Wanda and Lou travelled around Europe on their British passports but of course Uncle Joe only had an Australian one. They had not realised he would need a visa for one of the countries they planned to visit. Luckily there was an embassy in The Hague he could get that sorted with. A few days exploring Holland had been put at the front of the planned itinerary. Now a visit to The Hague would be included. Scheveningen beach and Rotterdam, thrown in for good measure.

Wanda, Lou and Uncle Joe finally set off in that green Italian wagon, heading directly east into Germany. Their first stop was to be Hannover. Uncle Joe was like a kid in a candy store. Everything was amazing. He did not close his eyes for one minute. Simple things were spotted ongoing and he had deep and meaningful things to say about it all.

Even though Uncle Joe had left school and home when he was just 13 years of age, he had grown up as an avid reader. Particularly interested in everything to do with Germany and the war, he was in absolute awe at actually being in those very places he had read so much about.

'Can you believe those images showing pre and post bombing raid destruction of this city? Unbelievable.' Lou had also been in awe but she was perhaps rather more unbelieving, that the human race could do such horrible things to its fellow humans.

Wanda had thought she might be able to share the driving with Uncle Joe. He had been driving for much longer than she had. As a taxi driver around Sydney, he faced the gambit of driving challenges. She let him loose when they had stopped at a motorway services. Pretty easy driving she thought. Lou and Wanda squirmed and winced, as Uncle Joe narrowly missed the trucks he passed. There had been plenty of room on this six lane motorway but he just could not get the hang of being on the wrong side of the car. Leaving the motorway to enter Berlin, he had totally lost the plot.

Onto the wrong side of the road and straight into panic mode. They all decided it might be better if Wanda got back into the driver's seat. Uncle Joe could try again in a few more days.

They were all amazed to relive the story of Berlin. How you had needed to drive through East Germany to get to Berlin and how Berlin itself, was then divided into East and West. Wanda had done that very drive when she first came to Europe.... going through Checkpoint Charlie to cross between the two very different parts of Berlin. American opulence in West Berlin. Poverty and military control across the wall for East Berlin. Families split. Shortages of just about everything for the East. What an incredible night it must have been, when that Berlin wall had finally come down.

Dresden would be their next stop. It had been completely annihilated during the war. Once the reunification of Germany had taken place in 1990, East Germany had been targeted for massive reconstruction. England's Queen played an important role in much of the funding provided. It had, after all, been the British who had carried out many of the bombing raids causing its destruction.

'The irony of it all,' said Wanda. 'See the special work required for the new bell? It seems there are few people with the skills to reproduce it, in the original style. The work is going to be carried out by the grandson of one of the pilots, from the British squadron that actually flattened it during the war.'

Lou, Wanda and Uncle Joe had read every word on the hoardings surrounding the site, where the cathedral was being rebuilt.

Lou sighed sadly, as she read the part about the bell. She knew that somewhere around 30,000 people had lost their lives in Dresden, during those infamous bombing raids.

It was, however, incredible to see the ornate structures of the baroque and rococo styled buildings having been reconstructed to perfection. The Elbe River providing a magnificent backdrop to this cultural treasure of a city.

Driving south, they had entered into the Czech Republic. Prague was a beautiful city but they had an encounter with the transport police, which overshadowed some of its charm. Wanda had gone to great lengths to work out what tickets they had needed for their underground journey. Tickets duly purchased, they boarded the train. Alighting at their desired station, they were confronted by a man wanting to inspect their tickets. No problem. Correct tickets had been purchased. But no…..they had not inserted their tickets into the machine on entry to the platform they departed from. A hefty fine was to be imposed. Wanda protested with all her might. They were almost escorted to the nearest real police station. After a half hour of heated debate, the fine had to be paid there and then.

Magical Vienna next. Schoenbrunn Palace .... a masterpiece. Originally named because of the artesian well located in its grounds, Schoenbrunn meaning literally 'beautiful spring'. For centuries, it had been home to the ever powerful Habsburgs. Wanda had arranged an extra special treat.

They had tickets to attend a Mozart concert in the Schoenbrunn Orangery. A venue that laid claim to having made the most important of contributions to Mozart's rise to fame.

'We have to make a sneaky call to Jay while the concert is on mum. So sad that he is missing all of this. I told him we would just dial his number and leave the phone running for a bit so he could hear some of the concert.' Lou was always looking out for Jay.

Another big highlight for Uncle Joe would be the Spanish Riding School. Over four hundred years of cultivating understanding on how a horse can move, through systematic training. Renaissance traditions captured and the magnificence of both the stunning white horses and their riders, on show to the world. Superb!

From Austria into Croatia, stopping in Zagreb en route to the incredible Plitvice Lakes. This mountainous lakes area offered up what presented as giant steps for the lakes to perch on. One lake cascading down to the next. Sixteen lakes in all. The unique azure colours changing with the light. Wooden pathways allowed visitors to make their way around the national park, without disturbing its wildlife or fauna. A world heritage site to be treasured by all.

Larry's wife Dee was from Croatia. She had been quite young, when her family immigrated to Australia. Dee and her family came from an island called Korcula. She still had family living there and they were expecting a visit from Wanda, Lou and Uncle Joe.

'We are booked on the ferry leaving Split the day after tomorrow. Only a few hours to sail out to Korcula. A nice cruise on the Adriatic. Think we call in at another island or two on the way. Really big car ferries and the weather report is excellent so all good.' Wanda was showing Lou and Jo the map and telling them all about the apartment she had rented on Korcula.

'Mum. Do you think Dee's family is going to feel a bit awkward meeting us? They haven't even met dad and they're going to meet his ex-wife and daughter.' Lou hadn't been sure about the family visit.

She could not have been any more wrong if she tried. Dee's family turned out to be so hospitable. Her uncle was teaching Uncle Joe how to make wine. They had been privileged to have been asked into his private vat. Bottles had even been entrusted to Uncle Joe to take back to Sydney for Dee's father.

What an amazing island Korcula was. It had recently been discovered by the rich and famous. Huge yachts had started making it an important port of call. The original walled old town and fortress very much still intact. Beautiful!

Back on the car ferry to Split and then straight onto another ferry for the crossing over to Italy. Their apartment in Korcula had water directly behind it so they had purchased lilos to float about on. Now the lilos were used to make beds on the ship's deck. It was an overnight crossing and they would sleep under the stars.

Venice for a couple of days and then up into Shakespeare country and the magic of Verona.

Arriving eventually in Milan, Uncle Joe was beside himself with excitement, at reaching the home of trotting horse races. The trots (harness racing) was born in Milan and the track at San Siro Hippodrome was legendary.

'I won! Did you see him shoot forward at the end? Bloody amazing! Should pay well too. I knew he was a goer. Should have just gone for the win. Bloody champion!' Uncle Joe had picked the winner. Wanda and Lou had wandered off, to take a look around the grounds, and returned just in time to see the race.

Much to his horror, Uncle Joe returned to the counter to collect his winnings and he had won nothing. Lots of arm waving and trying to communicate with the girl who had served him. He had told her number 2 in the 3rd but she had not understood. The ticket said number 3 in the 2nd. He had not checked. Damn! He could not believe it. The winner he thought he had backed paid brilliantly....but not for him.

It had taken some while for Uncle Joe to get over his San Siro mistake. Wanda and Lou had suffered in silence but Wanda's skin had always crawled, when the gambler came out in her big brother.

Crossing into France, Uncle Joe soon came back around and was taking everything in again. Perhaps the planned visit to Monte Carlo Casino helped. Even though he was not afforded an opportunity to place any bets, he had been enthralled by the opulence and had to pinch himself at being in the place he had seen in so many films.

Up into the hills from Nice, they had been fortunate enough to come upon a town celebrating its Corsican connections. Traditional musicians performed in the town centre. They dined on the local fare. A very special evening had been enjoyed and the weather was still absolutely perfect.

Uncle Joe was treated to a special bar-b-que lunch at Janet and Dan's house near Antibes. They all walked the Croisette in Cannes afterwards and noted the celebrities that had been there, for various film festivals. Dan also took the roof off his flash convertible and drove Uncle Joe onto the private wharf, where all the mega-rich folks had their gigantic yachts. Uncle Joe fancied the one with its own helicopter. He had been very impressed with Dan having this special access. Dan's years as captain of one of the big yachts, still kept him at the forefront of things in Antibes.

One day had been spent on the Cannes beach and Uncle Joe had even gone into the water. He couldn't swim but Lou had convinced him he would be safe on one of the lilos. More memorable photos for the family trunk.

'Jay, you need to call Ivan in London. He thinks he might have an opportunity for you at the agency. He was talking about the facilities department but I didn't quite hear what the role was. Getting a foot in the door is what counts. They are one of the largest agency groups in the world so this is an incredible opportunity. Yes. I know you do.

Even so, they have a huge department putting material together for radio and all sorts of media so that might pan out as something you're interested in. You haven't had any nibbles from the networks in Holland so I really think this is the best move forward to a possible career. Anyway, just call and talk it through with Ivan. You know he is a good friend and will only have your best interest at heart.'

Wanda was so excited when Ivan had contacted her about this chance for Jay. He was getting more and more despondent about not getting a good job and the video shop was giving him less and less hours. People killed to get into these big agencies. So lucky.

Lou was not sure she liked the idea of Jay moving to London but she agreed with her mum, that he was spiralling downwards on the job front. Her mum had also arranged that Jay could stay with some other close friends, if he did get the job, so that was good.

Checking out St. Tropez and the beautiful coves of the South of France, they had stopped one night in Marseille. What a vibrant port. Flavours of Africa everywhere. The next day they would drive on to Serignan to stay with English friends who had a holiday home there.

'Leanne's dad has been offered a job running his company's US headquarters but they have to move there straight away. They are looking at cutting their holiday short to rush back to Holland to pack up. They want to know if we can keep PJ?' Lou was shocked by this request suddenly coming down the phone from Leanne.

Jay had been looking after PJ but he had said she was not the sort of dog that would suit their family. He said she barked all the time and had gone to the toilet in the house. Having visited Leanne's family home and never been introduced to the dog, Wanda was a little concerned. Jay loved dogs. Strange that he would say such things about this pooch. Lou had stayed over at Leanne's several times and thought the dog to be lovely. Apparently when Wanda visited, they had locked PJ away in a cupboard. They had not liked her hovering around people when they ate. All of this led Wanda to believe this must not be a terribly good dog.

'When Leanne calls back, tell her we will keep the dog for now. When we get back to Holland we can see how she fits in.'

Wanda told Jay and Lou that, worse case scenario, she could liaise with Leanne's dad's office to have the dog shipped over to them in the States, once they were settled in. A back up plan, in case it did not work out for PJ to join their family.

The week in Serignan was broken up by a couple of nights visiting Barcelona. Their friends' daughter had accompanied them on that little side trip. Sangria, tapas, Gaudi ...... Barcelona was a favourite Wanda went back to time and time again. A cheap apartment right in the centre would do the job nicely this time.

Not like the visit to Barcelona Wanda had paid years back, with her crazy French/Italian lover. He was attending a conference and asked Wanda to join as his partner. They had a suite in the fabulous Hotel Arts.

Marco and Wanda had several encounters, in different parts of the world, over quite some years but she had been surprised to receive that particular invitation. They were really just friends at that point. Everyone at the conference would be there with partners. She figured he must just have been stuck to find someone else.

To her great surprise, it had been much more than she expected. Beautiful jewellery gifted, once they arrived at the suite. The most attentive he had ever been. After the first welcome dinner event, they returned to their suite to find fresh strawberries and champagne by the bathtub. He had arranged for the bath to be filled with bubbles and candles had been lit throughout the suite. Sinking into the hot bath together, he had fed her strawberries via longing kisses. Her toes were sucked for what seemed ages. He spoke to her of a future and how much he had been thinking they would be good together. Wanda had been caught up in the passion but knew only too well that was not the case. He was a playboy and that's how he would stay. She would enjoy the moment and nothing more.

'Brilliant Jay. Well done!' Everyone had shouted down the phone to congratulate Jay on being appointed to his new role with the ad agency in London. He would take the bus across with some of his things, the day after Wanda, Lou and Uncle Joe planned to arrive back in Holland. Just a week away. Two phone interviews had been all it had taken.

A couple more days back in Serignan and then they had travelled up to stay with more English friends, in their stunning cottage near Cahors. The coach house had been prepared for their visit. Such a beautiful setting. Sandstone tiling in and around their pool. Views to die for. They loved it.

Two nights in Paris were on the itinerary, to break their journey back to Holland. Their amazing trip had almost come to an end.

Thank goodness Wanda loved to drive. They had tried getting Uncle Joe back behind the wheel a couple of times but he just could not get it. All way too hard so they had decided back in Italy, that there was no point. Wanda would just do all the driving. No problem at all.

Setting off from Cahors that bright sunny morning, they had all felt very pleased with themselves. So many fantastic adventures. Little did they know, one of the biggest adventures was yet to come.

'The lights have all come on! I'm losing power.' Wanda was helpless. Luckily that green Italian wagon was able to coast to the other side of the roundabout and out of the way of the traffic.

It was a Friday at the beginning of a long weekend. They had planned to arrive back in Holland on the Sunday. Lou needed to go back to school on the Monday. Uncle Joe's flight back to Sydney was leaving on the Tuesday and Jay was booked on a bus, to go to London that same day.

Wanda used her best French to communicate with the road service people. She had never had to call them so needed to make sure she had the correct information first. The roads were full of holiday traffic and of course, that meant loads of people breaking down. Might be a while before they could get anyone out to them.

Quite some hours before a tow truck arrived. His best efforts to get the car going proved fruitless. Having decided what the major part was that would have to be replaced, the driver/mechanic had his office search for a garage that might have it in stock.

Wanda was happy she had taken out the full European road service cover for that green Italian wagon. The car had been doing so well. Now suddenly, right out of the blue, it had just gone to sleep.

Wanda impressed upon the road service folks, how urgent it was for them to get back on the road. She detailed all the various commitments of the people travelling in the car. It was however, Friday of a long weekend. Garages were closed and it seemed the part would need to be ordered in but that could not even be done until the Tuesday. Mon dieu!

There was one possible hope, at a garage in Toulouse. The road service people arranged a hotel for them and they all jumped into the double cab of the very large tow truck. If the car could not be fixed the next day, the road service would then arrange for Uncle Joe and Lou to make their way back to Holland by train. Wanda would have to stay with the car, in Toulouse.

'The train arrived into Paris at Montparnasse and we had to get right across town to Paris Nord, for the train onwards to Amsterdam. So glad you wrote out the sentences I might need to say. Can't believe the taxi driver actually understood me.' Lou was chuffed with her sudden command of French.

Quite an exciting way to conclude Uncle Joe's trip to Europe. He was disappointed they had missed out on looking around Paris of course but the car dramas, train journey and unscheduled night in Toulouse, had all been extremely entertaining. Never mind he and Lou coping so brilliantly with the parisienne taxi driver.

Wanda could not help but feel that fate had dealt her a good hand. There she was in a very lovely all expenses paid hotel in Toulouse, whilst all the chaos unfolded back at home in Holland. She might have been pulling her hair out, trying to get everyone organised. Without her there, they had all beetled along just fine to get themselves sorted.

That green Italian wagon would need to be in the garage a little while longer it seemed. The part had been ordered first thing on the Tuesday but would not arrive until Wednesday. It looked like it would be Thursday, before Wanda could begin her drive north.

Lou had started back at school without any problem whatsoever. Uncle Joe, also fine for his flight back to Sydney. Not quite so for Jay, with his trip to London.

'Mum. My bag was right there, on the floor between my legs. The mongrel ran up from nowhere, grabbed it and just kept running.' Jay had been picking up his ticket at the bus station counter in Amsterdam.

In a flash, the thief had whisked away his bag and was out the front door. Gone!

• CHAPTER SEVEN •

LUCKILY, THE BUS COUNTER ASSISTANT had already scanned Jay's passport. The police came really quickly and an incident report was completed on the spot. Having made a call to the British passport office for Jay, the bus company assistant confirmed he was OK to still travel. His money was safe in his pocket. Main luggage had already been put with everyone else's for loading onto the bus. Jay was happy he could continue on his journey.

Taking all the document copies from the assistant, he had the sudden realisation that over thirty of his favourite CDs, his CD player and new headphones, had all been in his small stolen backpack. The shock kicked in and Jay was devastated.

Wanda knew how much Jay's music meant to him. No way could she begin to replace the CDs but they did have travel insurance so she would get a claim organised, as soon as she could.

'You feeling OK to travel Jay? Difficult to believe people can do such horrible things heh? A young guy about to go on an international bus and another young guy swoops in like that. Just glad you didn't get hurt. Anyway, do give my love to Bern and Martha. Yes. They're picking you up at the bus station. Love you.' Wanda was glad that green Italian wagon was ready to rock and roll again. She drove from Toulouse straight through to Hillywood, stopping only for fuel and toilet breaks.

As Wanda opened the door to their Dutch home, a cute little pooch was sitting there on the stairs. PJ had gone to Wanda straight away and her big brown eyes, stared deeply into Wanda's. There was a strong and immediate connection.

The importation papers read mixed breed / Sheltie Cross.

PJ had a long dark blonde coat that bore a striking resemblance to Wanda's own hair. She even had the same 3-tone blonde effect Wanda paid hair salons to achieve with foils. The sweetest natured dog Wanda had ever met, with the cutest little face.

Leanne's family had given up an absolute treasure. After eight years, it seemed her mum could no longer cope with all the hair PJ shed. There had been a new baby and the constant shedding had been driving her mum crazy. Wanda also shed her own thick mop of hair so PJ would present no problem for her and Lou in that regard.

Wanda had cycled to Lou's school that afternoon, anxious to see Lou as soon as she could. Not wanting to leave PJ behind on her first day back, she had grabbed a backpack that PJ could fit snugly into and carried PJ on her back while she cycled. PJ seemed very happy to be going with Wanda and had not made any sort of fuss at all. Her little head was peering over the top of the backpack, as Lou came out of class. Lots of ooing and ahing from all Lou's chums. Very cute. PJ lapped it up.

They headed straight to the bike shop from school. Much more comfortable for PJ to ride in the little basket they then had fitted to Wanda's bike.

'See mum. I told you PJ was a lovely little pooch.' Lou was glad Wanda felt the same as she did. Neither of them could understand why Jay had not been as receptive.

Lou told Wanda how PJ would bark at the postman, when he tried to put mail through the letterbox slit in their front door. They both found this quite amusing really but maybe Jay had been sleeping in late and PJ was waking him up to be taken out. He loved dogs as much as they did. Weird that he had not taken to PJ as they had.

Leanne's dad had a work visit scheduled back in Holland so Wanda invited him over for dinner. He had clearly missed PJ and was really happy to be able to visit. PJ made an initial fuss of him. Then, as if to say this is my new home now, she planted herself right beside Wanda and did not move for the rest of the evening. There was no way PJ would be moving to the US of A.

Every morning Wanda had jumped out of bed, eager to get on her bike with PJ. Off they would ride to the forest nearby. PJ had sat there in her basket until they reached the woods, waiting for the signal that it was OK to jump out. Wanda then cycled as PJ ran along beside. When PJ saw another dog coming towards her, she would do a major diversion in through the trees. Miraculously, PJ had always managed to meet back up with Wanda further down the track. As soon as she was called, PJ would run to Wanda and leap up for placement back in the basket. They had become the very best of buddies.

'It's a house share with three other guys mum. Yep. They seem really cool. Into music and gaming like me. Think they all have pretty good jobs too.' Jay had been in London a few weeks and was settled into the advertising agency role. He had decided it was time he got out there. Great of Bern and Martha to put him up initially but he really wanted to live with people his own age.

Wanda and Lou had driven across to London for the weekend and taken loads of Jay's things to his new abode. They had also planned to celebrate Lou's birthday, whilst there. Theatre tickets booked and they would all go for a nice meal in the West End beforehand.

Jay's housemates seemed nice enough. Plenty of space for him to set up all his things in his room. Quite close to the railway station so the journey to work was fine. Wanda and Lou had a good feeling that things were going in the right direction for Jay. He even spoke of a girl he quite fancied at work.

Back in Holland, PJ had been staying with friends for the weekend. They had not wanted to give her back, when Lou and Wanda came to collect her on the Monday morning. This seemed to be a common problem. Did not take long for most people to fall head over heels for that pooch. No shortage of friends for PJ to visit, whenever Wanda and Lou went away.

Lou had decided it was time to find some casual work after school. Perhaps babysitting might be the way to go. She prepared a note in both Dutch and English and dropped it through doors around their neighbourhood. Low and behold if she did not discover an English lady, living right over the road from their house.

Denise had come to Holland eighteen years earlier, as an Au Pair. She had fallen in love with a local Dutchman. She and Jan married and had two sons. One called Jay would you believe. The other was Sam. Denise had split up with Jan and often needed a babysitter for her boys. She was a teacher, in the junior part of the International School.

Lou also found an Australian girl, just a little further along the street. She had an English husband. Genna and Neal had two small children that also needed babysitting from time to time.

The first night Denise had booked Lou to mind her boys, she had plans for a big girl's night out. Denise asked Lou if her mum might like to join them. Wanda had not hesitated. She had met Denise briefly and had thought straight away, that she seemed like a lot of fun. How right she was.

That first night out, had proven to be a turning point for Wanda. Denise's friends were all Dutch and the night was full on Dutch in every way. Wanda was in her element. She couldn't understand half of what was being said but she still had a feeling that she was very much at home.

They had been to several small Dutch bars, where everyone behaved as if they had known each other forever. Dancing wherever they stood. Singing all the old Dutch songs, laughing and generally having an amazingly 'boshy' time. The places were simply wall to wall with tall handsome men. Wonderful!

At one bar off Leidseplein, Denise gave the signal that she really fancied one chap in particular. Wanda was pleased to see he was with a friend she also found rather attractive. Once they were all dancing together, Denise decided she was actually not so keen. Wanda, on the other hand, thought her chap Alex was really good company. He spoke excellent English and made her laugh. Extremely charming. A couple of times grabbing her hand and kissing it. He took Wanda's phone number and she had thought it might be nice to meet up with him again.

Must have been close to 5am, when they finally arrived back home. Wanda wasn't fussed about drinking so she had been the designated driver for the night, as proved often to be the case. What a fantastic evening they all had. The only one thing that got to Wanda was the smoking. She stank. All her clothes had needed to go straight outside to air. Denise and her mates were all great fun. What a pity they all smoked. Not that there had been many people out and about that did not. The wall of smoke hit you, almost everywhere you opened a bar door.

'Mum. Is it OK if Danny sleeps over at our place on Saturday night?' Lou had been officially dating Danny for several months now. Having turned 16, she felt she would like to take the next step in their relationship. A deep and meaningful had taken place with her mum.

'We won't be having sex mum.' Lou had made that point very clear. It did not matter. Wanda insisted it was time for Lou to start taking the pill. She would also put condoms in her bedside drawer, just in case things got overheated.

Danny's parents had split up quite some years back. His father worked on large overseas pipeline projects and only visited Danny occasionally. His mum prided herself on being an excellent cook. No sooner had Lou and Danny declared themselves as a couple, than his mother had invited Wanda and Lou over for dinner.

A veritable Indonesian feast had been prepared. Her nasi goreng and sate were quite simply the best Wanda had ever tasted.

November hit with a vengeance. One of the coldest on record. Leanne's mum had given them a doggy jumper she knitted for PJ when they moved to Holland. Wanda and Lou had saved PJ the embarrassment of actually wearing it but now they were thinking it might not be such a bad idea after all. In fact, they had even put a small rug into her bike basket so they could shield her from the cold totally during bike rides.

As for Wanda, all the ski gear came in very handy for the winter bike riding. At one point, even the balaclava had been put into use. Burr. Affa frosty!

Early snow had been falling in the Alps and it looked really good for top Christmas skiing conditions for their confirmed group of thirty four. Friends were flying over from Sydney. Some would drive down from Holland and also from Germany. Others planned to make their way across to Switzerland from the UK by car, plane and train. Everyone had their own arrangements, for getting themselves to the chalet in Crans Montana. Wanda had organised the rest.

New central heating had been fitted throughout their new Dutch home. Thank goodness Wanda had also kept the old freestanding gas heater they had in the living room.

'Mum. That old gas fireplace makes such a difference. Instant massive heat straight away. Makes the room feel nice and cosy.' Lou's friends had all thought so too. Being so close to the town centre and school, it had been her house that everyone went to just to hang. Lou knew her mum was OK with that. They loved having people over and the fridge and cupboard, were always kept at the ready for any hungry visitors.

A couple of Lou's friends also had long train journeys to get home so there was often someone, other than Danny, sleeping over too.

Wanda always insisted on speaking to the parents of anyone sleeping over. She needed to know they were OK with it.

There had never been any problems with irate parents and she wanted to keep it that way.

One major challenge, on the parental front, came when Lou's closest girlfriend decided she wanted to have a declared relationship, with a boy in their group. She was from an Arab country and had really strict parents. No way they would let this happen. The casual meeting place was Lou's house. Her parents had been for afternoon tea and Wanda had also been to their house. It was clear they had trusted

Wanda to keep things above board. Lou had then asked Wanda to turn a bit of a blind eye to her girlfriend being able to meet up with the young man in question at their house.

Nothing more than listening to music or watching TV with the rest of the group but Wanda knew the girl's parents would be disapproving.

How to manoeuvre this one?

'Lou. He seems like a nice boy. Early in the New Year there is going to be a school dance. She needs to tell her parents about that and say she is really stressed that she won't have anyone to take. Everyone has to go in couples. She can ask her parents if they will help her choose a boy from your classmates. Invite everyone here to the house. He needs to get her parents thinking he would be the best date for her to take to the dance. It's the truth anyway. You know how that is always the best path to take.' Lou knew her mum was right.

Wanda was happy to have all of them spend time at the house but she really did not want to get sneaky situations happening that could cause strife. Engaging the girl's parents was the way to go.

'Yes Nan. No Nan. No. He's not from China. Danny was born in Indonesia. Yes. That's right. Up north from Australia.' Lou would talk to Nan every few days and each time she would have to go through the same rhetoric. Nan loved to know what was going on but had trouble holding the information in her head. She was happy though. Lots of visits from her sons that past year and she loved the food in the restaurant where she lived.

Jay had called his Nan from London too, maybe once a month. She always reminded him that her parents were born in London. The story of how they ended up in Australia had been told ongoing. Jay was always receptive. He would talk about food. Nan loved that.

Most of the time she made him laugh. Good old Nan.

This cold November day had been earmarked for several important meetings Wanda needed to attend. Then came the call.

Wanda had spoken to her mum just the day before. Same old conversation. Wanda had reminded her they were in Holland and that they would not be over to see her that day. Her mum had been in good spirits and particularly pleased with the meals that had been served that day. There had been talk of her being moved to a freshly painted and decorated suite. That would be nice.

'She could not have had a better exit if we tried Wanda. Doing one of her normal mid sleep visits to the toilet and she just fell over. They reckon it must have been a sudden and swift heart attack. She had pushed her buzzer and the nurse went straight in but she was already gone. I know. Yep. That's right. Never any problem at all with her heart. Strong as an ox. But there you go.' Joe was sobbing as he spoke. Wanda told him she would call him back in fifteen minutes. Then she burst into tears.

Wanda had half expected this call at any time. Her mum was almost 90. When they had left Sydney, Wanda had told Lou and Jay they would most likely never physically see their Nan again. Now it was a reality, they just couldn't believe it.

'Mum. What's happened?' Lou had just run downstairs saying she was late for school and needed to hurry. She sobbed uncontrollably as her mum finally managed to get the words out about Nan passing.

In between the tears and numerous phone calls with Jay and the family, Wanda had called school to say Lou would not be in. One call to Al and he took on calling the various people Wanda was supposed to meet with that day.

Jay was in shock. He felt isolated. Wanda said she would fly him over to be with her and Lou but he had such a busy schedule at work, he decided he had better carry on with that. Half way through the day he had realised he just couldn't function properly. Strange the effect shock has on you once it sets in.

Wanda discussed at length with Jay and Lou, about not going back to Sydney for the funeral. They all knew how much Nan hated funerals. She just would not go. Her mother, brothers, sister, a son and a daughter had all passed. It had been her desire to just be at home on her own, looking at old photos of them and remembering happy times. Nan did not believe in funerals in any way shape or form. Flying all that way back to be at hers, made no sense at all. They would have their own little ceremony in Holland.

'No. We won't be coming back. You guys need to do whatever you think the family want. It's not about mum. She hated funerals, you know that. It's now just about you all being able to grieve as you need to. Just do what works for you and I'm happy to chip in.' Wanda had spoken to her brothers several times and discussed funeral arrangements. It seemed people thought Wanda was the golden child and had some bottomless pit of access to funds. A lavish funeral had been unfolding before her eyes.

'Really? They're all coming up from Melbourne and want to see their Nan to say goodbye. Crikey! Mum would be horrified. OK. If you guys want to do that open casket thing, then at least tell the funeral director to perm her hair - and for goodness sakes, no fake smile added to her face please.' It was all getting way out of hand.

Wanda had already put in way more money than the others and now someone had another bright idea that would cost even more. Wanda had to say no.

'If you guys really want to do it.....maybe ask the grandchildren to put some money into the pot.'

Wanda phoned Joe daily at that point. He was the head of the family. She encouraged him to speak at the funeral. Larry went to represent Wanda and their children. Played his trumpet to see Nan off. Wanda wrote a beautiful eulogy for Joe to read. He delivered it perfectly and was glad he had spoken.

Jay was ever so spiritual. As the shock of Nan being gone settled in, he found a peaceful connection to her that eased his sadness. He decided not to fly over to join Lou and his mum for their own little Dutch church service, on the day of Nan's funeral. He was doing his grieving in his own way. Only a few weeks until he would be back in Holland and off on Christmas holidays with Wanda and Lou. He had switched his brain over to all the happy memories he had of Nan and would stay focused on those.

Wanda and Lou were on the phone to all the family at the conclusion of the Sydney funeral. They had been to church in Hillywood earlier that day. Prayers and quiet sadness now concluded, as they shared silly stories of life's moments shared with Nan. Lou was proud of her dad having played his trumpet for everyone. It warmed her heart that he was still close to all of her mum's family.

As the weeks passed, Lou and Wanda often found themselves off somewhere deep in thought and missing Nan. Those frequent and repetitive phone calls. The gifts they had been constantly choosing to send to Nan. Tears would well up in their eyes. They would sigh with heavy hearts and know there was a gap in their lives that could never be filled.

Nan was one of a kind. The eight children she had given birth to had produced twenty one grandchildren and twenty six great grandchildren…. so far.

PJ had a great sense for things. She had known something was up. No excited requests to be going out. The usual following Wanda around at all times but a quiet cuddle up to the feet, whenever she had stopped in one place for any time at all. Remarkable!

'Fancy a night out with the girls darling?' Denise had become a really good friend to Wanda. She had given her enough quiet time to reflect and now she thought it would do Wanda good to have a few laughs. Not too long before Wanda would have visitors arriving from Sydney so she had better start getting in the party mood.

That night Wanda also met up with Alex again. He had called several times since that first night out in Amsterdam and been very caring about the loss of her mother. The end of night review with Denise was however, not very positive.

'He is a laugh but I'm not sure I actually want to go out with him.' Alex had asked Wanda out to dinner the next evening and she had said yes but later wasn't so sure. She had called on Denise to reassure her. Denise thought he seemed really nice.

Wanda and Alex dated a few times. On the second date, he had cooked for her in his apartment.

'Really average sex I'm afraid.' Wanda confided to Denise the next day.

They did not go into the nitty gritty. Denise had not had sex for over a year so she was unsympathetic and could only retort. 'Better than nothing.'

Poor Alex knew Wanda could take him or leave him but he had decided, he would rather have it that way than not have her at all.

Why did December always get so crazy?

Not even the end of the school year in Europe but they still got into panics about end of year shows and things to be delivered before the first term finished.

Lou's drama group had been rehearsing their version of The Phantom of the Opera for what seemed ages. Lou had a lead vocal to perform. Pity the show took place before Jay came home but Denise had gone along to see the budding star with Wanda.

'Fantastic Lou. You are a born actor.' Denise was seriously impressed and naturally, so was Wanda.

Jay had the agency Christmas party to attend. The girl he fancied was giving him the cold shoulder and he had another girl from 'The Gallery' that seemed keen. Jay had discovered this squat full of artists, just near where he lived. He had often been DJ for their concert nights and this girl had come on to him big time. He might see where that led now.

Work was OK but Jay wasn't sure he liked the world of advertising. The pressure of short lead times had been getting to him a bit.

He was looking forward to flying back to Holland and being with his family.

Wanda completed her projects as promised and had now cleared the way for devoting all her time to Christmas, the close friends that were due to arrive and the big ski trip they had planned.

Cath and Rose arrived from Sydney, the day after Jay flew in from London. Lou and Rose had been to pre-school together, back in Sydney, and stayed friends all that time. Cath and Wanda were also the best of friends. Cath's son Bill had been a mate of Jay's too and they were all disappointed he had not been able to come along for this trip.

That green Italian wagon had gone in for a full service and extra winter treatments, for the big drive to Switzerland. There would be five of them in the car so Wanda had also asked the garage to fit a roof box, for all their ski gear.

'Oh no. You have to be kidding! I do not believe it!' Wanda listened to Cath, crying down the phone as she spoke. Cath had gone into the centre, to do a little shopping. There had been a lady looking around at clothes, in the same area Cath was exploring. Seemingly quite a nice chatty woman. Cath told her she did not speak Dutch and the woman immediately spoke to her in perfect English. They exchanged pleasantries.

Cath had put her handbag down on the floor for just a moment. Had not noticed anything until later, when she went to pay at the till. Stupidly, she had left her purse sitting on top of the open handbag. Cath had not seen the woman make her move.

The purse was gone.

• CHAPTER EIGHT •

CATH HAD SPENT HOUR AFTER HOUR, contacting companies about her various credit and bank cards. The travel insurance company had sounded reasonably helpful but there was no way she could have replacement cards, before they left Holland. She thanked her lucky stars she was with Wanda.

'Ridiculous they can't do something straight away. What if you were just out there travelling? You would be well stuck. Get onto them when you get back to Sydney and don't worry about it anymore. I'll cover whatever you need and you can pay me back later.' Wanda reassured her.

Cath and Wanda had become great friends, over the twelve or so years they had known each other. They met at the pre-school Lou and Rose attended in Sydney. Cath's husband had just gone off with another women and she was devastated. She had suddenly become a single mum with two children, just like Wanda. They both had a son and daughter, although Cath's were each eighteen months older than Lou and Jay. Throughout the years, they had been there for each other through thick and thin. The children went to the same schools and also became good mates. Ski trips to the Snowy Mountains or the simple Friday night pizza and movie gatherings. They enjoyed spending time together and had a real sense of extended family bond. They were all sad that Cath's son Bill had been unable to join in for this special ski holiday in Switzerland.

That green Italian wagon was equipped with a rented top box so they could fit in all their skis, boots and luggage for five people. It purred along the freeways, carrying the load with no trouble at all.

An early start and Brussels earmarked for a walk around the old town centre and lunch. Cath had travelled around Europe when she was young but Rose had only been to Scotland, to the borders town where Cath was born and her parents had also grown up.

They planned to make the most of the 1000km drive from Hillywood to Crans Montana in Switzerland. Two hours to Brussels and then just over an hour and they were in Luxembourg, taking a short walk. Soon they had crossed into France. A vineyard was chosen for their next break. They loved to explore new wines. Driving on through Metz, they saw the roman influence and 3,000 years of history they had read about.

That night they stayed in a beautiful youth hostel in Freiburg, Germany. Cheap accommodation and always fun to hear stories from other travellers. The next day they made their way to stunning Lake Geneva. More of an inland sea really and surrounded by the most majestic snow-capped Alps. A second night's stopover had been booked, at a charming little hotel overlooking the lake. They were in good time to enjoy its blue blue waters, before the sun set.

It never ceased to amaze them how quickly you could be in a different country in Europe. Such varied cultures, all highlighted by the speaking of different languages. Beautiful!

Wanda had 34 friends coming together for this special New Year week, in the snow covered mountains of Switzerland. Some of them had never met each other but she knew they would all get along. The majority drove across from the UK. Some came by plane and others by train. A few made their way from Holland and a couple from Germany.

American, English, Scottish, Dutch, German, Norwegian, Swedish, Australian…….. a mix of nationalities, ages and interests but all with a common desire to have fun. Wanda reflected on how lucky she was to have so many truly great friends.

The chalet was perfect. Parking at the front door. Two entire floors dedicated for their group. Each floor with its own large living room. The children were quick to claim one for themselves. That worked well. The adults got the upper level, with the largest balcony. A separate ground floor dining room had been allocated to their group and full catering was included. Fantastic food and plenty of it.

Everyone was more than pleased with the deal Wanda had made and had chipped in for a gift to show their appreciation.

'Oh wow. So soft. And I love the colour. Fits perfectly. You shouldn't have!' The pale blue zip up soft knit jacket was on Wanda in an instant and remained so for much of the trip.

'What did you bring for the Beach Party on New Year's Eve?' had then been a popular first question as the group started mingling.

Wanda had arranged a few different fun things for evenings. One night, a fantastic concert in the town hall. Another was tobogganing, which proved to be a big hit. Then the bowling night. What a total hoot that turned out to be.

'Leave this one to me Wanda. All those years of being a resort rep can finally pay off.' David beamed as he set about planning who should be in what team and even organising prizes. He was in his element.

Day two at the chalet the snow started to fall and fall and fall. The skiers were elated! Just a short walk down to the main cable car and there was even a little shuttle bus, if you wanted to wait. As day six came to a close, they had however not quite bargained for the blizzard that would take place that night.

'Good grief. The cars have totally disappeared! Mum. Come and take a look.' Jay was paying an early morning visit to the loo and most of the group were still asleep. He had not believed his eyes, when he took a quick look outside.

As Wanda listened to the radio news, she became more and more concerned. They had planned to ski for the morning and start out for the return to Holland, after lunch. They would only be driving a couple of hours before their planned overnight stop. Not skiing that day would be the least of their concerns. The blizzard had been causing havoc everywhere and showed no sign of letting up. Record snow falls were bringing traffic to a standstill, right across Europe.

'It looks so beautiful mum.'

Lou was right of course. But ……….

As everyone surfaced, it became clear it would be all hands on deck, to dig the cars out of the snow. They all set to work.

Nobody had snow chains. The snow cats had not made their way up to the chalet yet either. Some of the group had flights to make. Others had cross channel ferry bookings. They had planned to leave early morning but this was looking less and less likely, as the snow continued to fall.

'Franky! Look out!' Lou screamed, as the soft edge of the road suddenly seemed to suck Franky down the embankment. Luckily he had only fallen a short distance, having been stopped by a pole buried by the snow. The sheer drop below seemed endless.

Franky's dad was from Colorado. Franky had grown up with snow. He was in his ski gear and Lou was keeping him calm. She was feeling guilty that she had wandered off with Franky. They had gone out to help dig but could not resist playing in the fresh white stuff.

'They can't seem to hear me calling so I will quickly run back for help. Don't move an inch. OK?' Lou trusted Franky. He was only 9 but he knew to keep very still. All the same, Lou was shaking with fear. What if he did move? What if that pole was not secure? Way too many 'what ifs' for her liking.

Franky's dad Ken was a man of the mountains. Lou was confident he would soon have Franky up and she could make him a nice hot drink. Must be getting cold covered by all that snow. But where was Ken. Lou's heart sank when she saw their car was gone.

'Mum. Franky has fallen down the embankment! I can't see Ken anywhere!' Lou was starting to get a little hysterical.

'Their vehicle was the first one dug out. It's a 4 wheel drive so he went to organise a snow cat to get up here, to clear the road. Quick! Let's see who has a rope.' Wanda swung into action.

Franky's mum Clara and sister Lena, saw Wanda and Lou running off with a rope. They followed. A large noose was made on one end of the rope and carefully thrown down to Franky. He was a little slow with responses by now but managed to get the rope over his head and arms. The noose tightened, as the four slowly dragged him up.

Franky recovered with a warm shower but more dramas were unfolding. Snow was forecast to keep falling so, once the cars were dug out, everyone was loading up and heading off. Ken had been successful at getting the snow cat up to the chalet but they had left now and the road would not stay driveable for long.

The last of the bags had gone into Bern and Martha's van, when Martha suddenly lost her footing and went flying. The landing had not been a good one. A twisted ankle at the very least. They would need to stop at the medical centre, down in the valley. Quite likely Bern would need to do all the driving back to England.

David had left his vehicle down at the cable car the night before. One too many après drinks. He had planned to jump in the car with Bern and the family but now Martha was in the back seat with her leg stretched across to her daughter's lap.

'I'll drive you down to your car,' Jay was quick to offer.

That green Italian wagon was not a 4 wheel drive. David was not sure Jay quite understood the impact of all this snow.

No problem at all. David was at his car and soon on his way. Jay popped into the lift ticket office, to get the passes refunded. Heading back up hill to the chalet was quite a different matter.

'It just keeps stopping and next thing I know I'm sliding back down the road!' Jay shouted loudly to a kind man who stopped to see if he could help.

Lesson 'no high revving in these conditions' unfolded. Jay eventually got it. A suitable audience was on hand at the chalet entrance, when Jay drove back into the car park. They had all been very impressed. So had Jay.

Sally and her three boys had left really early in a 4 wheel drive taxi to the train station. They had arrived at Geneva airport only to find there would be no flight for them that day.

Traffic back to Lausanne moved at a snail's pace. Visibility very limited. Wanda was glad she had booked to stay at that same little hotel on the lake that night.

Bern and Martha ended up sleeping in their vehicle. All roads to Calais had been turned into parking lots. They were lucky to at least have pulled off the motorway at services, where they could eat and use the toilets. It had become their camping spot for the night.

Despite all the challenges making their way home, everyone was texting furiously to say was a great week they had spent together.

The snow stopped during that night and the following day broke with blue skies. That green Italian wagon was now headed for the Rhine River in Germany.

Stunning! So still. The beauty of snow covered forests, where tree branches sat decorated with high ridges of snow. Totally overwhelming!

Driving right alongside the river, they had been in absolute awe. One quaint village after another. So many fairy tale castles up in the rolling green hills, just back from the river on both sides. Massive river barges, carrying loads of gravel and grain. Generally a small car on the deck plus a small boat. Appropriate winch to get them ashore at routine stops. Some say these barge drivers have more than one family. Not spending long with any one of them. The river being their only true partner in life.

A 15th century Inn had been chosen for the next night. Secure parking a priority, as with any of the places Wanda booked. No fun having to unpack everything, when they stopped over somewhere. The Moselle River joined the Rhine near this village and a charming little restaurant held a tasting of the Moselle wines that night. Generally a bit sweet for Wanda's liking but the others seemed suitably impressed. Local stew with dumplings, proved to be a hit with them all.

Back in Hillywood, Lou and Wanda introduced Rose and Cath to the nightlife and local sights they loved. It was soon time for them to leave.

'I really miss Cath and Rose mum. And now Jay has gone back to London too. Just you me and PJ again.' Lou had been visited by her school chums and recounted her holiday adventures. After they had left, Wanda reminded her of assignment work due. Diverting Wanda's attention to the departed friends had seemed a good move.

Lou was doing really well with her International Baccalaureate but it had started to get much tougher, now she was in her final two years of IB. Her boyfriend Danny was still away so it was a good time for her to really focus and get that assignment done.

Only another year or so and they would be arranging their move to the UK for Lou to attend University. Wanda thought it might be a good idea, for her to start looking at work opportunities in London. She had quite some freelance work in Holland but not enough. With all the renovations to the house, travel and generally keeping fun at the top of the priority list, Wanda had drained all her reserve funds. The saving grace had been the block of land she had bought in Queensland when she was 20. That had finally sold, after a few years of trying. The money she fetched had strangely enough almost exactly matched the amount of overdraft facility she had spent. Excellent! She had moved back into the black again.

Wanda could not believe it when she landed a role with a major UK publishing organisation. As Director of Marketing for Europe, Wanda would be able to work from either their London or Utrecht offices. Perfect. A hefty salary and she could start straight away. Plan being to kick off in Utrecht. Just a twenty minute drive from Hillywood.

They would move to London the following year, once Lou was finished her IB. Al at the ready to take over any of the freelance business opportunities Wanda had.

'Marco was right. You are loads of fun. I was thinking this move to Amsterdam might be a tough one but now I think it's going to be great. All I need is for you to come and run the marketing communications for us. You already know my boss Bob. He can't speak highly enough of you. Would be a real bonus, if I could tell him you have agreed to join the team.' Patty was glad Marco had introduced her to Wanda.

Patty worked under Bob, at the General's headquarters in Paris. He had been moved to a different business, based in Amsterdam, and he wanted Patty to move up and lead his marketing. Marco once worked for the General in Paris too, some years earlier, running marketing communications for Europe. He and Wanda met in Singapore, when she was in the same role for Asia many years earlier. The affair began there but Wanda quickly saw he was a playboy and decided just to stay friends and work colleagues.

After Wanda left that position, Bob had gone across to head the business. He had not actually met Wanda but had heard from loads of his team, how good she was at her job. He would indeed be delighted if Patty managed to convince Wanda to join the team in Amsterdam, to lead communications. Wanda was flattered but it had only been 6 months since she started her new role in Utrecht.

Wanda felt pleased with her achievements for that business. The European business leader was demanding but goals were exceeded so all should be well, right? Not so. Head of sales lived with the boss it seemed. A lesbian couple. Individually, they were good business people but together they were explosive. Shouting and tantrums, not being things Wanda particularly cared to get used to.

It also seemed the boss had more than a business interest in Wanda. Eek. Luckily her boss was as large in size as she was in voice so Wanda would know when she was headed towards her office. Amazing how Wanda always seemed to be on the phone. As Wanda continually declined social invitations, the boss became more and more difficult. The opportunity to work in London, also looked likely not to ever eventuate. Meanwhile, Wanda was being pursued by Patty, for an excellent job back with the General. She finally accepted.

'It's quite different to the medical imaging equipment business Jay. This part of the General's business is about 70,000 semi-trailers across Europe. You'll like Damon. He does all our web development work. Sits right opposite me so I keep annoying him with silly computer questions. Takes it very well. You know how stupid I can be with computers. He's Belgian and he ran a nightclub there. You can compare notes on DJ equipment. Think he might be a bit of a computer gamer too. Next time you're over from London, we'll arrange a get together. His girlfriend is a real sweetie too.'

Wanda chatted with Jay a few times each week. She was happy to hear him well settled into his adult life in London.

'Sounds good Mum. I should be able to come over in a couple of weeks. Been frantic here. The agency won some new business and things are crazy at work. I've also had two gigs this week at the gallery and my mate and I recorded another track for the new album. All go.'

No sooner had Wanda started her new role with the General, than US global headquarters launched an all-out effort for businesses throughout the world, to carry the company brand fully and to detailed standards. Historically the General acquired a company and let them continue with their own branding. That was to change in a hurry.

The trailer business had been in the General's stable for over ten years, under a well-established brand. How fortuitous. This was right up Wanda's street. Second nature almost.

She developed a plan for maintaining current brand equity, whilst at the same time moving across to the General's requirements. She had done it so well in fact, that she was called upon by European headquarters to help other smaller operations, where there had been no specific expertise in the team.

As the year progressed, Wanda also led the opening of new offices in emerging markets like Latvia and the Czech Republic.

She worked with country managers in Germany, France, Spain and the UK to commission local suppliers for PR, Exhibitions and all forms of exciting promotions.

With the job came a whole new set of social opportunities. It seemed Wanda was always being asked to a borrel, a dinner, out dancing and to generally hang with fellow workers.

In the summer months, a group of them signed up for rowing lessons. The great Amstel River was on the office doorstep. Those balmy nights proved to be more about the drinks afterwards than the rowing. A good time was had by all.

Wanda loved life and led it to the full but the elusive Mr Right was nowhere to be seen. She had decided to stop seeing Alex after a few dates. He was basically a nice guy but just so average. There had been loads of other close encounters but it seemed not one of them could hold Wanda's attention for very long.

Her neighbour Genna had introduced her a builder friend. Good looking. English. Quite funny really. Liked to hug. Something that was indeed very important to Wanda. Sex had been OK. The trouble was, when he had a drink or two and started talking about an ex-girlfriend he had lived with for many years. It was all her fault he had come to Holland. Poor bugger. 'Why didn't he just go back?' Wanda would think. Way too negative for her.

Then there had been Ton. Met him out bopping with Denise, in Amsterdam one night. A totally gorgeous and very tall Dutchman. Great to look at but not much staying power when they got into bed. Wanda had seen him a few times, to see if things improved. It just got worse. Turned out he believed he only had a few years to live. Not sure why. Just had a feeling. How pleasant. Not!

Wanda had decided it was all just too hard. She had such a full life with work, the children and so many friends. Really no point interrupting all of that, for anyone she didn't find particularly special.

When Denise went through a reconciliation period with her ex-husband Jan, the bopping nights out came to a standstill. Wanda was happy to lay low for a while. Would be great if Denise and Jan could finally work things out. What a pair they had been.

Denise had moved across from London to work as an au pair with a British family, eighteen years prior. She and Jan met and fell in love. They travelled the world together and eventually got married in Holland, then had two sons. They had divorced a year before Wanda moved to the street but seemed to get back together on a regular basis.

'Well? He is here every day now it seems my dear. Is Jan going to move back in?' Wanda quizzed Denise on the phone, seeing Jan leave the house yet again that morning.

Jan did indeed move back in.

Their boys were so happy and things seemed to be going along great, for a few months. Wanda always thought they were well suited.

Denise was so happy when they were back together as a family. It was clear Jan loved her and the boys deeply.

'It's tough maintaining a relationship all these years and trying to keep the passion alive. Why don't you guys go off for a romantic weekend somewhere and the boys can stay with us?' Wanda had seen the strain coming back and wanted to help. She felt really close to them both.

'I see you hugging the boys all the time but never with Jan. Failed my own marriage so I really can't talk but it's so much easier when you're on the outside looking in,' she said quietly to Denise.

Denise booked a spa hotel, just an hour away by car. Wanda had a word with Jan the day before they were going, to give him a few tips on things that might make a difference.

'Fix a time to pick her up and make sure the car is sparkling clean. Be on time. Wear something new and make it clear you've taken care with your appearance. Don't forget the cologne she loves. It drives her crazy. Denise always dresses up and she's a stunning looking woman so you really need to let her know that you notice that. It can just be the way you look at her admiringly and call her beautiful. When you head to the car, just stop and hold both her hands. Tell her how happy you are about this escape together and how much she means to you. Give her the biggest hug you have ever given and don't let her go until you move to kiss her softly.

You know how much she loves to listen to Barry White so maybe have a CD in when you start the car. Talk about sex before you even get near a bed. Start to arouse her when you know it won't actually go anywhere. Words, looks and gentle touching.

The thoughts will linger. When you finally get to love making, ask her what she wants. If she goes quiet, then suggest things. Say them out loud and move slowly towards that point of connection. Make yourself really hot for each other and keep telling her how much you love her. What do you think?'

Jan felt pretty comfortable talking with Wanda and he knew she would say the same sorts of things to Denise. He was up for giving it his best shot. Just hoped Denise was too.

Wanda did say similar things to Denise. More really about the fact she had said them to Jan. All she really wanted Denise to do was stay open and not be her usual very demanding self. They had talked about it a lot. Wanda had a habit of being the same way in the past. They really did learn from each other.

The romantic weekend provided a new glue for Denise and Jan. No-one was sure how long it might last, once they were back to the strains of parenting and everything else life throws at people.

Denise and Jan were diverted by the horrors of cancer striking a very close friend. Just had her 40th birthday celebrations. Chain smoking had grabbed her big time. She was going downhill fast. So very sad. Husband sobbing most days and unable to drag himself to work. Two children that were too young to fathom what was really happening. Denise was at their house every day for two months, doing whatever she could. Jan was a brick and really kept their family and life together.

'Wanda, you should join us later at our house. It's New Year's Eve and Jan wants the boys to have their fireworks and do some laughing. I've done all I can do here today and they don't think she will come out of this coma so I'm coming home. A few other people are popping by too,' Denise said in a drained voice but with a determination to make the night a pleasant one for her family.

'Those friends of ours that arrived from Australia last month might be back here tonight. OK to bring them over too? Not sure what has happened but they decided not to continue the drive down to Marseille,' replied Wanda. No problem for Denise.

Lou was heading out with Danny to meet up with their friends, to celebrate Oud en Nieuw (old and new being the Dutch way of referring to 31 December celebrations).

Must have been around 7pm that New Year's Eve when Mel, Anna and Cindy arrived back at Wanda's. They had planned a big driving tour around Europe that should have taken months. Just a few weeks since they arrived from Sydney and only a week or so since they left Hillywood for their adventure.

As they entered the house, Wanda could see they were all in a bad way.

Mel went straight upstairs with Cindy. She just wanted to go to bed and knew where she would be sleeping. Wanda had given her Jay's room, when they arrived the first time. He had gigs so had not made it home from London that year.

'Cindy cut her wrist last night. She says she just wants to be dead!'

Anna was sobbing and shaking uncontrollably as she fell to the chair.

Back in Sydney, there had been some testing done on Cindy and medication had been provided. She was 21 now and had challenges identified since her early teens. Initially her behaviour had just been dismissed by Anna and Mel as being because she was an only child.

Once she hit puberty, it had all become increasingly dangerous.

Cindy's interest in boys had become a major problem and they had moved her to an all-girls high school. As if that would do any good. She had finally dropped out and had trouble finding work.

A year or so earlier, back in Sydney, Ann had received a call from Cindy to say she was in Bali. She had been out the night before and met a 'very lovely man who had taken her travelling'.

She had her passport with her as ID to get into clubs. He saw it and said they should take a mystery flight off on an adventure. After one day, and Cindy finally starting to feel she had done the wrong thing, the lovely man was putting her back on a plane to Sydney. She had freaked out on him totally.

Her inability to reason well, had been attributed to a disease with a very long name and drugs had been prescribed for that disease. They had done little to change her behaviour, accept to make her more insecure. Mel and Anna had become even more over-protective. Cindy's self-confidence had become non-existent.

'OK Anna. It's 9pm now and you and I are going over to the party at Denise and Jan's. We can leave a note for Mel to come over if he wakes up. Cindy is fast asleep too. We are just across the street if they need us,' Wanda had insisted.

Denise had the music pumped up and was thrilled to see Wanda and Anna. The bopping began. Jan was shaking a leg. Several neighbours had come in and a few of Jan's rugby mates. The house was rocking. Even Pat was dancing in his wheelchair.

Pat was English and lived around the corner. Poor guy had Leukaemia and was in a pretty bad state but still managed to laugh and enjoy himself.

At midnight, it was out into the street in true Dutch style. People everywhere sending off rockets and lighting fireworks. Magic! The first time Wanda had experienced this, she had been horrified. Back in Australia they had very strict controls and fireworks were only allowed in an organised group fashion. A difficult one. She could see how much the Dutch enjoyed their way of doing this and had always enjoyed it herself too.

Another hour of dancing afterwards, then they had all begun to fade. Pat decided he would head around the corner. Anna and Wanda thought they should make sure he got back safely. They had just wheeled him home when the phone rang. Ian was on the floor and couldn't get himself up. He had missed the bed when moving across from the wheelchair. As Anna and Wanda turned to go back, the phone rang again.

'I'm coming straight back now. You and Jan go straight away. I can sleep over with the boys. Anna will go sort Pat out', Wanda was trying to calm a tearful Denise. The cancer had taken its final hold on her friend. She was breathing her last breaths.

• CHAPTER NINE •

WANDA HAD WOKEN THE NEXT morning bright and early. The boys were still sleeping when Denise and Jan arrived home. It was clear they had spent a tearful and sleepless night. A beautiful young friend's dead body had been mourned over for hours. Tragic!

Making her way back across the street, Wanda found her own home to be in rather a state. Cindy had apparently woken up, shortly after Wanda and Anna went across the street to Denise the night before. New Year's Eve and Cindy wanted to party. Mel woke to find Cindy gone, just prior to Anna arriving back. He called the police.

'She is 21 and has gone out on her own to find some fun? Sorry sir but there is really nothing we can do. Let us know if you don't hear from her in 48hrs.' The policeman had sarcastically responded.

Anna and Mel looked like death warmed up, sitting there with coffees as Wanda arrived home. Then the phone call from Cindy.

'He is such a lovely guy mum. Think he said he was from Turkey originally. I'm still with him. Just about to come back there so I can change my clothes. He wants to take me to the movies.'

The few days that followed added nicely to this surreal week.

Cindy's new love ended within 24hrs. Mel and Anna decided they were crazy to think they could travel Europe with Cindy. She needed professional help. Mel's sister in England thought she might be able to get that. Their dog was due to arrive from Sydney and had to be in Europe for three months before it could go to the UK. It was agreed.

Anna and Ace (the dog) would stay with Wanda, Lou and PJ for those three months. Mel would take Cindy to England and get on with the testing his sister had suggested.

Ace arrived a few days later. Mel collected her from Schiphol. He was more traumatised than the dog. Ace had taken the travel in her stride but Mel was talking to her like a baby and carrying her just like one too. PJ had not been at all keen initially. She just barked at Ace when she came in the house, then ran to hide.

PJ had become very territorial. She would lay on the fourth step of the staircase going up, to keep a look out through the glass front door. Not that you could actually see through. It was a frosted type of glass. She still saw movements though and, when it came to the postman, she could smell him a mile away. As he put the mail through the slit in the door, she barked so fiercely that he had thought there was a big dog behind the door. He was really scared. Wanda had taken PJ out to meet him one day, holding her like a little child in her arms. So cute! He was still scared.

'Keep that dog away from me', he had exclaimed in his best English.

As Mel and Cindy drove off, Anna went into a sort of coma state.

It took four or five days for her to realise fully, they were actually gone. Coming back from the brink of a major nervous breakdown, would take a lot longer.

Lots of cycling and breathing the fresh Dutch air helped Anna loads. Being around the positive Wanda and Lou did even more.

One month into Anna's stay with Wanda, it was agreed they were ready for a night out bopping. Denise would of course need to join them. She and Jan had split up yet again. Anna had also told Mel that she didn't think she could ever live with him again.

Denise and Anna were determined to drown their sorrows ...literally. Wanda, the designated driver, had stayed as sober as a judge but just as keen to rock that night away.

'How cute is he?' Anna had exclaimed to Wanda as she came up for air. Snogging with this handsome young man, right there at the bar. Mind you. It was only 5ft from the bar to the far side wall so it really wouldn't make much difference where she had been snogging. Typical Dutch 'brown café'. So tiny and crammed pack with people.

Everyone singing and laughing. Great fun!

As the weeks progressed, Anna had seen that cute young man several times. They had grown closer and closer.

Mel had been over to stay for a weekend but there was no renewal of status. They had not had sex for over two years and it was not about to change now. In any case, it seemed Mel was less interested in seeing Anna, than he was in spending time with Ace.

Anna was pleased Mel's sister was looking after him and Cindy exceptionally well. Cindy was much better off without both parents constantly on her case. She had been diagnosed with Asperger's and was now in the system, to finally get the help she needed.

Another month passed and Anna had been over to stay at Mel's sister's so she could spend some time with Cindy. Things were so much calmer and Mel had gone out of his way to try and win Anna back. Although Anna missed her Dutchman terribly, she began to think she should try to make her marriage work.

Ace and PJ had become such good mates. They were now sleeping in the one large doggy bed.

'Just a few more weeks and you'll be making your way to England Anna. Let's do a little road trip before then and maybe do some skiing. Lou will be away on a school excursion.' Wanda enticed Anna, as she contemplated that green Italian wagon getting back on the road again.

Anna had told her Dutchman it was over. A fun trip with Wanda was just what the doctor ordered, to take her mind off him.

It was funny how Anna and Wanda had become such good friends. As Wanda thought back, it seemed like another life, when she had lived with Mel back in Brisbane so very long ago. Him being the smooth sophisticated Englishman. Her having moved up from Sydney to escape a teenage romance, which had come to a traumatic end after six years.

Wanda was 19 then and Mel had shown her that love making was more than just kissing and hugging, that led to sufferance of painful intercourse. He knew what he was doing. Foreplay was everything.

Wanda moved to England with Mel when she was 21. His mother became her adopted English mum. Even when she and Mel had split up several years into the relationship, his family remained her English family.

Years later, Mel met Anna. He had swept her off her feet and they had married within the year. Cindy was born a couple of years later and they had all moved to Sydney to live.

Initially Anna had been a little unsure of how she felt, being around Wanda. Family gatherings, when they were back in the UK, meant they would all be present. The more Anna spoke to Wanda, the more she realised how well they got along.

Once Wanda and Larry moved to Sydney with Jay and Lou, they had started to socialise quite a bit. It was clear that Wanda and Anna had a lot in common. A real friendship had blossomed.

Anna was such a chirpy little redhead. Always happy and positive. Mel could be fun but, more often than not, as soon as the audience had left, he sunk lower than low. When he was in Australia he wanted to be in England. Once back in England he wanted to be in Australia. Never satisfied. Always feeling he had missed the boat somehow. Wanda could never understand how Anna had stayed so positive and committed to Mel all these years.

'I found this great little bed and breakfast place, right in the centre of St. Anton. Really good price. We can take the drive along the Rhine River. A favourite of mine and I know you'll love it too.'

Wanda was full speed ahead making arrangements for their road trip to Austria. 'Maybe a night in Bregenz so it's daylight when we drive down into the Arlberg. It's on Lake Constance, which is just massive. Such a beautiful part of the world, that special point where Germany, Switzerland and Austria meet.'

Lou had asked if Danny could stay over for the week Wanda and Anna would be away. He already stayed a couple of nights each week so Wanda had no problem with that. Danny's mum was also fine with him helping Lou take care of things. Dogs needed to be walked and cared for. It might also help Danny get back on track with his school work a little. Lou knew that he was falling behind. She could keep him focussed for this week at least. At home, he seemed to always be caught up in computer games and unable to give his schooling the attention it needed.

That green Italian wagon was loaded with ski equipment. Anna had borrowed Lou's gear. CDs carefully selected to accommodate any of the changing moods this road trip might bring the girls. They loved to sing out loud and were hot to trot for an outrageous adventure. First CD up was Bon Jovi.

'My heart is like the open highway. Like Frankie said, I did it my way. I just wanna live while I'm alive. It's My Life!'

'Can you believe the size of this Youth Hostel and all the grounds it has? Can't believe we can actually have our own room for that ridiculously low amount. Only a short walk into the centre too. Excellent. I am starving. Where shall we eat?' Anna was ready to see what Bregenz might have to offer.

As it turned out, it had more to offer than either of them had bargained for.

A beautiful old town centre and loads of cafes for them to choose from. They would come back to the lake in the morning, when it was light, but the moon was full and the night reflections on the water were stunning. A maze of stars lit the sky and it seemed they were all sparkling on the deep blue waters below. Loads of people about. It was Friday night. Party time.

'Let's eat here Wanda. I really fancy a schnitzel and the price is good. Seems to be a nice crowd too. Check out those guys over there.' Anna was in the mood for some fun.

They had finished dinner by the time one of the guys finally had the nerve to come over and speak to them. He and his mates were going to a cocktail bar with live music and he thought it might be nice if Wanda and Anna joined them. Always the rock chick at heart, Wanda jumped at the prospect of live music. The guys weren't too bad either and Anna was certainly keen.

'I'm in this competition in a couple of days and need to create some new cocktails,' the English guy behind the bar had encouraged Anna to lend her support, as a taster of his new concoctions.

The band turned out to be just one guy singing and playing his guitar but he was a real talent. Wanda eventually got dragged into the cocktail tasting session too. The original plan had been not to drink at all but they were having such a laugh. An early start had been planned for the next day. Wanda normally had just one or two drinks on a night out. Not big into alcohol. Fruity flavours and lavish glass decorations, disguised the true strength of what they were drinking that night in Bregenz.

Anna was now enthralled by her conversations with the barman. Wanda was being captivated by one of the gorgeous young men, who had taken them to the bar. Tall, handsome and ever so sexy. He kept telling Wanda how much he would like to get her into bed. What a great body she had. The big blue eyes and the beaming smile. He loved the way she laughed and found her stories about life and love irresistible. He could not believe how he could meet this beautiful blonde Australian, in his home town of Bregenz.

As much as Wanda enjoyed his attention and flattery, she knew he more than likely said all of this on a regular basis. Something about him just did not connect with sincerity somehow. She looked across at Anna, who was totally absorbed and having a great time. A quick trip to the toilet and then she would see if Anna was ready to leave.

Standing at the basin washing her hands, Wanda suddenly saw her handsome young man enter the ladies. He locked the door behind him.

'What are you doing?' Wanda snapped at him.

'Just one kiss' he replied.

He was blocking her exit. Wanda's anger somehow turned to excitement, as he slowly unbuttoned his shirt to reveal his incredible torso. Erect brown nipples. Stunning firm body with an incredible six-pack. He just stood there smiling. Now he was the irresistible one.

'Just one kiss then,' Wanda finally responded.

Amazing soft and gentle lips. One kiss turned into several. He picked her up and placed her on the basin. It was almost instinctive for Wanda to wrap her legs around him. They were both aroused and aching. He sucked her nipples and touched her softly in every crevice. He had unzipped his trousers and released an enormous penis. Wanda couldn't help but admire its strength and form.

'Is anyone in there?'

'Yes. Sorry. Just coming out now. My boyfriend had a problem with his trousers so we were in here just trying to sort it out.' Wanda replied.

They had been in there passionately fondling and kissing for twenty minutes. As Wanda returned to the bar, Anna was nowhere to be seen. The barman said she had gone home to bed. Wanda raced off down the street and found Anna close to the hostel but looking very lost.

'Where the bloody hell did you get to?' Anna demanded of Wanda. She thought Wanda had gone off and left her there alone. Wanda of course had thought the same, when she got to the bar and no Anna.

They laughed so much they had almost been in tears. What a naughty night. Hopefully lots more would follow.

A quick coffee by the lake first thing in the morning. Not quite so early as they had wanted but it would do fine. Weather was good and the drive down through the mountains and into St. Anton should be pretty straight forward. Might have even missed some of the really early Saturday traffic. The lake had taken on a totally new look in the bright sunshine. Stretched out beyond what the eye could see. Sparkling in the morning sun quite differently to the night before. The girls would take exciting memories with them from their short visit to Bregenz.

Snow everywhere. So beautiful. Roads clear and in under two hours, they had reached St. Anton. Found their great little zimmer easily and could park without any problem at all.

'Let's get dressed for the snow and take our skis across to that flat area we saw coming in. You can get comfortable in the boots and we can do some gentle sliding and simple exercises, to get you feeling confident.' Wanda had promised to give Anna some lessons and not push her if she did not feel OK with skiing. She had only been once before and that was many moons ago.

Anna was a natural. Lou had a bigger foot than Wanda so she had given Ann her boots and used Lou's herself. All worked fine. They ventured up a small slope.

Anna had no trouble walking in the skis and had not freaked at all, when she started to slide back down the hill. The flat area stopped her nicely but Wanda still had her go into a snowplough position in any case. Best to get her in the groove for the slopes she had planned to take her on the next day.

That night they went for a quiet dinner, walked around the village pedestrian area and hit the pillow early. Still feeling a little weary from the night before and wanting to be on good form for the first day on the mountain.

'You really are a natural Anna. Can't believe you have not fallen over once. I know this is a beginner slope but you really are doing great. Might be ready to move up the hill a bit now. What do you think about lunch at that cool sun terrace we saw them promoting in the lift station? Looks like an easy blue run just in front of it.' Wanda could see

Anna was feeling confident and a nice sundeck lunch would also appeal.

It was March so the days were longer and generally more sunny. This Arlberg region of the Tyrol was popular with experienced skiers. St. Anton in particular, presenting some serious off piste back country opportunities and the highly desirable 10km long Valluga run. Lift facilities were first class. Wanda had never seen so many gondolas.

As Wanda and Anna ate lunch looking out across a never ending mountain range, they felt like they were in heaven. Stunning scenery. Perfect snow. Brilliant sunshine.

They were starting to observe just how many very fit looking men there were about. Way more men than there were women. They liked these odds. Anna would have been happy just to sit and observe but finally agreed with Wanda, that it was time to do a little more skiing.

'Not sure about this run Wanda. Might be a bit too steep for me. I don't do edges so definitely not going over that way.'

No matter how much Wanda explained that there were no sudden edges off this gentle blue slope, Anna was determined to limit her skiing to straight down the middle. Fine by Wanda. Bit boring after a while, just going up and down one t-bar. Eventually Anna had been happy for Wanda to leave her there practicing, while she did a couple of chair lift runs nearby. Hadn't been too long before Anna decided she had enough and settled back into one of the sun chairs again, with a coffee.

'This chap I was talking to, said we should go to BoBo's for dinner tonight. It's their special night for spareribs. Après drinks at the base of that gondola we came up too. Hope he shows up. Rather handsome.' Anna had kept herself well amused.

As it turned out, he had been a no-show at the Après bar. 'Never mind,' thought Anna. 'Let's see what BoBo's has in store.'

Once back in their room, they hadn't been so sure about having a big night. Suddenly ever so tired. Mountain air having the impact of immediate sleep, as soon as they lay on their beds to do some stretching.

'Good grief. Is it eight o'clock already Wanda? No wonder I'm starving.' Anna had stirred to the sound of her grumbling stomach.

A bit late to be arriving at BoBo's and expecting to get a table though. A quick shower and dress then they were out the door.

The head waiter just shook his head and grinned. Their happy smiling and almost begging faces had the required impact. He quietly squeezed them in, up at the bar.

All around them people were eating spareribs and they looked amazing. Huge portions so one serving between the two of them would be enough.

'Have you seen those two guys sitting at the table behind us?' Anna whispered to Wanda. She could see them out of the corner of her eye, as she turned slightly to face Wanda. For Wanda to actually see, she would have had to turn right around.

Anna had begun to exchange little smiles with one of the guys. He eventually walked up to the bar to speak to the barman, saying hello to Anna, as he parked himself beside her. He laughed and chatted with the barman for ages. All in German of course so Anna did not have a clue what they were talking about. When they laughed, Anna finally decided she would join in. He was almost leaning on her by that stage. Her 'Ya Ya Ya' with some very loud chuckling had been well received. Next Anna knew there were four shots on the bar.

Her new friend had introduced himself to them both as Hoopi and beckoned his mate to come up to the bar as well.

This exchange allowed the girls to turn around fully and check out Hoopi's mate. He looked totally disinterested and almost asleep. Just stared at them blankly. They had finished eating and he was ready to hit his pillow. Slumped back behind the table, he had even looked a little angry at Hoopi. Must have taken another 20mins or so for Hoopi to finally persuade him to join them. Wanda had begun to feel she would like to hit her pillow too by then.

The stools up at the bar were pretty high. Wanda knew Hoopi's mate had to be ever so tall for her to be looking up so much to make eye contact. He had finally moved to the bar. Wow. He was now smiling and he was gorgeous! Not able to speak much English but when he said 'please' with that cute Austrian accent, Wanda just melted. His thick black eyebrows and strong brown eyes had reminded her immediately of Robbie Williams. He also reminded her of a strong tall tree. So solid and upright. His name was Medwin. An unusual name to fit a mysterious and totally unusual man. Wanda was suddenly very awake and so, it seemed, was he.

The shots were peach schnapps. Served with separate slices of oranges, to have in your mouth as you knocked back the shot. Made for a sweet and fruity hit. Lekker. (they use that same word in German but not with anything like the same emphasis or in as many different situations. Also spelt differently. Lecker.)

BoBo decided the drinks for our little group were on him. It was party time. All food had been served and the singing could begin.

Hoopi apparently got his nickname because of his maniac skiing. Literally jumping through hoops on the slopes. Anna seemed well amused by his antics and little stories. It turned out the barman was actually BoBo and he had raced with Hoopi and Medwin that day.

'White Rush' took place each year. A 'fun' 9km downhill race, where crazy mountain folk lined up right across the mountain for a mass start. Around 500 entrants made of iron and coming from the absolute elite of the world's skiers and snowboarders. Named after a 1930's movie of the same name filmed locally, it was said only the toughest ever made it to the finish line. Anna and Wanda couldn't believe they had missed it. Watching people cross the finish line that is. Oh well. The stories would have to do. Nice to have their own personal up close encounter with the participants. Spring snow had been particularly good that year and end-of-season madness filled the air in BoBo's. Apparently BoBo had been this year's winner!

Medwin tried his best to converse with Wanda in English. She too tried a little of her very limited German. He was exhausted from the race and he and Hoopi were due to leave St. Anton the very next morning. Hoopi had nothing but fun on his mind. He was very clear that the train ride home could give him plenty of time to sleep. For tonight, they should all just party hard. Took some persuading to get Medwin interested in moving to a live music venue, where they could all dance. Once he was out in the fresh air and could take in the full picture of Wanda, a new man came to life.

Anna and Hoopi were straight onto the dance floor. The place was so packed that there had really not been anywhere else to just stand anyway. 'Great voice.' Anna shouted to Hoopi. The band turned out to be just one guy and his guitar with backing tapes. Brilliant though. Had the place jumping. Many were still in their ski gear. Even the boots. Loads of tall handsome men and very few women. Not a person who was not singing along and having a good time.

Medwin and Wanda had moved to the back of the room. She was standing on a step so she could see the stage. Medwin tucked himself right in front on the lower level and put his arms behind himself, then around the back of Wanda's legs. Wanda put her hands on his broad hard shoulders and held on to him tightly. The feeling of electricity was incredible. There they were, in the thick of this huge crowd, in just a simple hug and not even facing one another. It could not have been more arousing. The crowd seemed to keep pushing them even harder against each other. Medwin turned and looked Wanda straight in the eyes. The look went so much further. It was as if they were gazing into the deepest depths of each other's soul.

A slow song had begun. Medwin pressed himself against Wanda even more and they moved in a totally connected way. It was a favourite tune of his. Joe Cocker's 'You are So Beautiful'. He was whispering the words into Wanda's ear.

She felt as though her body had taken flight. As she soared to the music in Medwin's arms, she knew this would be the beginning of something totally unexpected.

The song ended with Medwin sweeping Wanda off the dance floor. Anna and Hoopi were snogging right in front of the stage at this point. Medwin gestured to Hoopi that they were moving to a different room. He and Anna were happy where they were and would continue bopping.

In the quiet of this lounging zone, Medwin suddenly seemed to speak much better English. He set about telling Wanda the tale of his life. His failed marriage and young son.

Medwin had grown up in a small Austrian town 60kms south of Vienna. His father had been the station master, as had his father before him. Medwin had also become the station master, after his father had taken early retirement. He married his childhood sweetheart and eighteen months later they had a much adored son. Downhill ski races, marathons, mountain biking and being a snowboard instructor, had taken Medwin to various places around Europe. Those trips had highlighted the smallness of his village and indeed his life. He had done enough time in his role as station master and been allocated a railway home, directly in front of his parents. His search for more had then led him to a head office job, designing railway signalling systems. And still he searched for more.

Once his son had started school, his wife went back to work. Medwin's parents did school runs and spent a lot of time with his son. He and his wife had grown further and further apart. Finally they had separated two years earlier.

All very amicable and they were not yet divorced. Medwin had moved in with his parents so still lived directly behind. Everyone had become much happier. They would divorce, whenever it became necessary. Medwin wanted desperately to leave the village and had been making plans to move to Vienna, to be close to his work. He had been out with a few different women but none had struck the right chord. Not that he had any intention of getting into anything serious just yet. Wanted to get himself settled in Vienna first. Anyway, he had been much too busy with all his sporting activities. The KTM motorbike had not even been ridden as much as he would have liked.

Wanda told Medwin about Larry and their breakup 16 years ago. He had been surprised to learn she had two teenage children. His son would turn 7 in a few months.

'Medwin. He's just about to play your song.' Hoopi shouted, as he finally found where they were sitting. 'Come back and dance you two,' shouted Anna immediately following.

Up they jumped. It was all starting to get way too serious anyway.

As they came close to the dance floor, Wanda could hear Bryan Adams *'Back in the Summer of 69'*.

'That's when I was born,' shouted Medwin as the rocking took hold.

'Shit.' Thought Wanda. 'Can he really be 17 years younger than me?!'

• CHAPTER TEN •

'I'M GOING BACK WITH HOOPI so you will have to take Medwin back to our room,' Anna informed Wanda. They had all danced until it was closing time. In just five hours time, Medwin and Hoopi would be on their train headed home. Wanda was ready to say her goodbyes as they left the club. Medwin had been sure to get her email address but she wondered if she would actually ever hear from him again. It had been a great night. Very special. Now she had expected a long goodbye and nothing more.

'Looks like we do not have an option here Wanda. Are you OK if I come back to your room for some sleep?' Medwin asked Wanda in a rather shy way, with cutely broken English. She nodded yes.

'Let's all meet for breakfast at the station around 8am,' Hoopi commanded.

'OK' everyone replied. Clear they had no choice in the matter really. Hoopi would throw Medwin's things in his bag and bring that along. Ski gear had already been put in the station locker.

Wanda and Medwin crept quietly in through the front door and up to the room. For sure the owner would not be at all happy, if she found Wanda in the hallway with a man. There were two single beds in the room. Wanda sat in one of the chairs opposite and offered Medwin a glass of water, from the bottle sitting on their small table. He sat in the other chair and they chatted for what must have been an hour. Silly small talk about the beautiful Austrian woodwork and hand painted edging that adorned the room. It was indeed beautiful but they were ever so tired. He talked about his father's talents with woodwork and how beautiful his village was. Eyelids had become like heavy weights on Wanda and she could see that Medwin was in a similar state.

'I might just fall asleep here in this chair,' Medwin had finally said. He was clearly waiting for some sort of sign from Wanda, before making any advance.

Wanda fancied him wildly but sensed that starting something with him, would lead to much more. More than perhaps either of them could handle. Even with the age difference, and the fact he lived in Austria and she lived in Holland, there was something incredibly intense going on between them.

The realisation that they were both falling asleep sitting up, had become too much for Wanda. She finally took his hand and walked to her bed. 'No point sitting up, when we can lay down comfortably,' she said.

As soon as she had taken his hand, her pulse began to race. They were like two young lovers on a first date. Awkward and clumsy. Wanda set the alarm to wake them in just a few hours. They were fully clothed. Side by side holding hands and sweating with emotion, Wanda could feel herself dropping off to sleep. She was afraid she would snore. When she heard Medwin snoring, she knew he had beaten her to it.

They both woke up well before the alarm. As they turned to look into each other's eyes, their lips locked. It was like New Year's Eve fireworks on Sydney Harbour. Flashes of light and colours swam around Wanda's head. Medwin had kissed her in the club earlier but now his lips were a totally different proposition. Not pursed and polite like they had been. Blood was pulsing through his entire body and his lips were full and soft. Wanda could hardly breathe, with the ecstasy that was filling her very fibre. His lips were not the only thing that had become full. As their bodies hugged together tightly, she could feel his penis bulging in his trousers and screaming out to be released.

He moved himself slightly back and began feeling her body all over. Exploring her every inch, with such soft and tender hand movements. It was as if he had entered a dark room and was trying to find his way. Wanda tingled all over, as she had never tingled before. Not a word had been said and they were holding back any sounds of pleasure. It had become daylight and the landlady might well have heard them otherwise.

Medwin removed Wanda's clothes, as if in slow motion. As bare flesh was revealed, he just stared for what seemed an age. He then kissed that bare flesh, with a passion Wanda had never experienced. He was sincerely revelling in each and every part of her body. Once Wanda was totally naked, he returned to kiss her lips.

Wanda ached to feel his naked body against hers.

She slowly began removing his clothes. As she revealed his pectoral muscles throbbing on his softly skinned chest, she was drawn to suck his hardened nipples. Holding his muscly arms at the same time, she was in heaven. He quivered with the sensation and pressed her even harder to his chest.

Undoing his jeans had been difficult. His enormous penis made them so tight, Wanda could barely open his zip. Medwin stood to allow his jeans to drop to the floor. Wanda could not believe her eyes. She asked him to just stand there for a minute. Unbelievable! Adonis came immediately to mind. In Greek mythology, he had been the God of beauty and desire.

Medwin's athletic form towered over Wanda, until he gently came down to the bed once more. As they renewed their all-embracing hug position, it was as if they became one. Neither of them had a condom so there would be no internal connection. Medwin opened the lips of Wanda's vagina, to allow his penis to be hugged as it throbbed against Wanda's clitoris. Hugging, kissing and gently rubbing against each other. They were both ecstatic. Wanda reached an electric climax, much sooner than she had wanted. The pleasure was so intense. Medwin was close behind and his whole body hardened as he peaked.

Rolling over onto their backs, they both knew they would have to see each other again. This was no casual one night of lust. Something very magical had been stirred in them both.

As Hoopi and Medwin's train pulled out of St. Anton station, Wanda and Anna knew they just needed to get some sleep. Very little had been said. Everyone had been light hearted and jolly about the night before. Hoopi was married and had made it clear to Anna that this was just a fling. Anna told Hoopi she had hopes of reuniting with her husband so that was fine with her. They literally did just enjoy the moment. For Wanda and Medwin, it had been a totally different matter.

Over the next few days and nights, Wanda and Anna had made the most of their time in St. Anton. Anna had become more and more concerned about the 'edges' so did less and less skiing. Most bars on the mountain had been explored by the last night. Their favourite was Krazy Kanguruh. That place sure did jump. Still a little way to go down the slope when you came out so that proved to be amusing. It claimed to attract the reckless. End of night skiing back to the village, certainly did demonstrate that in a big way.

Wanda had remained stunned by her encounter with Medwin, for pretty much the entire drive back to Holland. They had decided to leave St. Anton really early and do the journey in one day. A nice lunch break on the Rhine River, had broken it up perfectly.

There were two emails from Medwin, waiting for Wanda when she arrived home. He had obviously gone to a lot of trouble, to write his beautiful messages in English. So romantic. He had been captivated by Wanda and needed to see her again soon.

The feeling was entirely mutual. Wanda could think of nothing else. She had important meetings back at work. It had become more and more difficult to concentrate. She also needed to get closer to Lou's school work and make sure that was all on track. Just a couple of months and Lou would be finished the school year. Then, come September, Lou would enter her final year of high school. She was determined to go to University and would need a high number of IB points, to get into the study she wanted to do in England.

'Mum. He sounds so special. I have everything under control for school. I can run through it all with you tonight. I'll be finished that painting by the weekend too. Just go and have a great time.' Lou had been so happy to see her mum glowing, when she told her about Medwin. It had been a long time. Anna also raved about him. The one photo they had was not so good but Lou got the general gist. Tall, dark and handsome. Perfect!

Wanda had spoken to Medwin on the phone that day for the first time. She had been home three days and sent and received emails with him at least once each day. They still had not exchanged phone numbers. That day she had added her mobile number at the bottom of the email and he had called straight away. Would she please spend the next weekend in Bratislava with him? He had already arranged accommodation and wanted to keep that a surprise. All she needed to do, was work out what flight she could take and he would arrange that too.

'Damon. Are you OK with covering that meeting with the agency on Friday afternoon? I might leave the office around mid-day, to take Medwin up on his offer.' Wanda knew Damon would cover for her. He had been so excited about the St. Anton encounter. So had Patty. She gave her the afternoon off, without hesitation. They could not wait to meet him and made the only proviso that the next time Wanda met up with Medwin, it should be in Holland.

Beautiful Bratislava! Just over the Austria/Slovakian border and so close to Vienna, that many people took the cheap flight options to there, with a short bus ride, for getting to the Austrian capital. The one and a half hour flight from Amsterdam, seemed to take a lifetime for Wanda. Why was she so nervous? It was only ten days since she had been with him in St. Anton. They had felt a little strained with his broken and limited English but she was really comfortable being in his company. Even with the seventeen year age difference.

Medwin had been in his office by 6am that morning. Quite some things to do and he had wanted to be clear of all thoughts of anything to do with work, before he picked Wanda up from Bratislava airport. It was quite normal for Medwin to be in so early. The 60km drive from his village, was a nightmare if he left later. His day would start with a sharp awakening at 4am and a fast mountain run.

There was a good place right at the back of his parents' house. He wore a hat with a big light fixed to it, for visibility in the dark.

The run was steep and rocky. Certainly not a good place to be falling over your feet, not seeing properly.

His mother would have breakfast all laid out for him, when he got back to the house. She would bake for him most days. Freshly ironed shirts sat waiting in his wardrobe. He would peel off sweaty and very expensive lycra running gear, jump into the shower, dress for the office in a rather nice suit, then head off in his car for the high speed drive to Vienna. Mother would then scrape the sweaty clothing up and wash it all by hand, pretty much each day. Not that she needed to. He had so much designer sports gear. Most of his money had traditionally gone on his sports. If it was not on things for skiing, running and mountain biking, it was for his hot KTM motor bike.

'Oh my goodness! He is even more stunning than I remembered'. Wanda thought to herself as she approached Medwin, at the arrivals gate.

During the flight from Amsterdam, Wanda had been remembering Medwin's likeness to Robbie Williams. She recalled the deep and dark eyes. Medwin did however have much broader shoulders and a taller, more solid body. Standing there dressed so smartly, he had a sultry star look about him. She could not believe he was actually waiting for her.

They both seemed a little shell-shocked and speechless, once they were in Medwin's car. The welcome hug had lingered on and on, with enormous intensity, but the kisses that followed had been rather formal. In Austria, it was two kisses to the cheeks. In Holland, it was three. They had both gone in for a third and then fumbled over whether or not to hold hands, as they walked off from the gate.

Medwin had opened the passenger door for Wanda, as they reach his car. He waited and closed it after her. An absolute gentleman.

'Perhaps he is having second thoughts and wondering what the hell he is doing here.' Wanda thought to herself.

He had never asked Wanda her age but maybe he was now thinking, she was a bit too old for him. He had looked at her deeply and lovingly though. Or was she not reading things right. Of course he was nervous. She had also been very aware of her own body quivering, as they hugged earlier. The hug had been truly amazing. Wanda felt herself melt into his arms. She felt his heart beating quickly, as he tightened his hold. It would have been just fine with her, if he had never let her go. What more could she ever wish for. This gorgeous man, holding her with so much passion that she felt she might burst.

Age had never been an important factor in relationships for Wanda. People were so different and the number that was attached to them, because of when they were born, often bore no resemblance to the energy or mind set of that individual.

Some people were old and lifeless, by the time they were thirty. She knew others that were in their eighties and still full of energy. That said, she had actually only ever been out with two people that were older than her. Her ex-husband Larry was seven years her junior. Tim the fireman had been thirteen years younger. Now she was moving right along, to a seventeen year difference. Did not matter to her, if it did not matter to Medwin. Not actually looking that much younger anyway. The mountain man had more wrinkles than she did. Out there in the wild all those years, his rugged face had become quite weathered.

'I hope you really like this special place we will stay at,' said Medwin in his cute broken English, as they turned off towards the centre. 'Before we go there, I was thinking to stop for a drink by the river. OK with you?'

Everything was OK with Wanda. Very OK. He had put his Joe Cocker CD on. It had been pre-set to play 'You Are So Beautiful'. He had remembered that song he sang in her ear, the first night they met in St. Anton.

She began to relax and Medwin gave her a brief history on Bratislava. As they came to the river, he told her it was the Donau but she would most likely know it better by its English name, the Danube. Ah yes. The very famous river of that Johann Strauss waltz, the Blue Danube. They pulled into the car park of this stunningly quaint boat café, right alongside the Donau's very blue and sparkling waters.

It was early afternoon and the light could not have been better. The river was said to have lost its 'blueness' of late but that day it seemed to almost shine. One of the world's great rivers, the Donau began to wind a path from Germany's Black Forest. As it made its way through several countries in Central and Eastern Europe, it eventually emptied into the Black Sea in Romania and Ukraine. That weekend it would provide the perfect backdrop, for a very special and passionate coming together of hearts and minds.

Wanda ordered a nice glass of red wine and Medwin chose a beer. The staff at the boat café, could not have been more hospitable. Nibbles were provided with the drinks, without ordering, and the platter had been explained in detail, as it was placed on the table. Beautifully presented. A second drink would be needed indeed. A good move by the proprietor perhaps but a most enjoyable taste sensation for the recipients too.

An hour had passed. Medwin seemed a little nervous again.

'Maybe we should go to check in now Wanda. I told them we would arrive early evening so it is OK but maybe also nice to get settled, before we go for some dinner.'

They walked towards the car. Wanda waited for Medwin to approach the door but he went straight to the car boot and took out their small suitcases.

'Now let us see how you like the boat next door my beautiful Wanda,' said Medwin as he gestured to the vine covered archway, on the other side of the car park.

It was quite perfect. Passing through the archway, the hidden boat hotel had suddenly become visible.

A porter met them, as they reached the entrance to the boat. They had travelled lightly and it was no trouble at all to manage their own suitcases but he would not have it. So friendly and just wanting to give 100% quality service. On the deck of the boat, they were serving cocktails. Two violinists did a wandering minstrel thing, entertaining the six or so guests in attendance. What a stunning old craft. An enormous river boat that was ever so grand. They joined the other guests for one cocktail, whilst the porter took their bags to the room.

Room! Well … it turned out to be a suite! Simply stunning! Medwin had gone all out to impress. Wanda could not help but think he really did not need to spend all that money. That was just how she was. A reflection of her poor upbringing perhaps. At the same time, she could not help but feel overwhelmed by his efforts.

He had even brought along the very same peach schnapps they drank that night with BoBo….. as well as the fresh orange slices. It had been a very long time, since Wanda felt so spoiled. It was also very clear that these things came from the heart and that made a world of difference.

Sunset meant completely different lighting. The lamps on the boat had been turned on. Reflections from the lights bounced around the river outside and made their way into Wanda and Medwin's line of sight. They were sitting at their table enjoying a schnapps. As the water rolled and surged with any passing craft, they could feel their bodies gently sway.

'Across the street, there is a really good Italian restaurant. I made a reservation for dinner but if you don't feel like Italian, I can cancel.' As Medwin said this to Wanda, he stood up to see where he had put his phone. They had both been very careful about keeping their distance, until that very moment. Wanda stood up to say that Italian would be lovely and she might go take a shower and get ready. He grabbed her and gently pulled her to his chest.

'This is the hug I keep recalling so vividly,' Wanda said to herself. She wished she could say it to Medwin. They had not really said all that much so far. She had not wanted him to feel uncomfortable about not understanding or being able to speak English terribly well. Looks and gestures. Light comments. They had managed fine. Emails had been different of course. Medwin must have taken hours to write them. Much easier with a computer translation program to hand.

Wanda melted into Medwin's arms. Her head rested onto his chest as he hugged her with the deepest and most sincere warmth she had ever felt. It seemed an age, before he finally lifted her to lie on the bed. Horizontal hugging then allowed their lips to meet effortlessly.

A gentle and short first kiss, quickly followed by longer and softer meetings of their lips. As they pressed together, the kissing took on a greater depth. The swaying of the boat seemed to have a massaging effect on their bodies. The kissing and hugging sent their heads into a complete state of longing. They wanted each other but both held back, unsure of what should come next.

As was often the case when things got serious, Wanda resorted to laughter. She pushed slightly back from Medwin and reminded him, she was on her way to take a shower. The foreplay had begun.

Medwin moved immediately towards the bathroom, as Wanda came out of the door. He paused to take in the sight of Wanda wrapped in her towel and bent over to gently kiss her legs. Shivers went right through her. Medwin carried on into the bathroom, leaving Wanda to dress in private.

'The restaurant booking is in twenty minutes so I will be very quick,' he said as he closed the bathroom door behind him.

It took Wanda a few minutes to get her mind back onto what she was doing. Thank goodness she had planned what she would wear. Before she packed her small suitcase, she had tried pretty much everything in her wardrobe on. With all the travelling she had done in the past, it had been a trick she learned long ago. Pack only what you know you will wear. Spend time beforehand playing with clothes in front of a good mirror so you feel very clear on having achieved the look you want. Have the right shoes and any other adornments you need. Too late to think about these things once you're out there.

Wanda was dressed and ready, by the time Medwin emerged from the bathroom. He looked suitably impressed. Already wearing his boxer shorts, he moved to his suitcase and took out a perfectly folded shirt. Wanda could not take her eyes off him. Her very own Adonis.

'Did you buy new shirts?' she enquired. The shirts were all buttoned and folded, as if they had just been removed from store packaging.

'No. That is just how my mother likes to have my shirts, once she has washed and ironed them,' he replied.

Wanda could not help but wonder if his wife had also prepared his shirts for him in that way. One would imagine she had. He seemed to think that was totally normal. Wanda on the other hand, prided herself on never ever ironing anything. She would shake things well as they came out of the washing machine, to make them as wrinkle free as possible, before hanging them to dry. Shirts and jackets generally went straight onto coat hangers. As soon as they were dry, they were hung in the wardrobe. She did not buy things that had to be ironed to be worn. A total waste of time and effort, as far as she was concerned. May not be quite the time to tell Medwin though. Keep that one for another day.

Split with his wife for two years and still back at home with his parents. She could not help but think he must really like being looked after. A bit odd that he had wanted to move up to Vienna and, in all that time, he had still not managed to do so. She guessed easy access to his son would be an important factor.

Food in the Italian restaurant was outstanding. The setting, so incredibly romantic. Al fresco dining under beautiful green vines that took on a fresh new look for the spring, with the smallest of yellow flowers starting to bud.

A warm spring evening. Good food and wine. Wanda and Medwin had mellowed, to a new state of comfort and ease with each other. They were getting better at understanding and responding, to the many questions they each wanted to ask. Past relationships seemed to dominate the conversation initially. What were those people like? Why had it ended? What were the things they each felt were most important in a partnership?

Wanda discovered the cutest thing with Medwin. Whenever he had not understood what she said, he would simply look at her with a slightly tilted puppy dog face and his big big brown eyes, then just ask 'Please?' He clearly loved the smile that word brought to Wanda's face.

The conversation continued, as they walked back across the street to the boat. Such a balmy evening. They stood on the deck, to fully take in the stars and continuing movement of reflections on the river. A complete peace came over them both. Medwin had his strong arms wrapped around Wanda once again. She remarked how 'huggy' he was. There was apparently something about Wanda, that made him want to hug her endlessly. It was quite a new thing for him.

They stayed hugging on the deck, for what seemed an age. Medwin's mind was going crazy. He was running through different scenarios of what might happen, when they got back to the suite. The day before, he had searched the web for all the English words he might need, when it came to love making. One website was very graphic. His mind went wild thinking about it now. 'Fucking Her Brains Out' was the heading and at the top of each of the pictures below, it had said 'Fuck Position 1' …. 2 …. 3 …. etc. Went right up to 69. Umm. He found that picture particularly interesting.

Medwin had never used that word before but he did have a friend, who had occasionally talked about the way he liked to fuck. Medwin wondered if fuck was a word that Wanda used. The website had talked about how stimulating it was for people to talk dirty to each other before, during and after love making.

Medwin was also recalling, how sedate his love life had been with his wife. She did not even like to have him see her naked. Not that she had a bad figure or anything. Maybe just too young at first. They had known each other since primary school. Played at arousing each other fully clothed, right up until the day of their wedding. He had been in agreement, that she should be a virgin bride. The wedding night encounter had been totally traumatic. He did not know how to stop her being so rigid. Kissing and hugging just seemed to make her even stiffer. He had read about the clitoris and how girls liked that to be licked. She would not let him near it. In the end, they did have intercourse but it was a nightmare. Blood everywhere.

As the years progressed, he and his wife had grown to understand what they could do to turn each other on. He had loved her deeply and by the end of the second year, she had given him a son. After that, it was very quick sex maybe once every month. By the time they separated, it had been almost a year since they last had sex. She looked after him really well. Maybe he could just do without the sex, he had thought. No. It had led to the eventual demise of their relationship.

For him, there had been one encounter before his marriage. With a teacher. His mind was flashing back to that afternoon when she kept him back, because his work was not finished. Had not taken much effort on her part at all. Before he had known anything, she had his penis out of his pants and erect. The door had been locked and she had him behind her desk. Next thing he knew, her skirt was lifted and she was pulling his penis straight into her vagina. She thrust him back and forth and in moments he had come. It was quick and surprising, to say the least. She had not looked at all pleased about the speed of his ejaculation and immediate shrinkage. He had just been directed to lick her where she had her hand, when there was a knock at the door. He had been caught up in her hot desires and found her really attractive but remembered how relieved he felt, when their progress was stopped by that knock. The next day she finished at the school. He never saw her again.

Medwin's head span, with exciting hugging and fucking thoughts. Watching Wanda gaze across the water, he felt his penis grow.

• CHAPTER ELEVEN •

THE POWER OF THE MIND. Wanda was off in fantasy land. Each movement of the boat, seemed to make her rub up against Medwin even more. The hugging was so intense. She had always felt hugs to be an important part of relationships but this was incredible. The heat he was generating, had started to make her a little sweaty. She wondered what he might be thinking about. Funny how shy he seemed to be. She had even felt a little shy herself.

Wanda's mind started to connect all the different views she had seen of his body so far. Coming out of the bathroom in his boxers, jumped straight to mind. Then she was back in St. Anton. The sight of his body that morning, as his jeans had fallen to the floor. The hard nipples on solid pects. His enormous charged penis, that seemed to point directly at her. Those soft soft lips, that kissed her with amazing intensity.

What was it going to be like, when they went back to the suite this balmy night? Getting a little late and there they were still hugging on the deck in the moonlight.

Wanda thought about the hugs, that led to the quick climax back in St. Anton. He had such a huge penis. Maybe it would present a size challenge, when they finally had intercourse. She knew they would be using a condom. Never had liked those but of course she knew it was a must. Difficult to really have the full sensation of becoming one. Hopefully he will have brought some lubricating gel.

Wanda had looked at edible condoms but had decided she might look a little too basic, for their first quality time together. Her mind went wild, with all the things she would like to do to and with Medwin but, this time, she would let him take total charge.

Wanda stopped herself thinking about different sexual positions with Medwin and brought her mind back to the simple pleasures of hugging. It was often adopted by people in only superficial ways. Polite hugs, as a friendly form of contact. No hugging and very little holding of hands in relationships had, more often than not, been clear signs that people were struggling to connect. She was amazed at couples missing out on the deep connections hugging could bring. Such a great way to express and truly feel the love between two people. That feeling when you are hugged so tightly, you lose all breath. The deepest of sighs, as oxygen is refreshed and a person looks into a partner's eyes and feels them look right through to their very soul. So beautiful!

Many other sorts of feelings, also came from different hugging scenarios. Loving hugs with children for instance. Nothing better than cuddling up in front of an old movie with the kids and feeling the love. Priceless. The hug a child gives to their favourite cuddly toy. A grandparent's hug, as they entertain with stories of days gone by. Hugging of a pet, often attributed to better health and a more positive state of mind. The hug of a tree, to show one's connection with nature. All so very beautiful.

Medwin turned to kiss Wanda gently on her forehead. She twisted around and lifted her lips to his. Those New Year fireworks were back. Soft lips finding each other, as the boat swayed a little harder under the surge of a passing river cruiser. Even with high heels on, Wanda stood on tippy toes as Medwin bent his head downwards. The kiss lingered and intensified. Medwin finally took Wanda by the hand and led her back down to their suite.

Visits to the bathroom, were followed by the pouring of a small schnapps. Medwin had cut some orange, while Wanda was out of the room. They had both then laughed, as they recollected their BoBo's first meeting over orange pieces and schnapps.

'To us! ' Medwin toasted. 'A long and deeply fulfilling partnership.'

'Wow. That sounded really serious,' thought Wanda. At this point, she might normally have wanted to run. This time, she knew it was very different. She was not wanting to go anywhere but into the arms of the amazing man standing right in front of her.

Medwin made the first move. Wanda had already slipped out of her shoes and jacket. The dress she had worn was rather low cut, with a padded bra section that encouraged her breasts to peep over significantly at the top. Wanda very rarely wore an actual bra. Felt way too constricting for her and she had figured her breasts were small and pert enough to manage without. The sunken chest had also provided the appearance of cleavage. Medwin gently drew one breast out from inside the dress, to suck it.

They had not spoken at all about what they each liked or did not like in bed. He wanted to tell her about the fucking website he had seen but he did not know how she would respond. Images of that site were coming into his mind all the time. He was, however, very clear from that first night in St. Anton, that she loved her nipples to be sucked. So did he. He recalled how he had almost come, just from the way she had sucked and licked his nipples. It had been a first for him. A total surprise that he had been so aroused, just with his nipples in action. He also recalled Wanda's two nipples being very different. It had taken much more time, to encourage the inverted nipple to harden and stand tall with its counterpart.

Standing there very still, now with both breasts exposed out of the top of her silky dress, nipples hard and erect, Wanda did not move a muscle. Medwin stopped sucking her nipples, stepped back slightly and just looked. Her blonde hair sat just below her shoulders, almost touching the nipples. Big blue eyes focussed totally on him. He observed the deep breaths, that lifted her nipples even further. Medwin took in every inch of her and loved what he saw.

Removing his own shirt, unveiled his nipples ... already hardened, without any effort on Wanda's part. Wanda put her shoes back on and stepped towards him. Standing high on her toes again, she was able to gently connect her nipples to his. A gentle swaying sideways, allowed their nipples to flick against each other. What bliss! They held on tightly to each other's arms and started to shake in anticipation of what was to come.

Unzipping Wanda's dress happened in perfect concert with her unzipping his trousers. They soon found themselves lying on the bed naked, in their horizontal hugging position. Website images and words span around Medwin's head. Kissing stayed focussed on lips, as they pressed into each other's body. Medwin reached for a condom. A definite moment stopper. Wanda lay totally still. Nothing was said out loud. Vivid images of his penis came into her head and she recalled her concern, about whether it might be too big.

'Thank heavens for the sounds coming from the river,' Wanda thought to herself. 'Nothing being said is making my head spin.'

Medwin had been with three women, since he split with his wife two years earlier. None had lasted more than a couple of months. Even then, he had only seen them a few times. Sex had been frantic and rather basic. It was totally different with Wanda. She clearly had more experience and had a worldly way about her.

Medwin had expected Wanda to be a little more in charge when they got into bed but, to his surprise, he was enjoying his position of power. He had been able to arouse Wanda throughout the night. She reacted to his every touch. He had loved that she was as huggy as he was and sensed right from that long passionate hug on the deck, she would be his for a long time to come. It was a confidence that made him a lot more bullish than he had ever been before.

Wanda was so wet by the time Medwin moved deep inside her, his size was no challenge at all. The penetration had been slow and loving. Soft kissing had continued throughout.

Wanda and Medwin had become one. Locked in ecstasy, the speed of movements stayed slow and deep, until Medwin could hold back no longer. He came with the power of an earthquake. Wanda did not. The silence was deafening. Medwin rolled onto his back, trying to regain his breathing. Wanda had been left floating. Close to a thunderous climax but now feeling perhaps a little left behind.

He found her hand and held onto it tightly. The energy Wanda felt, just lying beside him holding hands, reminded her how passionate the entire evening had been. As she came down off the peak, she felt no lack of overall satisfaction. She basked in the impact she obviously made on Medwin and felt confident their sharing of pleasures would be more than equalised, as their partnership developed.

Medwin was asleep in moments. He had not moved an inch. No snoring or even heavy breathing now. Wanda had taken a very close look and spoken quietly, to ask if he was awake. Nothing. That was a relief. Wanda knew she would be snoring in no time at all. Best if he was already asleep so she did not have to think about keeping him awake. They were both elated but totally exhausted.

Waking to find themselves in 'spoon' position, the hugging had obviously continued even in their sleep. This pleased Wanda no end. She reflected on some of the men she had dated. Pretty much wanted to be off in another part of the house, after they had sex. She loved to start her day with that hug connection. The warmth of a loving body held close, as you both joined a new day.

Wanda moved one hand down to hold onto Medwin's firm buttock. The other arm was lying in between both their bodies. She then gently ran her fingers up and down his strong back. He started to arch with pleasure. An erection then pushed itself onto Wanda's dormant arm. He was ready to play again.

Medwin had woken feeling a little unsure of how to begin the day. The fucking website fully occupied his thoughts. How could he find out what would please Wanda. He knew he had not completed things the night before. Now he was quickly aroused by her simple touches on his body.

'A penny for your thoughts Medwin,' Wanda said sweetly as she raised herself up onto one arm and moved a little back, to take a better look at his aroused body.

Medwin had not quite understood this silly English expression. They both had a good chuckle at Wanda's explanation and then went through other similar silly English sayings. Now they were really laughing. Almost in fits of giggles. Medwin felt a door had opened for him to talk more, about the things he had seen online. He became more and more relaxed, as he went through all the fucking positions he had read about. As they discussed the pictures, the giggling grew in intensity. They had become like a couple of teenagers, who just found their first dirty magazine.

Medwin talked about how much he liked hugging and had been so pleased that Wanda loved to hug too. Fucking was definitely not the be all and end all. He used the cutest English to explain himself.

Wanda felt more and more close to him. She had not been one to swear and it had been a surprise to hear him suddenly talking about fucking. They talked for what seemed an age. Eyes rose, when he finally admitted that his favourite picture on that website had been fucking position 69. Medwin told Wanda how his wife would not entertain much of anything, other than straight intercourse. He really wanted to please Wanda and hoped she would help him to explore new territory.

'So we are agreed. Let's get started on our hugging and fucking discoveries straight away then,' Wanda said lightly to bring him back from what had become a serious moment, at the mention of his wife.

Medwin's thoughts of the website became even clearer. Vivid images of people, doing different and very sexy things with their bodies, span around frantically in his head.

'I like to hug and fuck with you so much Wanda,' said Medwin with an absolute sincerity in his voice.

'Hug and fuck,' said Wanda. 'Sounds like that ice cream. What's it called? Bit of a Swedish sounding name as I recall.'

They both went into fits of laughter again and eventually needed to visit the toilet. As Medwin left the room to go in first, he asked Wanda to think about how she would like to start with some hug and fuck adventures. It sounded to Wanda as if he had said hug and fug.

'Any sort of hug and fug will be wonderful with you I am sure,' Wanda had replied, not wanted to correct his English.

As Wanda took her turn in the bathroom, she decided she really enjoyed the sound of these two new characters that had come into their lives. Hug and Fug would play big roles in their future together, she was sure.

'Maybe we can start some more Hug and Fug with a nice shower together,' Wanda suggested coyly, as she looked towards the big massage shower head standing over the large bathtub.

They soaped and rubbed and felt the heat of the water caressing their bodies. Exploring each other with their eyes and hands, Medwin then sat on the edge of the bath. Wanda was still under the water, taking on a seductive wet look that drove him crazy.

Medwin started to kiss Wanda's belly button. He moved to nibbling her hips then turned her around so he could kiss her buttocks. Water ran over his face when his mouth was against her body. Turning her again to face him, he gestured for her to lift one leg up onto the bath edge. The kisses, the sucking, the licking into every part of her pussy drove her into a frenzy of excitement. She was holding his head tight into her, as her body began to shake. The warm water ran across her breasts. It can't have been many minutes at all before she needed to lean back against the wall, reaching with her total body into a head spinning climax.

Medwin's desire to be inside Wanda as quickly as possible was unstoppable. The thought of a condom flashed past quickly but he felt helpless to alter his course.

The full strength of Medwin's athletic body was in motion now. Thrusting of his penis into the deepest depths of Wanda, was at maximum power this time. Seeing Wanda in a total state of euphoria had driven him more frantically than he had ever experienced. The loud groan that came forth from Medwin, as his juices burst out of his body, was also something he had not encountered before. They both collapsed into the bath tub, unable to move for what seemed an age.

Eventually making their way back to the bed. Wanda and Medwin had soon fallen back to sleep. Wrapped in a passionate hug. Still spinning from their love making. Whispers about their new best friends Hug and Fug, sent them to sleep smiling.

Breakfast had been missed completely. Room service brought them food around 1pm. More Hug and Fug activity, once they had eaten. Watching a little TV followed, to see if there was anything happening in the world they should be aware of. They both liked music videos so the music channel had finally won out over the news.

Only a couple of hours of daylight left, by the time they finally dressed to go out for a walk along the river. Medwin had planned loads of things for them to visit. Bratislava had a long and interesting history. He had wanted to show Wanda so many things from its rich cultural heritage.

Now it had seemed they could not walk very far at all, before they needed to just stand and stare at each other. Wanda could not believe the way Medwin made her feel, just by staring at her. He would turn her to face him, give her an amazingly powerful hug. Directing her chin up to his face, he would give her the most loving kiss. Then he would hold her back at arms-length and first of all stare straight into her eyes. It was as if he was trying to see right through to her heart and soul. He would slowly move his gaze, to look at her hands. His eyes went down to her feet and moved slowly, all over her body. He would then finish by hugging her head to his chest and more often than not, just saying 'unbelievable'.

Wanda felt more special with Medwin than she had ever felt before. He made her feel truly beautiful and incredibly desirable.

Buskers entertained them on their walk. Medwin told Wanda how he sometimes played trumpet in a Guggamusik band, some guys got together in his village. He had a CD at home and would bring it the next time he saw her. They laughed so hard when he was trying to explain the way the band dressed up in silly clothes, often even in animal suits. She told him about her ex-husband Larry being a professional trumpet player. Even though she had told him back in St. Anton about Larry, Wanda was aware of him going a little quiet, at the mention of his name there in Bratislava.

'I have a booking at this traditional Slovakian restaurant for dinner at 7pm. We can go back to the boat to get ready now if you like?' Medwin said, as if to change the subject.

The walk back was very quiet. Wanda had been a little surprised at Medwin's reaction to her comment about Larry but she took it on board. Maybe she had ruined his moment of fame so to speak. He had been telling her about his own trumpet playing attributes and she had referred to Larry being a pro. A mental note was made, not to do that again.

They constantly had Hug and Fug coming into play. No sooner had Wanda removed her jeans, once they were back at the boat, than Medwin had grabbed her and lifted her into the air. This had been the first time, for a very quick and frenzied Fug. Medwin placed Wanda on the small table and quickly released his beast. He had moved her underwear to one side and placed his penis inside her, in a matter of moments.

'You drive me crazy Wanda,' had been all he could say.

They were kissing and both pushing hard into one another. Medwin's pelvic bone seemed to be in just the right position to rub against her clitoris. Wanda lifted herself, to increase the pleasures coming from both inside and outside. She sighed ecstatically as she came. Moments later, Medwin gave out an almighty moan and thrust himself even deeper inside of her, as he reached orgasm.

They hung on tightly for some time, until finally Medwin lifted Wanda and they both fell onto the bed. Still locked together, they would have stayed right there on the bed, if Medwin's phone had not rung.

A quick look at his phone and Medwin could see that it had been his young son trying to reach him. He had not answered quickly enough.

Mino was just 7 years old. He had not seemed overly traumatised, by his mum and dad breaking up when he was 5. Dad still lived with Oma and Opa (Grandma and Grandpa), right next to his house. Mino spent as much time in that house, as he did in the house he lived in with his Mum. Mum went to work five days a week so most of the time Opa was the one to take Mino to school. Oma would collect him in the afternoon. She always had something nice baked for afternoon tea. Mino really liked that. His mum had not even seemed all that emotional, about his dad moving out of their house.

After Medwin phoned Mino back, he quickly dressed for dinner. Wanda had not wanted to ask about the call. He was quiet and obviously in deep thought about whatever had transpired.

The traditional foods of Slovakia proved interesting. Wanda started with a sort of cheese-filled dumpling and Medwin had the soup, with sausage and sauerkraut.

Not that she needed a second course after that but Wanda had already ordered the potato pancakes. Medwin had to finish it off for her. Delicious as it was, the dumplings had been very filling. She had also tasted some of Medwin's pork stew, with sour cream and dumplings. Absolutely mouth-watering. Now they were both totally stuffed but Medwin said she really could not get away, without trying his favourite Slovak desert. Trdelnik was a very traditional cake and sweet pastry, with a hollow centre that came from being baked on a cylindrical spit. Looked stunning and tasted amazing.

During dinner, Medwin had told Wanda about the call from his son Mino. He had wanted to know if his dad would be there tomorrow, for his try-out with the village football team. The fact he could not be there, had made Medwin feel very sad. He was also annoyed that his wife had clearly approved for Mino to call him. He was 7 years old. Medwin could count the times Mino had ever called him on one hand. What was she playing at? His parents would have told her that he was away for this weekend. Not like her to play such games with Mino. Maybe she had seen how different Medwin looked, when he had come back from St. Anton. She had not met anyone since they split two years earlier. It had been work or Mino for her. She got along well with Medwin's family and spent a lot of time with them. Maybe someone mentioned he was meeting up with a lady this weekend. Maybe she suspected, Medwin had finally met the someone that would take him away from the village.

• CHAPTER TWELVE •

SITTING ON THE PLANE headed back to Amsterdam, Wanda felt as though her entire world had been turned upside down. Hug and Fug had been in play for several hours earlier that day. Sleep the night before, had been a little restless. Medwin had taken quite some time to recover, after the call from his son. Wanda was so tired. He must be tired too. She worried about him doing that long drive home.

Medwin's son clearly meant the world to him. Wanda was happy he did. What sort of father would Medwin be otherwise?

Larry had disappointed her often enough in that regard. She knew that he loved Jay and Lou deeply. 'Why then had it been so difficult to keep him engaged with their lives?' she would often think.

They were only four and two, when she and Larry had split. He had a key to the front door of the new house they moved to and he was free to come and go as he liked. Turning up for dinner had been no problem at all. Bath time regime after dinner, was his for the taking. He always knew there would be enough food for him to join them in a meal. Singing songs and reading books took place after the bath. Then it was lights out. In the early days of the split, Larry turned up often.

As the years progressed, it seemed more and more difficult. Getting him along to school events had been an enormous challenge. Birthdays had however been something he was really good at. Generally playing trumpet for the pass the parcel games. A big hit with the kids. Thinking about it all, made Wanda feel even more emotional.

Wanda had never led Jay and Lou to have false expectations. As difficult as it had sometimes been, she always talked in a positive way about their dad. When they had not heard from him in ages, she would just tell them to call him. The most important thing was that they knew he loved them very much.

Being a musician, there was no point having any schedules for weekends on and off. Larry could just see them whenever it worked. They were also lucky to have no money issues because of the clear settlement, with an agreement for no maintenance. This had all suited Wanda just fine and worked really well for Larry too. They both knew split couples who had so much anger in their lives, all due to arguments about money.

It seemed Medwin had almost normal contact with his son. Mino even had his dad living in the house he spent most of his time in. With Oma and Opa. Wanda could not help but wonder if that was all a little like having your cake and eating it for Medwin. The folded shirts and being so well taken care of by his mum. No wonder he had not moved to Vienna yet.

Medwin found it hard to focus on his driving. The road was very familiar and weather was good but his new friends Hug and Fug would not remove themselves from his thinking.

How could Nina have given Mino her phone, to call him like that last night? That was really not nice. This had never happened before. Apart from him being made to feel so bad about not making the football try out, Medwin knew that he had not been such good company for Wanda afterwards.

His love for Mino was overwhelming. It confused him to be thinking about Wanda and their Hug and Fug activities, at the same time he had Mino come into his mind.

Medwin had never been at all huggy, with either Mino or Nina. His family were all the same and so was Nina's. Respectful kisses on the cheek, to greet each other and say farewell. Even the early kissing sessions Medwin and Nina had, were very short and sharp.

With Wanda, Medwin became a totally different beast. He hungered for her body. Just to look into her eyes and know that she was his. The life she led, was a life he had always seen himself living. They could be so happy together. He would make it happen and there was nothing Nina or any of his family could do to stop it. Early days to be telling them about Wanda though. She might get back to Holland and wonder what on earth she had done. He really needed to get himself moved to Vienna and being more independent. Wanda must have thought it really odd that he still lived with his parents.

Back in Hillywood, Anna was preparing for her departure in just a few days. She was keen to get the full Bratislava story from Wanda.

Anna could see that Wanda had been totally captivated by Medwin. He certainly was a 'spunk', she would say. (A good Australian word for an attractive and sexy looking person ..... male or female.)

Wanda felt as though she must have dreamed the weekend. It could not have been so perfect. Medwin was like this shining knight, who had come to save her from sexual obscurity. He had brought her senses to life so strongly, that she could still feel his presence. Her skin took on goose bumps, when she told Anna about their very special new friends Hug and Fug. Anna laughed to think how Medwin must have sounded, saying Fug when he meant to say fuck. How unbelievably sexy and cute was that?

Having met him personally, Anna felt that extra bit special and involved.

Not a mention of age difference from Anna. Wanda had thought about it momentarily but then looked at a picture she had taken on her phone. They looked totally suited. Her Adonis mountain man looked like the perfect match. Lou thought so too and was so excited that her mum was in such a spin. She had not heard quite the detail that Anna had but she could read all over Wanda's face, that she had quite an amazing time.

Medwin had sent Wanda an sms, as soon as he arrived home safely. He had signed off simply. *'I am yours and I am in love.'*

Later that evening, Medwin emailed such a long and beautiful message. Words of love so tenderly written. Talk of Hug and Fug, bringing such vivid recollections that Wanda became totally aroused.

Medwin suggested that he would like to visit her in Holland, on her birthday in a few weeks. He would need to ask about taking some holiday from work but first wanted to know if it was OK with her.

OK? Wanda could not have been happier.

The day came for Anna and her pooch to leave for the UK. Mel had driven over to pick them up. They seemed fine with each other. Cindy had stayed back in the UK, to attend medical appointments. They were on track for a pleasant reunion. Mel had taken the trouble to colour his hair and was dressed to impress.

PJ was sad to be seeing her buddy leave. They had become good doggy mates. Wanda and Lou were also a little sad to see Anna go. She had fitted in with them very nicely indeed. Fingers crossed it would all work out for her, back with Mel and Cindy in the UK. No doubt they would see them all, when they visited next time.

Back in the office, the General was keeping Wanda very occupied. Just as well. She might otherwise have sat around all day, thinking about Medwin. Only a couple of weeks and he would visit her in Holland. She could hold on until then. Really did miss him though. They must have exchanged at least three emails a day and a great many sms texts. Little messages of love. Funny things that happened during the day. The miles were keeping them apart but their hearts and minds, still felt totally connected.

Wanda had put a brief together, for three agencies to pitch for a new marketing communications campaign for the General. Al's agency was one of the contenders. All of the European business leaders, would be in Wanda's office to receive the presentations. Wanda wanted them all to play a role in the decision making process. Her team knew that Al was an old friend. That just meant he would have to work even harder, to convince them of his company's merits. After all three presentations were seen, she would be operating a very simple secret vote. The business leaders would be the ones to choose the final winner.

'Great work pulling all this together in such a short time Wanda,' said Patty when the final time was set for pitches. 'You have Medwin arriving a few days. Good idea to make the pitches for after he leaves. Let me host a dinner party at my apartment, to thank you for all of this hard work and to also make Medwin feel welcome. Can't wait to meet him. My old boyfriend is coming up from France then too. He can cook for us all. Let's ask Damon and his girlfriend too. It will be your birthday around then. Even more reason to celebrate.'

Wanda agreed and thanked Patty, then they got back into the discussions at hand, about where the marketing communications should be heading. The re-branding was in place and a new satellite tracking component had been added to their product portfolio. All very exciting. A launch needed to be planned and she had just the venue. The European Space Agency expo centre in Holland.

Medwin loved to hear all the stories about Wanda's work. She clearly had a great deal of respect from her colleagues and really enjoyed what she did. It unfortunately highlighted the fact that he did not like his job, in any way at all. Designing rail signalling systems would be fine, if the hierarchy would let him do his job. There was always someone interfering.

Many of his colleagues had left for better roles at other companies. Some had taken the last voluntary redundancy package that had been offered. Now he wished he had also taken it. The only thing that kept him going when he was in the office, was the constant contact with Wanda. He had fallen madly in love with her. All he could think about, was the passionate Hug and Fug experiences they had shared.

'All sorts of other Hug and Fug moves yet to be explored.' He would think to himself. Then he would look at that website on hugging and fucking again and plan which numbers he hoped to prioritise, for future encounters with Wanda. He still had not had the courage to talk to Wanda about his desires though. It would need to wait, until he had her right there in front of him.

Meanwhile, he focussed on words of love in his messages and tried to explain how deep his feelings for her were. The translation program continued to support all his email and texting efforts so very well.

Jay was also not happy in his work. The advertising agency world moved at a fast pace and he had found it all way too commercial. If only he could just focus on making his music and supporting the Gallery's art exposure. The DJ gigs had increased in number but that would still not pay the rent. Money was good at the ad agency but he found the experience a little soul destroying.

Wanda's friend, that got Jay the interview, had saved Jay through a couple of rounds of people being made redundant. At the time, Jay had been happy about that. He enjoyed living in London and had a lot of other things going. Now he was in a similar boat to Medwin. Wanda had them both telling her down the phone, they wished they had been the one made redundant.

Jay finally had his wish.

'You need to sign straight on for unemployment Jay and get out there to find another job.' Wanda had been supportive but now Jay was an adult, he had to make his own way in the world.

'Mum. I've actually seen this excellent IT study program but it is full time for three months. Do you think I could do that? I think I can get a grant for the course fees so I will only need a little financial support towards my living costs. Should get some study support money from the unemployment office too.'

Wanda had always told both Jay and Lou that she would support them through any serious studies. This looked like a good course and Jay had done all the background work so that would be fine.

It should enable him better, for a decent job at the end of it. Started really soon so no time for Jay to be idle.

Lou was busy finishing two paintings that needed to be handed in to her art teacher by the end of the month. These were to be her main pieces for the entire school year and her teacher had been giving her some grief. His idea of good art, was anything that took on a totally abstract form. Lou on the other hand, was a master of creating art that made live objects present in such a way that you felt you must reach out and touch them. Her use of colour was magnificent. Brush strokes brought things to life in the most vivid way. With Anna and one dog less in the house, Lou was able to set up the dining area completely for her painting needs. No problem for Wanda. At least that was for the two weeks, until Medwin was scheduled to arrive. Lou wanted them finished by then in any case. She wanted to be able to join in some of the things Wanda had planned for showing Medwin around Holland. He would stay for a week. Her mum was so excited but Lou could see she was also a little nervous. How sweet was that? Probably wondered how he would feel about Wanda having such a grown up daughter. Her mum would have also been keen for Lou and everyone else to like him. Lou felt sure she would. No way her mum would have fallen so hard for someone, if they were not really special. It was very clear, her mum was totally smitten.

Jay and Wanda had talked about her upcoming birthday. It was a tradition for the three of them, to always make sure they celebrated each other's birthdays together. Jay was in March, Wanda in May and then Lou in October. A nice span of dates across the year. This year, Wanda's birthday fell during the week. Medwin would be visiting until the day after. The following weekend, was therefore agreed for Wanda and Lou to fly across to London for celebrations with Jay. Maybe some other friends would join in for a theatre visit. Excellent!

Medwin had free rail travel, because of his job, so he would take the train to Holland.

'I arrive in Utrecht on Thursday at 10am. Should I take another train to you?' he had asked.

No way had Wanda wanted to wait any longer than she had to. She would be at Utrecht train station to meet him.

Medwin had sent several sms texts during his journey. Looked like the train would be on time. He was nervous. Not much sleep for him on that train ride. Questions ran through his head like wildfire. He would be staying in Wanda's house and her daughter would be there. Different to being on neutral ground, away from home. He had spoken to Lou once on the phone and she sounded very nice. What if she did not like him? She and Wanda were really close. There had not been a man staying at this house with Wanda before.

Lou might feel strange and even a little jealous maybe. Although, she did have her own boyfriend who stayed over so that helped.

Hug and Fug came to Medwin's rescue. His head had cleared totally, of all thoughts around Lou's acceptance of him. Good old Hug and Fug. Umm! He was feeling very light headed now. Position 24. Oh so clear in his head. Wanda's hand was reaching down to feel his pulsing penis? Hug and Fug were at play. He let them take over. In moments of greater clarity, he became aware of his own hand being the one actually on his penis. It was no stranger. They understood each other very well. Masturbation had seen Medwin through many years of quick release, not having a partner.

After several changes of clothing and last minute panics to have everything just right in the house, Wanda had been amazed to actually reach Utrecht station before Medwin was due to arrive. Not much sleep for a couple of nights. Really needed Bon Jovi to energise her first thing that day. She had every intention of living while she was alive and she had total confidence that Medwin was the man to help her live it to the full.

Stunning!

It seemed the hustle and bustle of a busy station, just drifted into a slow motion backdrop. There he was. Her Adonis. He had not seen her yet. When their eyes finally met, smiles went from ear to ear.

Wanda quickened her steps, to reach his arms as quickly as possible. Medwin lifted her high in the air and she instinctively wrapped her legs around him. They stood sighing into each other's ears, for a good five minutes. Neither wanted to let the other go.

'I can't believe you are actually here in Holland,' had been all Wanda could say. She was speechless and so was he.

That green Italian wagon was parked under the station. Wanda had planned a little visit to the nearby lakes, with a stopover at one of her favourite cafes. Not for too long though. She was keen to get him back to her house, with a good couple of hours up her sleeve before Lou would be back from school. Hug and Fug thoughts had been driving her crazy.

Medwin proved to be the perfect tourist. He loved everything. So excited about the smallest of details. It was the first time he had been to Holland. In fact, the most distance he had ever travelled before, was when he had been to Portugal with his wife for a holiday. She had not enjoyed travelling so far. Other holidays, had only taken them as far as Northern Italy. He wanted to see the world. Holland was a great place to start. Wanda was the perfect person to do it all with.

'What a beautiful house,' remarked Medwin as Wanda gave him a little guided tour on arrival. 'The way you explained the renovation, I thought it was much smaller. All this space on your top floor.

You made it all work very nicely.' He was particularly impressed that it seemed so quiet on the top floor. This was Wanda's bedroom and they had their own bathroom. He was feeling more comfortable already.

Wanda had walked ahead of Medwin, as they climbed the steep stairs. He admired her beautiful strong calf muscles all the way up. She had great legs. Her buttocks moved in front of his face. They were narrow and very steep stairs. Hug and Fug thoughts had her clothes removed and he was pushing her to the stairs and taking her from behind. Maybe he would do that for real one day, before he left. Now, as they both stood staring at the bed, Medwin moved gently and took her hand to kiss it. He took the other hand and did the same. She melted to sit on the bed and he followed. They fell back, into a tight hugging position.

'This is where I am meant to be Wanda. Tightly together with you. Holding you always in my arms. I am in love with you so very much,' Medwin tried hard to find the English words to say what he felt in his heart but the kiss that followed said it all.

'I am in love with you too Medwin. I am so happy to have you here. It feels so right being with you.' Wanda replied, light tears of happiness filling her eyes.

Wanda had special massage oil beside the bed. She lifted it to show Medwin and asked if he would like her to take some of the strain of travelling out of his back. 'Yes please', he replied.

His naked and muscly body was soon face down on her bed. She stood to take it all in. What an incredible form. Legs like strong tree trunks. Buttocks standing high and solid. As the oil drops hit his cheeks, they squeezed tight and made small indents on each side. The drops had found their way into the crevice of his anus. Wanda could see the oil running through and knew it would reach his balls. She gently followed the oil with one finger. Medwin groaned.

Wanda had taken her clothes off. She straddled into a kneeling seated position, across Medwin's buttocks. Poured oil over the upper part of his body and began to massage him deeply. Muscles to the side of Medwin's spine, were large and hard. She moved up and down them with her elbows, to try and loosen their grip.

Taking a short rest, she leaned forward and softly kissed the side of his face. Her tongue gently circled his ear and lobe. He continued to sigh and groan with pleasure.

Knuckles were manoeuvred into his shoulder blades. It was clear they were a big source of pain. Having worked on those for some time, Wanda decided on gentle rubbing down each arm. Deep and soft work on the hands, then ended with individual finger pulling and clicks to draw the bad energy out of each meridian. Legs followed.

She lifted herself off his buttocks and turned to re-straddle in the opposite direction. Gently encouraging his balls and penis out from underneath and down to sit between his legs. They were enlarged and throbbing. So beautiful to see.

She slowly dropped the smallest amounts of oil on them and did little butterfly finger movements all over. He began to shake.

Each hand worked hard, to massage up and down Medwin's upper leg in unison. To reach his calf muscles and feet, she needed to slide herself a little forward. One slide was not enough. Her clitoris was now fully engaged with his buttocks.

'A little more massage oil and just another slide or two,' she thought to herself. It was clear that Medwin enjoyed this massage feature, almost as much as she did.

The thickness of Medwin's athletic calves was astounding. Wanda massaged them from every angle. Finally down to the back of his ankles, into the highly sensitive pulsing area behind the ankle back. Pressure to the arches of his feet initially caused a small tickling sensation. When she went into the gaps of his toes, he stretched the entire foot and leg with pleasure. Individual toes were extended with meridians released and clicked for closure. The back massage was complete.

'Shall I do the other side?' Wanda asked pensively.

The massage had been heavenly but Medwin could not hold back any longer. He managed to roll over, still keeping Wanda in her straddled position. His penis was inside her in an instant. Hard, throbbing and ready to explode. She was already so close to climaxing, from the rubbing on his body. They simultaneously went into an orgasmic explosion.

It must have been at least half an hour, before they stirred back to a conscious state. Hugging and simply pointing towards the bathroom. They needed to wash and dress. Lou would be home soon.

Back in Bratislava, they had both agreed they would give condoms a miss. It was highly unlikely that Wanda could fall pregnant again and very clear neither of them would be having sex with anyone else.

Wanda thought about that conversation, as she watched Medwin at the washbasin in the bathroom. Hug and Fug took them over, way too quickly for having to think about condoms. She was pleased they had agreed to exclude those.

Wanda was relaxing in a hot bath, soaking in eucalyptus oil. The aroma and mere sight of her lying there in the mirror, aroused Medwin yet again. He turned to face her with another massive erection. Before she knew it, he was in the bath with her. He lifted her onto his lap and they sat wrapped up hugging, with his penis deep inside her. The warm water and soapy eucalyptus bath, splashed out onto the tiles. This time it was a slow and lingering movement back and forth together, with her on Medwin's lap. He came with a quiet and deep pleasure, while Wanda needed to continue just a little longer in the sway before joining him.

They had dressed and were downstairs, well before Lou appeared through the front door.

Wanda had already arranged for dinner out, at one of her favourite restaurants in town. She thought that would be a little more relaxing for everyone. Danny had gone straight from school to do some chores but would be with them in good time to join in. A nice little foursome.

Conversation was initially stilted but once it got around to talk of skiing, Lou and Medwin clicked. His stories of downhill races and different competitions he had taken part in, amused everyone. Lou also recounted some of her funny little episodes on the slopes.

The dinner was a great success. Medwin felt right at home. Danny was a keen cyclist so he had been particularly interested in the stories of mountain bike races Medwin had taken part in. Danny had been in a few races himself. All most entertaining.

'I just need to spend a couple of hours in the office tomorrow afternoon remember, then afterwards it's drinks with folks at work followed by dinner at Patty's. OK with you?' Wanda was reminding

Medwin of plans for the next day, before they hit the pillow. He had decided he would like to visit a couple of sports shops and Wanda had made plans to drop him off where there was a few next to each other, while she went to the office.

The Friday night work borrel had been a little too busy for Medwin. He had resorted simply to his endearing 'Please?' over and over again. Everyone had however enjoyed his company. He always listened intently and laughed appropriately at people's stories.

Once they were at Patty's, a few of her guests had spoken German and he was much more at ease. It seemed Patty herself spoke good German. Wanda had not observed that before. Most odd. Every time Wanda turned around, Patty was leading Medwin out onto her balcony for a quiet chat. He was way too polite to pull away. Wanda had been amused initially.

Patty and Wanda had been out dancing and to see bands a few times. They were quite good friends, she thought. Patty had been the one to hire her back into the General. Wanda was grateful.

She had shown Patty around Holland and on one occasion they had even been skiing together in France. The old boyfriend visiting from Paris, was in fact the guy they had stayed with in Val d'Isere.

Michel was old enough to be Patty's father and still married. He had children older than Patty. Their relationship was indeed, very strange. All Patty really wanted in life, was to get married and have a child but she just kept finding herself spending time with the wrong man. Michel had been her most important boyfriend in ten years. How on earth did she ever think she would find that someone special, if she kept this going.

The dinner had been exquisite. What an amazing chef Patty's Parisian friend turned out to be. He had also brought along some incredible wines.

They all drank far too much to be driving home. Or so Patty thought.

She was insisting that Wanda and Medwin should sleep over and had forgotten that Wanda always made a point of managing her wine intake. Michel was fast asleep by now and the other guests were up dancing.

Totally capable of still driving that green Italian wagon out of there, in a hurry, Wanda could not leave soon enough.

Patty seemed to have her sights set on seeing much more of Medwin. He had been oblivious and polite but Wanda could see the glint in Patty's eyes, as she looked his amazing body up and down constantly. A ménage a trois had never been for Wanda. She would keep her beautiful man all to herself.

Driving home that night, Medwin talked excitedly about all the different people he had met. Wanda thought about the unacceptable attention that Patty had paid Medwin. She would have to mention it to her, when she went back to work post Medwin's departure. He clearly had no interest in anyone other than Wanda and that made her feel very special. All the same, Patty had behaved badly.

Wanda felt very pleased with herself, driving home with this amazing man by her side. He kept looking across at her, with such loving gazes.

Suddenly those naughty little Hug and Fug characters started jumping through her mind. What were they up to? It seemed a ménage a trois had struck quite a chord with them.

• CHAPTER THIRTEEN •

'HAPPY BIRTHDAY,' Medwin and Lou shouted as they entered Wanda's bedroom with breakfast and presents. Wanda's eyes tried to open fully. She was smiling from ear to ear and had eventually managed to sing along with them. 'Happy birthday to me.'

She was still not totally with them. Quick thoughts to the night before. Pleasant thoughts of the love making she and her gorgeous man had, after the drive home from the party. Just the two of them.

The half sleep haze was soon lifted, when Wanda saw all the beautifully wrapped gifts being laid out before her. But first to eat some of that lekker breakfast Lou had made. The three of them sat on the bed. Lou had put some of Wanda's favourite music on downstairs. Aretha Franklin could be heard in the background, as they chatted and ate fresh fruit and croissants.

'This one first mum,' said Lou as she pushed one of her gifts towards Wanda.

It was a CD. Something new that Wanda had mentioned she liked. Lou ran off downstairs to put in on. Lighthouse Family. Excellent!

She had also given her mum some new ski gloves and a book. How very thoughtful.

Now for the cards. Wanda loved cards. She read each message fully and talked about the people who had sent them. Her friends were very dear to her. A couple of friends in the UK had also sent gifts. Cute slippers from one. A little bicycle ornament from another.

Medwin wondered if she would ever get to his gift. She kept picking it up and putting it back down. Maybe she wanted him to hand it to her and say something. He could do that. He lifted the small box and put it behind his back. Leaned forward and gave her a big slow kiss on the lips. 'Happy Birthday my very beautiful lady,' he said as he placed the package into her hands.

She had been saving the best until last. Medwin had already demonstrated how thoughtful he was. The weekend he arranged in Bratislava. Bringing along the BoBo's schnapps and songs that had made an impact on their first meeting. When he arrived in Holland, he had given her special chocolates from Vienna. That had been quite enough. Now this precious looking box. So beautifully wrapped. The heartfelt card. He must have searched forever to find it. Two people on the deck of a boat in the moonlight. The most incredible words of love inside. In English.

Wanda took the deepest of breaths. Her eyes enlarged and one hand went to her mouth. She could only stare at Medwin and felt tears come into her eyes as she said, 'It's so beautiful. You shouldn't have.' She reached over and hugged him, as she beckoned for him to put it on her wrist.

'Wow mum. It really is beautiful. Good taste Medwin. I love it,' said Lou as she gently touched the silver bracelet now adorning her mother's arm. 'Big chunky solid silver. I love the way each section loops across and over the next. A real work of art.'

Lou took away all the breakfast things and told them she was heading out to catch up with some friends at the library. She would get the shopping from the market, on the way back. People were scheduled to arrive for a birthday bash around 3pm.

Medwin ran a bath and he and Wanda spent the next hour or so making love in the bathroom. She had bought two new super soft bath robes. At one point, they found themselves lying on the bathroom floor in their robes just hugging each other. So so soft and huggy. It sent them both to sleep briefly. Such peace and tranquillity, just lying there in each other's arms feeling totally loved. Hugged by the soft robes. Hugged by each other.

Denise and the boys arrived just before 3pm. They could not wait to finally meet Medwin. 'Ooh La La! Very nice indeed,' was all Denise could say when she had a quiet moment with Wanda.

Lou had several of her friends over for the celebrations. Most of Wanda's local friends came. Around thirty people in all. Highlight of course being their chance to meet the lovely and talented Medwin. He had quite some difficulty with understanding people but it had not dampened his spirit. 'Please?' was heard often. Everyone loved it. They were then encouraged to use less words and talk more slowly. A couple of people did speak German but he asked if they wouldn't mind sticking with English. It would help him to learn. Very sweet.

It was quite late by the time the last guests left the house. Lou and her friends had been gone a couple hours already. They headed into town, to play some pool. Denise had wanted Medwin and Wanda to go into town with her. A good band on in a local bar. Should be a good bopping night. They had said they might meet her in there but all they had really wanted to do, by the time everyone left, was curl up in front of the TV. The motorcycle grand prix had been on that day and Medwin discovered it would be shown on Dutch television that night. Wanda was more than happy to sit and watch it with him.

As they sat watching the bikes roar around the track, Wanda nodded off slightly. How perfect could life get? What a fantastic birthday. Now they were sitting wrapped around each other hugging. She had bought special new super soft 'caress' cushions for the sofa. Their heads were sent into an almost trance-like state, as soon as they hit them. Wanda drifted off slightly. Hug and Fug jumped straight into her head. Next thing she knew, her hand was on Medwin's penis. It was soft and sleepy but still just as wonderful to behold. He lifted himself to free it slightly, then put his hand down Wanda's pants. They stayed totally intent on the Grand Prix and just sat there holding each other's genitalia. Even as Medwin's penis enlarged, they sat still and stayed focussed on the TV. Very magical!

The race was coming to an end. Crowd was going wild. One minute the Australian was in the lead and the next it was the Italian. Medwin wasn't quite sure which rider he wanted to win.

They zigzagged to cross in front of each other continuously. Medwin had historically favoured the Italian. Since he had met Wanda, he felt his allegiance had swayed towards the ozzie. How amazing that he was now looking like he might win this race. Medwin had sat with a quiet erection through all of it, hugging one of the cushions resting between him and Wanda.

Yes! The race was won! The ozzie had taken his championship racing machine over the line first. Incredible!

Medwin might have jumped to his feet, had he been able to move. Instead, at that precise time of elation, Wanda had taken his penis out of his jeans and placed her mouth over it. It was a first for Medwin. Her head rested on the 'caress' cushion. Just seconds and he was over the line with an orgasm. His head span. Tissues were to hand, to mop up the sperm on his stomach. Wanda had never been one to swallow.

Over the next few days, that green Italian wagon helped Wanda show Medwin Holland. Spruced up with a good clean and polish, both inside and out. Several CDs sorted to play during the planned sightseeing adventures. Medwin had seemed to like that Wanda had a station wagon. Good for all those interesting trips they would go on. Plenty of room in the back for all the gear they would need. He had ideas of camping trips. Wanda had only ever once in her life been camping. That had been a mother/daughter thing with the Girl Guides in Sydney. She and Lou had shared a two person tent.

It completely zipped up but they had still been terrified snakes and bugs might get in. They were not terribly rugged.

Zaanse Schans was the first stop on Wanda's sightseeing list. An amazing purpose built tourist destination, for exploring some of Holland's heritage. Their working windmills sat right alongside the beautiful and very wide River Zaan. Some visitors arrived by canal boat but the majority took the 15km ride from Amsterdam with a bus tour. At certain times of day, there could be 16 or so coaches in the parking area. Plenty of parking for cars too. That is where they made their money. Although you entered the mini village through an actual gated area, no charge was made for that. Photographers placed themselves at that entrance, to snap happy tourists as they arrived. Photos were ready and fixed into a souvenir frame, by the time they went to leave. A large wall holding all the images for visitors to view. Buy if you like. No problem if you don't.

First into the clog making house and museum. 'Klompen' being the Dutch word for clogs. Stop for a quick photo, standing in the giant clogs outside perhaps. An amazing collection of clogs displayed inside, from many centuries past. Brilliantly crafted wooden shoes that had kept Dutch feet dry and safe for a very long time. Demonstrations on how they were made, took place on the hour. Started with a block of Poplar or Willow wood. Antique machinery used by the craftsman to hollow out. Very sharp cutting blades to shape. Blowing on one end of the clog, showed just how much water the fresh wood held. Final shoe requiring significant drying time.

Blue Delft china and pottery museum. Farmhouse with cheese making demonstrations. Toy shop. Lace making. General store. Such an array of interesting things to see. All presented in old wooden buildings, painted the traditional dark green. Over 35 houses, buildings and windmills dating back to 1574. Laid out in a little village, running beside the river. Exquisite!

'The paint making windmill is my favourite Medwin. Apparently the only remaining truly working windmill in the world. With this wind, it should be operational,' Wanda was excited about showing him this beast in action. The large central section would be pounding on stones and chalk, to make pigments for paint.

That day's sightseeing concluded with dinner in Volendam, the quaint fishing village a little further north. Old fishing boats sat alongside modern river cruisers. Looking out across the Zuiderzee (South Sea), it seemed the water went on forever. Wanda explained how this section of water had been closed off from the North Sea a long time ago. Land had been reclaimed to provide new opportunities for housing. A great trick of the Dutch. Very clever engineering. On the road to the north of the village centre, it was easy to see that the land to the left, was much lower than the sea to the right. Most of Holland was below sea level and this was clearly in evidence here. The original salt water inlet, changed to fresh water as it became the Ijsselmeer (Ijssel Lake – named after the Ij River that drains into it). Average depth was just six metres and it spanned almost 1100 sq.kms.

After dinner, they sat in the car looking out across the sea. Wanda continuing her tour guide facts and figures. Medwin was captivated. It really turned him on to watch her speaking in such an animated and informative way. Hug and Fug started to play in his brain as he tried to focus on what she was saying.

He lifted her shirt. 'Keep talking. I really am interested but just need to play with you a little if I may,' he said to Wanda as he started to tweak her nipples.

Wanda kept talking and tried to act nonchalant. Medwin had his hand inside her jeans and was kissing her neck, as he rubbed her pussy.

The words left Wanda. As she relaxed back into the car seat, he moved her a little further back for better access. The fondling and kissing all over had Wanda reaching a gentle climax in minutes. She had closed her eyes and gone off into dreamland.

Medwin kept his hand hard pressed against her pelvic bones, as he moved to kiss her lips tenderly. They hugged tightly and a wave of sleep swept over them.

Quite late by the time they reached their bed that night. Tired of course but there had not been one evening where they had gone to sleep without first making love. This night would be no different.

They had only to hold each other and they were aroused. Wanda had thought she might be sore with all the activity but not so. Medwin was insatiable and it seemed Wanda was too.

Keukenhof gardens and their world of spectacular tulips. Canal boat tour around Amsterdam. Cycling in the local forests. A favourite beach restaurant, by the sea in Zandvoort. The fun filled days had passed by so quickly.

It was soon time for Medwin to leave Holland. They squeezed each other more tightly than ever, as daylight broke that morning. Wanda's head was nestled on his shoulder. Medwin pulled her over to lie on top. He pushed her shoulders upwards to lift her breast to his mouth. Kissing her shoulders and chest, as he licked and teased her nipples. He knew how much she loved all the foreplay. He did too. They would play and touch each other's sensitive areas throughout the day, not just when it came to actual love making.

She was soon sucking his nipples. Medwin had incredibly strong arms. He seemed to lift her with such ease. Pulling her up to a sitting position on his chest, he had slid down the bed somewhat to be able to focus completely on the licking of her entire crutch area. Finally it was just her clitoris. Gentle slow licking, with his wide soft tongue. As she burst into climax, he moved her body back down and thrust his penis deep inside. Neither of them moved. They just hung on tightly, as if they were afraid any movement might part them. Wanda was totally ecstatic and tears had welled in her eyes. He would be leaving soon. It took very little movement at all for Medwin to reach a climax, by which time Wanda had moved to a second. They came together and squeezed tighter even still.

'The train seems to be on time and I bought a few things for the journey. Thank you for an unbelievable week. Speak later. Love you so much X,' Medwin's text message had read.

Wanda was already on her drive to the office. They had decided she should just drop him at the station and not come in. Did not want to be leaving each other in a state. Plans had been made to see each other again soon, in Vienna. They had also discussed a possible visit to Australia and the Olympics later in the year. Lots of forward thinking to focus on and be happy about. Did not help Wanda hold back the tears though. She missed him so much already.

Two days back in the office for Wanda and then she and Lou would fly over to Jay in London for the weekend. Plans had been made for more birthday celebrations and she was really looking forward to that.

Agency pitches were to take place on the second day back so she really needed to get her head into gear again.

Patty had been a little annoyed that Wanda had not managed to find any other time to catch up while Medwin was in town. She had sent texts most days, inviting them to one thing or another. It had been pretty clear to Wanda that Patty had less than honourable intentions, when it came to Medwin so she was keeping him well away.

'Fantastic pitches Wanda. Will be interesting to see what the secret ballot reveals. Good you included this democratic process.

No doubt in my mind though. Al and his team are clearly ahead of the game, with understanding our business,' said Bob as they all walked out of the room for a stretch break.

Brilliant. The vote was in and it was unanimous. Al's agency won the pitch. One of the biggest budgets they ever had and high profile work Al would definitely be able to exploit, for other new clients.

'Will we be taking pot luck for theatre tickets tomorrow night mum?' Lou asked as the plane took off from Schiphol.

They had always managed to get good tickets from the half-price ticket booth in Leicester Square. Arrived mid-afternoon and then just went for whatever looked interesting for that evening.

'I would really love to see Blood Brothers. Had excellent reviews. Let see how we go heh,' replied Wanda.

This visit to London, they had decided to stay in a hotel. Jay joined them. The friends they had wanted to catch up with had gone out of town. Nice to be tourists for a change. Just the three of them.

Any visit to London would of course have to include passing by St. Thomas's Hospital. Both Lou and Jay having been born there, facing Big Ben and the Houses of Parliament directly opposite. Thames River carrying all manner of water craft in front. The entire area so steeped in history. Most important history of all to Wanda, was the fact she had given birth to her children there.

Having found a well-priced hotel on the edge of Regents Park, they had also planned to visit the colourful Camden Markets and Lock. Possibly rent bikes to ride around the park also.

Wanda and Lou told Jay all about Medwin. Lou spoke very highly of him, which pleased Wanda no end.

'He is such a good runner Jay. So funny. We took him into the forest. Mum and I were riding our bikes as fast as we could, while he and PJ ran. So fit.' Lou recounted. 'He wants to teach mum and I to ride mountain bikes and use gears. Can't see that happening. We do not do hills.'

Having mentioned the mountain biking to Lou the last time he saw her, Medwin had now actually found just the place. A perfect little trip for that green Italian wagon. He suggested plans be made for a time when Jay was in Holland, at the same time he would be. Maybe Danny could come too. It was just a couple of hours drive from Hillywood. In the Ardennes. A short way over the border into Belgium. The hotel had bikes and helmets so we had no need to take anything. Beautiful mountain lanes all around it.

Wanda had not been too sure about the mountain biking but the hotel certainly looked appealing and she was prepared to give it a whirl, at some point.

'Great catch mum,' was Jay's initial reaction. 'Love the sound of the mountain biking in the Ardennes too. Let's work out dates.'

Blood Brothers had been even better than they all expected. So moving. Twin boys separated at birth. Tragic mining town in the Midlands. Love of the same woman. Finally realising who they were, after knowing each other for so long. Such a sad ending. Brilliant music. A real tear jerker.

Wanda had then been on the phone to Medwin straight after. If they got to London, he would have to go and see it with her. Musical Theatre at its best. So emotional! She wanted him to be there with them. She needed so much to just hug him.

Medwin had not seen much theatre. Loved music though. Would be great to see these shows with Wanda. He was pleased that Jay had been keen to do the mountain biking trip too.

That weekend for Medwin was pretty much 24/7 with Mino. Took him to his football that day. Only a two month pre summer holiday competition series. Really just to get the young boys interested and thinking about football for the next season. Medwin thought back to that Bratislava phone call. It had never been mentioned by Mino and he had not at any point seemed bothered by the fact Medwin didn't make it to those try outs. He had never raised it with his wife Nina either. Decided instead not to tell any of his family what he was doing in future. They never talked much anyway so that was not difficult. He was either at work or out with Mino. Conversations with Mino were always about school or the different sports activities they both did. If his dad was not about, he didn't seem bothered.

Mino had not even asked where his dad was that week he went to Holland. The life of a 7 year old, it seemed, was way too busy to be wondering about such things. Medwin's parents had been told there were work things taking him abroad. No questions had been asked. He did not want them discussing movements with Nina.

As Medwin sat there watching the football, his mind drifted to the apartments he would be looking at the following week in Vienna. He really did need to move out from his parents, as soon as possible.

'Mum. It's huge. A bit painful now too,' Lou was pointing in between her legs, at this very large and red blister looking thing. Being in the crease of her groin, it had been difficult to look after. Always a hot and sweaty place on the body. Wearing jeans had not helped. Wanda had wanted her to wear a skirt and get air on her blister the day before but no.

'I think we had better take you to casualty at St. Thomas's. It really looks awful now,' Wanda replied. The blister looked infected.

They were due to fly back to Holland very early on the Monday morning. Sunday night was going to be a chill night, watching TV in the hotel. They had been busy with Jay all weekend. Had an early dinner that Sunday evening. Then Jay had gone off on the tube, to his house share, so he could prepare for his IT classes the next day.

Doctors decided it was quite a dangerous cyst in Lou's groin. They needed to admit Lou so they could administer intensive antibiotics via a drip. The scheduled morning flight would need to be changed.

'Damon. Really sorry matey but can you tell Patty I tried to call her. I was actually relieved she didn't answer, to tell the truth. Finding her a bit painful lately. There is a risk of poisoning the blood stream so we can't discharge Lou from hospital here, until they are happy that risk has passed. I already changed our flights to tomorrow evening. Let's hope the drugs work OK. I'll call again tomorrow when we know more,' Wanda informed Damon. 'The agencies all need to be told. Patty should maybe make those calls. Good coming from her anyway. Especially with it being Al's team that won.'

Wanda then focussed on her little girl. She hated seeing her laid up in a hospital bed like this. So pleased she had taken her in though. Hopefully all would be clear by the morning. Meanwhile, Wanda would play slave and run around catering to Lou's every whim. Lou would do exactly the same, if it was her mum in the bed.

Wanda and Lou chatted and played silly games. They recalled the time Lou had been is hospital with a broken leg, when she was 10.

She had been ice skating back in Sydney. They had an au pair living with them who was a little dim, it seemed on reflection.

When Lou had taken the fall on the ice, the au pair had called Wanda at work straight away. Wanda had been told it was nothing. She would have raced home otherwise. The au pair had then driven home, given Lou food and drink and put her to bed. Told Wanda there was no pain and she must have just pulled a muscle. Wanda had come home early from work that night, just in case.

One look at Lou's leg and Wanda could see all was not well. Straight into the car and down to Manly Hospital. Ages in emergency waiting to get an x-ray. Main bone broken in not one but two places. A week in hospital followed. Then another six weeks of wearing a full leg cast and hopping around on crutches. At least Lou had been able to choose a colour for the cast. A very pretty pale pink.

Within two weeks, that cast had some fabulous artworks drawn or painted on it. Endless messages from well-wishers too. Luckily the break recovered well and she had no impacts from it later. Skied like a demon. Did competitive dance classes. All was well.

The au pair had been totally distraught by her mismanagement. Wanda bought her a couple of books on what to do in case of incidents. Good lessons had been learned. Neither Lou nor Wanda could now remember the au pair's name. Needless to say, she had not lasted all that long.

On her way out of the hospital that night, Wanda popped by the intensive care ward in maternity. She recalled her two weeks sitting there beside Jay after his birth. Him all wired up for tests. Her expressing milk from her full breasts, to be fed to him through tubes. Wondering if her first beautiful baby would be OK. Looking at all the other babies come and go. Some had been in there much longer than Jay. One premature baby had been there two months. His mother came every day to visit. A couple had come in and not lasted out the day. New-borns not getting their chance for life. So sad.

Wanda had her bed on a four-bed ward, for the two weeks Jay was in special care. Running an advertising agency, with so many large corporate clients, Wanda had been sent enough flowers to start a florist. Her bed was one of two alongside the large window, looking down to the Thames and across to Big Ben. The very wide ledge along that window had been completely filled with incredible flowers. Extra drawer units had been brought into the ward to hold flowers. There were plinths with flowers at the entrance to the room. Flowers had gone to the nurses sitting rooms on that ward and also in intensive care. It had been a sight to behold. Beautiful messages and so many strong and loving thoughts being sent their way, to get them through that very difficult time.

Larry had been fantastic. He had stayed at the hospital the first few nights. Work had been put on hold, as long as it could be. On top of his trumpet playing gigs, he had become a specialist joiner. He worked for himself and had clients waiting in the wings, for jobs to be finished. He worked his butt off, under the stress of not knowing what was happening with his first little baby boy. Came to the hospital early in the morning for an hour, before going to the job. Then back to the hospital in the afternoon. Stayed until it was lights out on the ward. They had been so close then. What had happened?

Medwin's concern for Lou being in hospital had meant a lot to Wanda. He called a few times, while she had been with Lou.

Talking on the phone was difficult for him but he chatted to Lou and made her laugh with silly ski stories. Receiving such a good reception, he went for a second round of laughs by playing her some of his oompah-pah guggamusik down the phone.

'Wanda I think I found the perfect place in Vienna,' said Medwin excitedly later the next day. His Monday had been spent viewing apartments to buy in Vienna.

Lou had been quick to respond to the intravenous drugs and by morning she had been given the all clear. They had made the late afternoon flight Wanda rescheduled and were now back in Holland.

Danny had been at the house when Lou and Wanda arrived home. He had been looking after PJ. Lou had called him a few times from hospital and he had been extremely worried. There he was, a bunch of flowers in one hand and PJ's lead in the other. A great welcome back for Lou. Very sweet.

'We just got to the front door. Let me get everything inside and make sure Lou is settled, then I can call you back,' responded Wanda.

The apartment sounded perfect. It was being promoted on line so Wanda could look at the images and information, as she spoke with Medwin. He was desperate for her to come and see it. Having been on the market for a couple of months, he felt sure it would still be available when she could make it. Weekend after next would work.

Medwin then went to great lengths, to tell Wanda how he had decided not to tell his family what he was doing. He had not even told Mino. Kept saying how he did not want 'his wife' to know his plans. Wanda hated him referring to her as his wife. She knew that her name was Nina.

Why did he not just call her by her name? Why had they been separated for two years and still not made any moves towards a divorce? What had led her to asking Mino to phone his dad that weekend in Bratislava?

Wanda was feeling really uncomfortable with all of this. If she raised the questions with Medwin, he would only feel as equally uncomfortable. Maybe another time.

Hitting the pillow that night, Wanda had a million thoughts running through her head. She hated the way negative questions about Medwin, seemed to take lead position. Laying there in bed, she decided that would not do. More stretches were required with focussed deep breathing. She would look to her middle eye and take herself into a state of positive calm.

The brain had started to clear and her eyes were feeling heavy. Just then the phone rang.

'Wanda. Our little friends Hug and Fug are being very active with me tonight.' It was Medwin having difficulty getting to sleep.

'They are replaying that incredible time together on the sofa, watching the motorcycle Grand Prix.'

Wanda and Medwin had phone sex for the very first time that night. She asked him to tell her what Hug and Fug were doing. As he recounted every detail, he finally reached the part where her mouth was over his penis. She told him his hand would have to play the role of her mouth.

Wanda had Hug and Fug in her mind too. She was under the shower in Bratislava with her leg up on the side of the bath. Her own hand now became Medwin's tongue. The brain can do amazing things.

They kept telling each other what was playing in their own minds. It was like an orgy of sexual activity and deep deep love making.

Finally a huge sigh came down the phone from Medwin. Seconds later, his phone was providing sounds on a groaning nature from Wanda.

'Good night my love. Sleep well. I miss you so much.' They each seemed to say at the exact same time.

• CHAPTER FOURTEEN •

THE OFFICE WAS ABUZZ THAT following week. Excitement about all the new marketing plans, had given the team a real lift. Even Patty had taken on a more light hearted self. She had apparently met some tall handsome man over the weekend too. Just the job to brighten her horizons.

Wanda had been given full approval to run with pretty much everything Al had presented. Some brilliant stuff. The new website would go down really well with customers. Interactive portals had been planned, to give quick access to information they needed on a regular basis. They had been crying out for such a tool, for way too long. Damon would take charge of all web activities. Right up his street.

A new branch opening in Prague, would be backed by a major launch. Al had a local Czech PR agency working with his team on the event plus media coverage. He and Wanda had a meeting with them, that coming Friday in Prague, and would stay over that night. Their Managing Director wanted to show them the live music he had in mind for the launch. This new branch would serve much of the Eastern European country's needs so it had a high priority. Al's designs, for new promotional material, all had to be ready and printed for the event and it was scheduled for just four weeks' time.

'Damon. I've written the final copy for the website now. Bob just needs to take a quick look one more time. Patty is happy with it. Then over to you to implement with Al's guys,' Wanda confirmed.

Writing had always been a forte of Wanda's. Marketing blurb could often take way too long to cut to the chase but she had mastered the art of getting to the point, quickly and with impact. No point paying writers to do the copy. She could do it much more efficiently. There was enough work to be done with all the translations, once everyone had signed off on the English text. The website would be put together in fifteen different languages. Damon arranged all of that and needed to get in-country team members, to confirm their language read well. Then on with the build. He certainly had his hands full with all of that.

'Did you say this Friday you and Al are in Prague?' responded Damon. 'Guess that means no borrel for you Madame.'

Wanda loved the way Damon was so laid back about everything. His super-efficient self had been totally confident of achieving all that was required of him, for getting web pages live and happening.

Lou was happy to be in her last few weeks of school for the year. Most of her teacher reports were in and they had all been fairly positive. She had done a good job and was on track for her final IB year, when school resumed end August. In September she would visit Universities in the UK with her mum and decide what her options were for degree studies. There would be no gap year for her.

Loads of her school chums, seemed to think about nothing else. Grand travel plans for post IB completion, was all they could talk about. Lou could not see the point. She had already travelled a great deal and would much rather get straight on with her University Degree. Having to go back to school, after taking a year out, would be way too hard. Nice to have this little trip back to Sydney coming up for the break though.

'So cool of you to pay for me to visit Dad and the kids over the holiday mum,' Lou was saying to Wanda, as she handed back her credit card. 'Think I did pretty well with this deal I found. All booked and confirmed for me to leave the day after school finishes. Will be funny being there without Jay.'

Jay had to carry on with the IT course so there would be no trip back to Oz for him for a while. Wanda had planned to get them back to Sydney to see their dad and family, whenever she could. Not that Larry had ever asked. It was more for them than for him. Of course he did love to see them though. This time there would be a third child from his second marriage to meet. Lou was really excited about that. A little sad that she would not see Danny for all that time but she knew it would be a great trip.

'Fantastic band. They will be perfect for the launch,' said Wanda reassuringly. 'Dinner was also excellent so we can lock in that catering too.' Everything had gone perfectly, that Friday in Prague.

Al was over the moon with his Czech PR partner choice.

Al could not believe it! Wanda had made plans to go to Vienna the following weekend and he was going to be there too, speaking at a conference. How cool would it be if she and Medwin could attend some of it? Might be good for Medwin's networking too. He had been talking about maybe setting up his own business, arranging travel for sports groups.

For the remainder of that weekend, Wanda focussed on Lou and PJ. Interspersed, of course, with several calls and emails with Medwin. He was definitely keen to attend the conference Al was to speak at. Even keener to have Wanda in Vienna soon.

Danny had gone off with his mum for a little break so Wanda had Lou all to herself. Lou's girlfriends had even been put off so that she could spend quality time with her mum.

Dinner Saturday night would be at a favourite local restaurant. They had already decided on food, before even entering the door. It would be the Chef's Surprise. All they had to do was choose meat or fish. Both were happy with either but Lou made the final choice. Fish it would be. Three courses, more than enough. Nothing further to think about. Over to the chef.

Amazing! They started with taste sensations served in tiny glasses ....one a light lemon sorbet and the other a Carpaccio. Simply delicious! Fresh out of the oven, the accompanying seeded rolls were also a delight. Four completely different types of warm bread. A choice of pure butter or Italian olive oil to the side.

Next a starter of scallops. Pan seared with a slight ginger twist and served on a bacon and asparagus bed. Mouth-watering!

Then the piece de resistance. The colours alone were a delight to behold. Such a shame to actually eat this beautiful work of art.

Thick salmon roasted with tarragon and mustard, resting on a bed of baby spinach leaves, prepared with an orange glaze. Pesto potatoes and baked cherry tomatoes to the side. It glowed with an enticing appeal. Totally delectable!

Quite some time was needed before they could interrupt their taste buds and move on to the final pleasures.

Breathtaking! The dessert platter lived up to all expectations.

A black slate tray framed small servings of four different sweets. Fresh coconut shavings rolled into a tiny ball and coated in chocolate mousse. A mini lemon meringue pie. Succulent strawberries, with a light sponge cake base. And last but most certainly not least …. a mini kiwi Pavlova. Delicious!

They thought they must have died and gone to heaven!

What better way to end such a perfect evening, than to cycle home and cuddle up in front of a favourite movie. A special moment for PJ too. Love story or animation? Lou had decided, for that night it would be 'Enchanted'. The best of both worlds.

They finally crawled up the stairs and into their respective bedrooms. Lou had her text message to Danny half written, by the time she got to her room. Wanda had a call lined up with Medwin.

'I have one group of marathon runners, for a three day trip into Switzerland. Pretty sure they will go with my offer.' Medwin's excitement, over an early win for his new travel operation, was infectious. He and Wanda discussed other possibilities for getting his business up and running. The name had been chosen and he had done what he needed to do, to register things. Business cards and a small website were all in place. Fitting things in with his existing job had proven a little difficult but he was managing.

'So glad you like the apartment I rented for next weekend.'

As they chatted on the phone, Wanda had looked at the website link Medwin sent through. Such a quaint old building and right in the centre of Vienna. One very large bedroom, with super-sized bed. They would put that to good use. The living room had a separate little office area, with the most stunning antique mahogany desk and two chairs. A small balcony would allow them to take breakfast in the fresh air, looking down to the pretty garden that several of the old houses backed onto. Might even catch the morning sun. Only possible challenge perhaps, the fact their apartment was on the second floor and the building did not have a lift. Often the way with these old properties. Amazingly beautiful central staircase and entrance though. Just as well there would be a very strong and athletic man to carry the bags up. Medwin had no problem at all with that.

The week that followed, presented one nightmare after another. So much work for everyone to get done in Wanda's office, in such a small amount of time. She had left six people tearing their hair out in a production meeting, to get her flight to Vienna that Friday. They were not amused.

'The flight is two hours late my darling,' said Wanda a little frustrated down the phone to Medwin. She had rushed to the airport, only to find her online check for flight departure time confirmation had been wrong. 'Could have put that extra time to good use in the office. '

'All good at this end,' replied Medwin. 'Just can't wait to see you. Maybe I can tell you what I would like to do to you tonight. It might calm you a little. I know how you like me to get inside your head, with thoughts of our love making. Our little friends Hug and Fug are already very busy in my mind. They want me to lay you flat on the bed face down. You have to pretend like I tied you to the corners of the bed. Are you sinking into the bed?' After Wanda gave a light sigh, he continued.

'I have this very beautiful white feather. Can you see it? Quite a large feather and so soft. It is going to caress the back of your body, until I can sense you are sinking even more deeply into the bed. First the feather will gently touch your ears and neck. Then down each arm. Quite some attention to your fingers. I might have to also suck a finger I think. I will be kneeling on the bed, across your body.

The feather will make its way down the centre of your back. Lightly down your legs. Not to tickle your feet though. Sweeping across your toes slowly and then to make its way back up and around your butt cheeks. As it circles your beautiful bottom, it will slide further down the join between your butts and around your pussy. At this point I will turn you over. The feather will start to sooth your eyes and face. The arm and across to each nipple, for much extended touching. Some sucking now perhaps. Me to your nipples. You to my penis, as it is hovering over the top of your body. Just some quick teasing. When the feather finds your clitoris, you will need to hold the sides of your pussy clear so it can fully do its job. The feather is going to take you to a climax. Oh so slowly. I will know when your back is arched and mind is filled with pleasure. This is when my penis will go deep inside and we will be one again.'

Wanda was speechless. She felt like everyone in the airport must have heard Medwin. It seemed all eyes were on her. Could they tell she was almost near orgasm, just listening to her love on the end of the phone? Of course not. Don't be so silly, she told herself.

A little cough to clear her throat. Sweet words of adieu to Medwin. Then for a drink at the bar. Might be nice to have a little quiet time before the flight.

Medwin had been true to his word that evening in Vienna. Hug and Fug were definitely on good form!

As Saturday morning broke, Medwin and Wanda were at it again. They had planned to take a quick breakfast and get to Al's conference by 10am. Seeing Medwin naked in the bathroom mirror had been all it needed, for those plans to be changed. Wanda had been lying in bed, looking through the bathroom door. Medwin was shaving in front of the mirror. She had gone in, simply to kiss his butt and tell him how handsome he was but it turned into sex at the sink, before they knew it.

'Al, we will not make it for kick-off. Is that OK? You don't speak until after morning tea anyway right? We will be there in good time for that.' Wanda knew all would be fine for Al.

A leisurely walk along the river, through the park and into the classic venue that had been chosen for the conference. Attendees were amongst some of the most creative and industrious people in Europe. Gathering to share ideas and learn from each other, the three day conference presented serious networking opportunities for all. Medwin was prepared to tell people about his new venture. Wanda had every intention of supporting him, as much as she could. They would both support Al, in his efforts to connect with possible new business.

As it turned out, Medwin became quite shy when faced with discussing his sports travel operation, amongst serious business people. Wanda was surprised. She tried to encourage him but to no avail.

Thank goodness they had an appointment at 5pm, to see an apartment Medwin was considering buying. They would see a second one early on the Sunday too. Al knew they had planned to leave early. They would join him at the event dinner later.

Medwin became even quieter at the dinner. Al had been as effervescent as ever and seemed to overshadow Medwin. Wanda asked Medwin if he was OK and his reply had been rather abrupt.

'You and Al have so many things in common. It makes me feel a little bit left out.'

The scornful look was a first.

Wanda tried to just change the subject and lighten up the conversation with talk of the apartment they viewed. That seemed to make Medwin even more uncomfortable. Not really a very nice apartment and asking way too much. He apparently felt silly about having even chosen it to see in the first place.

After a visit to the ladies, things had become even worse. Wanda returned to their table, to find Al quizzing Medwin about his sports travel operations. He had no answers for many of Al's questions.

'I am ready to leave whenever you are,' he had whispered into Wanda's ear. He was not a happy chappy.

That night, was the very first time Wanda and Medwin had gone to sleep without making love. Not a word had been spoken, on the journey back to their quaint little rented apartment.

By the time Wanda had returned to the bedroom, after a quick shower, Medwin had fallen fast asleep. Surprised but also feeling incredibly tired herself, Wanda curled up into his arms and also went to sleep.

They woke the next day, in a full spoon hugging position. Medwin was kissing Wanda's neck. Not a word was spoken about the night before. Soon they were making love and a new day had begun.

'Wow. This apartment is fantastic,' Wanda confirmed, as they left the viewing that Sunday morning.

'I know. Can't believe it is also in my price range. Do you think we need to see more? I really would like to put an offer in, to buy this one.' Medwin was over the moon. This apartment was twice the size of the one they had seen the day before and it was the same price.

Lunch by the stunning blue Danube. Such fun how they have pretend beaches, at cafes along the banks of the river. A great atmosphere. The sun was shining and they were in love. Talk of Medwin's apartment purchase, dominated the conversation. First thing the next morning, he would put in an offer.

It was a late flight back to Amsterdam for Wanda but she needed to be in a meeting first thing Monday. In a couple of weeks Medwin would join her in Prague, for the new branch opening and launch parties. Over the weekend, they had further discussions about a visit to Australia and attending the Olympics in Athens on the way.

Lots of fun things on the horizon. They would start looking at options for all of that. Medwin might have a couple of sports travel groups and that could impact things too. Lots to sort out.

'I do not believe it! Why on earth did they even show us the apartment if it was already under offer?' Wanda had been as upset as Medwin that Monday morning. The apartment had officially gone off the market on the Saturday. First person that saw it bought it. As the appointment had already been made for Medwin to view, they let him go ahead. He had not been at all impressed, with this incredible waste of his time. Had his heart set on that place. So disappointed!

Wanda had wanted to reach out and hug him. He, on the other hand, wanted to keep the call short. She had felt a little cut off by his abruptness. The worst of his German nature came to the fore, when he did not have things go his way.

Wanda had expected a late night call from Medwin that day but nothing. Best to leave him if he needed to be in a negative state about this, she thought. A simple good night text and she was in her bed and dreaming herself to sleep, with flashes of happier moments of passion between them.

'Mum. After you take me to the airport, are you dropping that green Italian wagon of ours in for a service? You wanted me to remind you that was the day you booked,' said Lou as she sifted through the clean washing, to grab things she wanted to pack.

'Thanks bubs. I did almost forget. Only remembered when they were booking flights for Prague. Now it is all lined up, like ducks in a row. Drop you for your flight to Sydney. Then take the car in. They keep it to do the work while I'm in Prague and drive me to the office. I will already have my bag at the office for Prague and can take a taxi to the airport later that day. Dad has your flight details and said he will be at the airport to pick you up. All sorted.'

'So exciting to be meeting a new little sister mum,' said Lou.

'Yes. Very exciting,' replied Wanda, as her mind drifted off to thoughts of Larry.

Could it really be almost ten years since he married Dee?

Wanda still found it hard to believe, he had not even told her and the children about the wedding. They had arrived at Grandma and Grandad's in Scotland for Christmas that year, only to be asked by Grandma what they thought about Larry getting married. It had been a total surprise to them. They knew nothing. They had left Sydney in the September for Wanda's one year contract in Amsterdam. A month later Larry and Dee had married. Larry had mentioned her name briefly but they had never met. Wanda and Larry had been divorced for four years by then so no problem but it would have been nice to know.

Prague was exhausting. Not just the opening events for the General. Medwin had driven up from Vienna and things had been a little strained.

Might not have been such a good idea, having him there when Wanda was so busy. He had also had some bad news about a sports group that would now not travel with him. The event had been cancelled so nothing to do with him but he took it all very personally. Lots of hugs on first sight but then a bit moody.

Wanda had never been good with moody people. If someone could not be positive about things, she felt challenged to be around them. What to do?

"Sorry about leaving you to chat with other people so many times tonight my love. That was so nice of you, to organise the pack down of the promotional material. Would have taken us much longer to get out of there otherwise,' Wanda had found a way to occupy Medwin and was truly appreciative of his energy change, when it came to mucking in with her team to help.

Back at the hotel afterwards, they laughed and shared little stories about some of the interesting guests that night. Laughter moved to petting and soon they were in each other's arms again. Making love like there were no tomorrows. Extreme passions shared, in such a desperately wanting way. The times they were apart, seemed etched into their flesh so strongly that when they were finally together, they never wanted to let go.

Sunday was theirs to explore Prague. The sun shone and they started their day with breakfast at a café in the middle of the beautiful Vltava River. A perfect day.

Sitting there holding hands, they looked out to views of the famous Charles Bridge. Always so busy with tourists, buskers and artists showing their works. A hive of activity.

Having Medwin's car, meant they could venture outside of the city. Bohemia began in Prague and was still evidenced by some incredibly abstract buildings and cafes. Several were recommended to visit. They concluded the day with a visit to the majestic Karlstejn Castle. One hour by car, to the amazing woodlands that surrounded this 14th century Gothic work of art. This fairy tale castle was built 1348-1368 by the King of Bohemia and Holy Roman Emperor Charles IV. Quite stunning!

During the day, Wanda and Medwin discussed fine details about their trip to the Olympics and Australia. Wanda had friends living in Athens, who were working on the Olympics. They would get them tickets to events. A room in their house was also available for them to stay in.

Medwin was pretty sure he would be competing in a half marathon in Switzerland, just prior to the Olympics, so they might include that as part of the trip. Mykonos had always been a favourite Greek island of Wanda's. She would love to show Medwin that, if plans fitted. Heading straight to Australia afterwards, meant they would be there in winter and skiing could be an option. Fantastic!

Medwin was not driving back to Vienna until first thing Monday morning. He would drop Wanda to the airport for the first flight to Amsterdam and then take his three hour drive to his office. Should still make it for 9am.

Over the weekend, Medwin had also talked about leaving his job. He hated working for the railway. Designing signals had its interesting moments but the bureaucratic environment was soul destroying. He knew that it drained his energy and made him negative. If only he could focus on his new enterprise with sports travel needs.

Buying an apartment in Vienna had also fallen flat.

After getting all excited about the apartment he and Wanda had loved, everything else had seemed either too expensive or just not right.

He needed to get away from his village and living with his parents.

He needed to be with Wanda on a more regular basis.

As much as Wanda loved Medwin, she felt uncertain about living with him full time. What they currently had, worked fine for her. She missed him badly when he was not there but it had made getting together so much more special. Thinking about his moods, and the way he was so well looked after by his mother, Wanda really had her doubts about being able to cope with it all every day. She also knew that he would miss Mino enormously.

When Medwin complained about things at work and at home, Wanda offered up positive suggestions for coping or changing things. She reassured him that, when he had his own place in Vienna, everything would be different. He really needed to stay with the railway for the time being so he could have his mortgage approved. Great to have the opportunity to build up his sports travel business on the side but there was no way anyone would lend him funds for his property purchase, on the back of that.

Seemingly endless hugging, as they said farewell at Prague airport that morning. Both laughing and talking about nothing else except positive fun things. That was the way Wanda liked things. She had a Prague launch review meeting, soon after she would arrive at the office. Her flight time would be fully occupied with planning for that.

It had all gone exactly to plan so everyone should be happy. The PR agency should have sent through a report. At the end of the review, Wanda would have them on the phone to present to the team on media coverage. Having managed to get a good turnout of media to the event, they should be pleased with things and able to talk about loads of positive activity hopefully. Everything had also managed to come in under budget. A fantastic result all round. Should be a good meeting.

'I am just out of the Prague review meeting Medwin and we are all going to lunch. Are you OK?' Wanda enquired nervously. She could see that Medwin had tried to call her four times. Not like him. If he called once with no reply, he knew she would call when she could. Trying her another three times, was totally out of character. Something must be up.

'It is what we both wanted my darling. I have been made redundant!' Medwin was almost shouting and spoke at twice his normal speed.

He was so happy. Wanda wanted to be happy for him too but all she could think of was, 'What now?'

• CHAPTER FIFTEEN •

'I KNOW. I SHOULD BE OVER THE MOON. He is such an incredible man and I love him enormously. Why do I have this feeling of dread, about us actually living together full time?' Wanda had confided to Damon.

The lunch chats were always interesting but this one had taken Damon totally by surprise.

'Most of the time it's always how much you miss Medwin', he replied.

Damon was a good listener. Wanda told him about her concerns, with not being in the same league as Medwin's mother and most likely his wife when they were together too. They clearly waited on him hand and foot. She could never be like that. He would need to pull his weight with cleaning, washing and cooking or whatever needed to be done around the house. She had her doubts that he could cope. None of this had been said to him of course. All the time they spent together so far, had been way too precious for such seemingly unimportant things.

Wanda also told Damon about the moody and abrupt side of Medwin, she had seen both in Vienna and in Prague. She really could not do moody.

'Not sounding too good right now, is it?' Damon finally chipped in. 'Maybe you should tell me again, about all the great things you love with him. Seems to me these things you don't like could be sorted.'

It was never hard for Wanda to switch into positive gear. That was her normal functioning state.

'Ah. He is so gorgeous. Just the sound of his voice and I am a quivering wreck. Then when I see him … I turn to jelly. Those huge dark and loving eyes, seem to look right through to my very soul. That funny laugh he has. His cute way of speaking broken English. Excellent singing voice and he loves music as much as I do. Don't need to tell you about the amazing body. You have heard loads on that before. Sex is extraordinary and the hugs could most likely be the most important thing of all. It really is incredible. When he lifts me up into his arms, it's like nothing else exists. He hugs me so tightly that I feel his heart beat against mine. Our hearts even seem to beat in unison. We hug all the time. It is so beautiful.'

Damon then went on to remind Wanda, there was no such thing as a totally perfect relationship. It sounded to him like this one came pretty close though. She would just have to adapt to living with a man again. How bad could it be?

That night, when Wanda and Medwin spoke on the phone, she told him about the reservations she had. He totally understood. There was no way he would just move in on her. He also reassured her, that he had no problem with doing things around the house. Might need some training but he was more than willing to learn. Just two more weeks and he would be finished his job. Lou was in Sydney. No current plan for Jay to visit. They had the house to themselves.

By that time, it would only be a few weeks before they left for their big trip to the Olympics and Australia. He would just bring a suitcase with clothes. Definitely had to take his own ski boots, if they thought they might ski in Australia. Actual skis could be rented. Maybe they would have some new super-fast ones for him to trial. Should be able to wangle one more train ticket to Holland through the job so no problem to bring one of his bikes with him too. He would no longer have a car.

It was agreed. They were now happy at the thought of being together and could not wait to start sharing their lives fully.

'Wow mum. Fantastic.' Lou was a little surprised but happy for her mum, as she told her about the plans on their Skype call. A definite first though. Mum talking about someone actually living with them. Would be a lot easier now that Jay lived away from home, she guessed. Medwin was such a lovely guy. His visits had been really nice.

'We will just see how it goes?' Wanda replied. 'He is going to be looking for a job here in Holland and, at the same time, trying to get this sports travel business going. Apparently has quite some savings to see him through for a while but will need to earn some money eventually. The big trip to the Olympics and Oz, is going to set him back quite a bit. Weird how we look like just missing you in Sydney. I really can't do more that the two weeks there though.

That flight I found, has us arriving the day after you leave. Really difficult to get flights out of Athens during the Olympics. Oh well. You need to be back and getting yourself organised for school anyway. It will be almost four weeks away from work for me. Medwin has his half marathon in Switzerland and then we go straight on to Athens. Hopefully a few days in Mykonos on the way back, if we can work it. Fly back via Athens so might as well.'

Wanda casually omitted to tell Lou about the possible ski excursion in Australia. That would have been way too hard for Lou to take. She could not wait to have a ski with this Austrian racing dude, after all the stories she had heard.

'Can't believe I am also going to miss Pete and Mary visiting us in Holland mum. All this time they have been making their plans for the big world trip and now I am actually in Australia, when they get there. They leave Melbourne in a week or so. Must at least give them a call and say hi.'

'Yeah. That is a real pity. Think it was just the big bus tour they ended up booking from London. Had to fit in with those dates. Medwin knows that I promised to take them away for a few days, to visit Bruges and Paris. He will be at the house when they get to Holland and do some of the Dutch stuff with us. A couple of days later, he flies back to Austria for Mino's birthday. I will take them travelling while he is away.'

The big move in day soon arrived. Wanda had played it all very low key. She told friends and business colleagues that Medwin had come to spend a few weeks in Holland, exploring job opportunities. Everyone knew of their plans for the Olympics and Australia.

'It is OK if my bike stays indoors I hope?' Medwin asked shyly, as he propped his ultra-lightweight and super expensive bike, up against the rear wall of the dining room.

Wanda had wanted to say no and have him put the bike in the shed with hers but she held back. He told her how much the bike had cost. Mon dieu! She could not believe anyone would spend that sort of money on a bike.

True, it had helped him win several races. BUT.

This was just his mountain bike. The road bike was of course a lot more expensive. Eeekk was all Wanda could think.

She had met him at the station and taken charge of the bike, walking to the house. It had not felt even a little bit precious but what did she know.

All clothes in the suitcase were perfectly ironed and folded. Mother had clearly packed for her beloved son.

Wanda had made space in her walk-in robe for his things and given him a set of drawers. Once he had put everything into place, she felt quite happy with the prospect of having him about all the time. He was at that point, standing totally naked and heading for a shower.

'So beautiful,' said Wanda as her gaze stood fixed on his perfect body.

He took her hand and beckoned her into the shower with him. It had been a couple of weeks, since they had been together. Phone sex and relaying of Hug and Fug thoughts, had kept them going. Now they were in each other's arms again. Warm soapy hugs, eased the tensions of the day. Wanda had purchased some new shower oil and the scent summoned up a need for deeper breathing, to fully explore the arousing nature of the exceptional aroma.

Medwin quickly had Wanda's clothes off and they were soon under the hot water. He lifted Wanda up, into their full heart throbbing hug. Her legs were stretched wide and held on tight around his waist. He slid her upper body from side to side and the warm shower oil increased the tingle they felt, as their nipples connected.

They kissed softly but with incredible intensity. Medwin held on to Wanda with one hand. The other hand reached under her bottom and along to her clitoris. He needed only a few short strokes. Lips still fixed to one another, Wanda gave a deep outward breath and gasped as her orgasm hit.

Within moments, Medwin had a deep and slow penetration inside the longing body Wanda had pushed forward.

The connection was complete. Thrusting was gentle and deeply emotional. Wanda came for a second time, just as Medwin reached a climax. His tree trunk legs stood firm, as he held Wanda in that connected position for what seemed an age.

They felt totally complete. They had taken the next step in their relationship and it seemed to impact their love making positively.

For the next several minutes, all they could do was hug and keep saying how much they loved each other. Eventually Wanda felt tears well in her eyes. She began to sob. Medwin started to weep too. The tears of happiness, made them both realise how exhausted they were.

Medwin lay Wanda on the soft bath rug and dried her gently with her huggable towels, as she loved to call them. He placed her gently into bed. Dried himself and joined her. Hugging themselves to sleep, they could not have been more content.

Over the week that followed, Wanda and Medwin could not get enough of each other. Not a morning or evening passed that they did not make love. On a train ride to Amsterdam, they even found themselves masturbating each other in total silence as they appeared to others as a sleeping couple in the back row, nestled under a jacket. That green Italian wagon even had its first love making experience. On a long drive home one evening, Wanda and Medwin decided they needed to connect. They had been so aroused, they had to find a hidden parking place in the forest and were soon in the back seat, like teenagers on a hot date.

Medwin had several meetings, about different jobs. He even met with the head of the General's Rail business. Two opportunities presented themselves but they might take some time to pan out fully.

'The group from Zurich have confirmed for Lauterbrunnen,' an excited Medwin relayed to Wanda down the phone. He had been chasing this group for some while and finally, they had accepted his proposal. Some decent money to be earned for him but also a really good deal for them. They would participate in the same race he had signed up for, only they would do the full monty. He would only do the running part of it. Only! That meant a 21km run, up the rocky Schilthorn Mountain. This group needed to swim across a very cold lake first, cycle to the village where the race started and then run their little hearts out up the very steep mountain.

Wanda could not help but think they must all be quite mad. She had, however, been ever so excited for Medwin to have this win for his Sports Travel business.

Nothing had come of the groups he approached in Holland so far. Wanda thought there might be some problem with him not speaking Dutch. Next year they would all move to the UK for Lou to go to University so not really much point him taking lessons. His English was passable so best to focus his energies on people who were happy to work with that or German.

'Nice to have this deal through, before you head back to Austria next week darling. Something positive for you to share with your family. Everyone should be pretty up anyway I guess, with all the planned birthday celebrations for Mino.'

Wanda knew his family were not at all happy about his move to Holland.

'Pete. Mary.' Wanda shouted out, as her nephew and his wife came through the busy Schiphol arrival gate. She had been fully entertained by all the comings and goings. The joys and sadness expressed, as loved ones arrived or departed at airports, had always been a fascination.

Shrieks were followed by big loving hugs. Pete had always been a close nephew and Wanda was so excited, to have an opportunity to show him some of Europe. Mary was also lovely. Wanda had only met her on a few occasions but they had always been very pleasant. They wed in Melbourne some years earlier and had been planning this big trip overseas ever since.

Pete's mum was Wanda's sister Elizabeth. The second youngest of the eight children, of which Wanda was the youngest. Elizabeth had suffered badly with all the different homes and no father growing up. By the age of 15 she was going off the rails. One tragic weekend, she had decided to take herself off with not a word to anyone. Eventually their mother had discovered she had gone to their Nan's.

A friend drove Wanda and her mum to try and bring Elizabeth home. She had already left Nan's by the time they arrived. A cousin and her boyfriend had also gone to Nan's and they had taken Elizabeth to visit her uncle out in the country. Wanda and her mother arrived there, also to find they had just left to go somewhere else. Shortly afterwards, a neighbour arrived to say there had been a car accident. Everyone rushed to the hospital trying not to panic.

The cousin and her boyfriend were in the waiting room, with no injuries. Elizabeth had been trapped in the back of the car, when it rolled down into a ravine. Those in the front thrown clear. Elizabeth had to be cut free. She was on life support in intensive care. It took six weeks for her to come out of the coma. Brain damage meant she could not speak and it was very unlikely she would ever walk again. Several months in the hospital, various operations and a whole lot of therapy, helped her regain simple speech and learn to walk with a calliper on one leg. She would be paralysed down one side for life.

A few years later she married and the years that followed, brought forth three children. Pete was the youngest and all that more special being a boy, after two little girls. Elizabeth managed them and life, with a totally unsupportive husband. Old fashioned material nappies, with large pins, were manoeuvred with just one hand. The dead arm used as a weight.

Wanda had endless admiration and love for Elizabeth, giving her as much support through the years as she possibly could. Being there for her children, was also important.

Medwin had stayed home to cook dinner for their arriving guests. He had become quite a dab hand at his special pasta with salad. Pete and Mary were sure to love it. That green Italian wagon had no problem coping with all the luggage and they had arrived home to dine, in no time at all.

Pete had been trained as a motor mechanic, then changed career to take up bus driving a few years back. Now just over 30yrs of age and deeply in love with his young wife, he was feeling very happy with his life. He had dreams about driving in Europe and Wanda was more than happy to let him take the wheel of that green Italian wagon, when they all set off the next day to explore some of Holland.

Pete insisted on giving the car a quick mini-service check, before they left. All perfect. He was most impressed.

Medwin and Wanda took the back seat and watched as Mary and Pete beamed happiness across to each other, at every opportunity.

Mary had been just 24 when she found her prince charming. They made a beautiful couple. Her parents being Egyptian, she had beautiful olive skin that complemented her long curly dark hair perfectly. The smile reached from ear to ear and her big brown eyes took in every inch of the Dutch scenery, as did Pete's. He also had dark hair, big brown eyes and a happy smiling face. They were positive and energised. Loads of fun to be around.

Being even shorter than Wanda, Pete and Mary had to strain their necks somewhat to look at Medwin. Their faces were such a sight, staring up in awe at Medwin's cute way of speaking English. They loved to just listen to him. So funny!

Out in a bar that night, they soon realised there were a great many more extremely tall people in Holland. Neck strain could be the order of the day but they just loved it all.

'How were they going to top Holland?' they thought out loud.

A fantastic few days that they wished had been longer.

'Gefeliciteerd for Mino's birthday my love,' said Wanda down the phone to Medwin, as he confirmed his flight to Austria was on time and due to board shortly.

'We have everything packed into the car and will leave for Bruges soon. Lunch in Antwerp is first on the agenda. Pete and Mary are so excited. Me too of course. Have fun with the family and good luck with that presentation too.'

Medwin had lined up quite a good opportunity, with a large sports group in Vienna, for a big event in Portugal the following year. Not much he could prepare for at that stage but the phone conversations and emails, had been extremely positive so he was hoping to get a firm brief, once he presented his capabilities to them officially.

Boarding the plane, Medwin realised he was nervous about seeing his family. He and Wanda had agreed he should not tell them about her yet. They had been so distressed about him leaving Austria. He told them he had an amazing job opportunity, with the rail division of the General, and also leads for some sports travel groups so he was going to live in Holland for a while. He was renting a room with an Australian family he had met through contacts at the General. Nothing more. It was enough for them to take in. Especially 7yr old Mino, who had trouble coping with the fact his dad did not live close to him anymore. Medwin tried phoning Mino but conversations had been difficult.

Wanda let all thoughts of Medwin's visit to Austria leave her mind. No doubt Mino's mother would be included in celebrations and her behaviour, still made Wanda feel uncomfortable.

Now for some more fun in that green Italian wagon with Pete and Mary. 'Antwerp here we come,' thought Wanda.

It never ceased to amaze Wanda how this very small country called Belgium, could be split into the French part in the south and the Flemish part in the north. To her untrained ear, Flemish also sounded the same as Dutch but do not tell an Antwerp local that. A bit the same as Canadian and American being confused she guessed or even Australian and New Zealand perhaps. Incredible to find that when you drove just a short distance from Antwerp to Brussels, you would find everyone speaking French. Good for the sign makers. They had to do everything in two languages.

'Quite tricky getting off at the right exit from the Antwerp Ring Pete. Lots of exits point to the Centrum but you can end up going miles around, through very confusing small streets. I will know which one is best when I see it so just be ready. OK?'

Pete was more than OK. He was loving it. No problem at all, getting into the wrong side of the car to take over the steering wheel and then being on the wrong side of the road. He likened it to some of the car computer games he had played. Antwerp Ring would certainly sharpen his future gaming skills. At least they were hitting it at a decent time of day. Not too frantic with traffic.

'Great work Pete. Only a short distance and we should come to my favourite car park. Next to the beautiful main square (Grote Markt).

We can have lunch in the square, looking out to its stunning 16th Century Guild houses. Take a walk through the lanes and check out the 14th Century Cathedral. Would be great to show you the incredible collection of 14th century musical instruments in the Vleeshuis Museum too, if we can. Then walk from there down to the castle on the river for a quick look. Could spend our entire four days in Antwerp of course but this time three hours will have to do. Need to get back onto that Ring, before the rush hour.'

Wanda was in her element, playing the tour guide. She never tired of new discoveries and loved to show people her old discoveries too.

It was a brilliantly sunny day and the Grote Markt (main square) cafes were filled with people, just sitting and watching the world go by. They could have happily sat there all day but there were things to see, places to go. Pete and Mary were enthralled by it all.

Once that green Italian wagon had them back on the Antwerp Ring, it was just an hour's drive to Bruges. Stunning! UNESCO lists Bruges as a World Heritage Site for its unique historic centre, built on a maze of quaint canals. Its medieval architecture incredibly intact. Numerous squares holding different and unique attributes. Tiny cobbled streets, echoing with the clickety clack of horses hooves from the many carriage tours of the city. Picturesque canal scenes. A totally charming city, that captured the hearts of Pete and Mary.

They had two nights booked at a very reasonably priced hostel and would share a triple room. Wanda hoped her snoring would not keep the others awake. She had plans to let them fall asleep before she did but that was not to be. They were all exhausted after a very full and exciting day. Wanda had nodded off before Pete and Mary had even managed to brush their teeth.

Bruges being renowned for romantic escapes and honeymoons, Wanda had suggested Pete and Mary head out on their own the next day, to be alone. No way.

'We've scored the best guide ever. Not missing out on that,' retorted Pete sharply. Mary quickly followed with a similar line and it was agreed. They convinced Wanda, they would have plenty of time for romance over the coming couple of months of their travels. Being with her was a high priority for this part of their trip. Nice.

'OK. Let's do strawberries and waffles with hot Belgian chocolate sauce for brunch. I know just the place!'

Driving out of Bruges the following day, they were on their way to Paris. Viva la France!

'I can't believe I am actually going to be in Paris in a few hours,' said Mary. 'A dream come true. Think I started the dream way back in my first year of high school. French class was standard. I was terrible but loved it. When they taught us about places in France, I fell in love with the idea of Paris. All the films you see that make it look so amazing. Hope the reality lives up to it.'

'I am sure it will,' replied Wanda. 'We have a little apartment for our two nights. Just a short walk from the Latin Quarter. What a find that was. Even has parking, which is quite unheard of in Paris. We can do a little drive around when we get there but then just walk or take the metro after that.'

'Might be an idea if I take over driving just before we get to Paris Pete. Probably need to busk it a little for finding our way. Do not want to be telling you to turn suddenly, with all the crazy drivers of Paris,' said Wanda a couple of hours after leaving Bruges.

Having driven in Paris on many occasions, Wanda felt quite familiar with its different neighbourhoods. They would hit the Peripherique just after lunch so traffic should not be too ugly. She would take them off that major ring road, to the Avenue des Champs Elysees, and drive around the Arc de Triomphe a few times. Always fun going around the eight driving lanes that stem from the twelve roads leading onto this incredible roundabout. Down to the Seine River, where the Eiffel Tower will be right in front of them. They will definitely know they are in Paris then. Could drive along the river and soon be at their little apartment. A quick snap in front of the tower first perhaps. Ah! Paris!

The apartment was magnifique. One cute bedroom for Pete and Mary. A larger than average sitting room, with a fold-out bed, for Wanda. The cutest of little balconies and it looked out onto the gardens of the building. The sun shone and the world was perfect.

That night was a highlight for Wanda. One of her favourite little jazz clubs had two of her most favourite French jazz musicians playing. For dinner, they sat outside in a café facing Notre Dame. A balmy summer's evening. Excellent food and incredible people watching, followed by amazing live music. A text from Medwin to say how much he was missing Wanda and loved her beyond all else. She was in seventh heaven! Hug & Fug played in her head. If only she had Medwin in reach! Ooh la la!

The Louvre, magical Montmartre, a cruise along the Seine, the late supper Can Can Show at the Moulin Rouge. They had managed to do so much. Even so, the two days in Paris seemed to have slipped by quickly. Pete and Mary were taking the train to London and Wanda would drive back to Holland alone.

Pete and Mary could not thank Wanda enough. What an amazing way to start their world adventure. A few days in London would follow, then they would join an organised bus trip across southern Europe and eventually into Greece. Later they would fly to Canada and travel right across the country. No fixed plan for that. They would rent a car in Vancouver. Once they finished travelling around that side, they would head east to wherever the mood took them. A young and happily married couple, with the world at their feet … and they planned to enjoy every minute of it.

Relaxing on the train from Paris, Pete and Mary reflected on the night before and how Wanda opened up to them about Hug & Fug.

Wanda's comments about these two little characters, span around in their heads. The way they had been born out of Medwin's cute English. The innocent and open talk of hugging and fucking that gave these wild inner voices real faces, in the world of passions shared between two loving people. Hug & Fug allowing loving couples to excite their senses to the max. Freeing them to be as wild as they liked. Also demonstrating the power of simple hugging. Encouraging caring and deep love making, in a relationship where both parties agreed fully on whatever they decided to explore.

Hug & Fug provided the voices to say the things people had only ever thought in silence before. They empowered people in new and exciting ways.

Just talking about it on the train, Pete and Mary had found themselves to be incredibly aroused.

'What are you thinking now Pete,' asked Mary in a most seductive voice.

'Umm. Hug & Fug are telling me I need to go to the washroom and that you need to follow me,' replied Pete.

They both smiled a deeply sexual smile and stared into each other's eyes. Hug & Fug were clearly in play.

Pete was up and off down the aisle. Mary followed soon afterwards.

'Half way back to Holland. Drive going well. Can't wait to see you. What time does your flight arrive? Should I drive straight to the airport maybe and pick you up?' was Wanda's text message to Medwin.

The message that came back left Wanda a little puzzled.

'Need to change my flight but all is OK. Give me a call when you get home and I will explain.'

• CHAPTER SIXTEEN •

THE PHONE CALL BETWEEN WANDA and Medwin, was a very different one that night. Could she be imagining things or did Medwin sound strangely distant? Wanda had not asked how much his wife Nina had been included in the weekend's activities and he was not offering up any comment about her whatsoever. All he could talk about, was how happy Mino was to have him there and how desperate he was for his father to stay an extra day and come to an event at his school.

'Fair enough,' thought Wanda. The call ended with a very quick 'Love you' and that was that.

A couple of super busy days at work followed for Wanda. She had enjoyed the little travel adventure with Pete and Mary but things had piled up back in the office. It was also the week she had chosen to speak to Patty, about the planned move to the UK the following year. Several people in European lead roles, worked away from that Amsterdam head office so she did not expect it to be a major problem, if she continued in her role from the UK's main branch.

Things with Patty had not been so friendly since Medwin had moved in though. Patty had only a few months to go until her 40th birthday and the big plan to be married and have a child before then, was looking more and more impossible. She seemed to get grumpier by the day. Wanda had declined several invitations to her house for dinner too. Patty's behaviour with Medwin on previous occasions, had put her right off them all getting together.

'Do you think today might be a good day to raise the subject of me working from the UK office next year Damon?'

Wanda had told him of her plans ages ago. He could not see why there should be any problem but recently, he too was finding Patty extremely difficult.

'The witch has not signed off on so many things for me. I really do not know when might be a good day. Think I heard her talking to a guy she went out with on the phone yesterday so I guess today might be as good as any,' replied Damon.

Wanda scheduled some time in Patty's calendar. That day would be the day.

'So. How did it go?' asked Damon, when they popped out for a coffee afterwards.

'Not sure,' replied Wanda. 'She agreed it seemed to work OK with other people but she also came up with some specific tasks that she thought might be challenging. She asked me to write a proposal, on exactly when I was thinking of moving and how I saw the role being managed efficiently. She would then have to put that in front of Bob.'

'I mentioned to Bob really briefly yesterday about going to see Universities in the UK in September with Lou. He asked me if I would want to live there then and I said yes. All he said was OK. Did not seem to stress him at all. I am probably being silly but I really got a sense from Patty, that she hated the thought of me living happily ever after with the lovely Medwin, in the UK and with my two children. She really had this strange look on her face.'

Medwin's arrival home, turned out to be extremely pleasant indeed. He had flowers, wine and chocolates and could not have been more excited to see Wanda. Love beamed from his longing gazes and he did not take his eyes off her. She had driven straight from the office to Schiphol, to pick him up. As planned, they headed from the airport to a favourite restaurant at the beach so they could really talk and catch up on the week they had spent apart.

Medwin had his hands all over Wanda as she drove. He kept kissing her hand and telling her how much he missed and loved her. She felt silly about any of the doubts she had. None of which would be relayed to Medwin.

The week that followed, was filled with exciting plans for their upcoming trip. Adrenalin was high. Medwin ran every evening in the forest, as Wanda tried to keep up cycling while PJ ran alongside at full speed. Medwin's serious training had mostly been done through the day, when Wanda was at the office. He felt more than ready for the 21km run up the Schilthorn.

Wanda did her proposal around continuing her role from the UK. She presented it to Patty with a totally positive mindset. Hopeful Patty would get a chance to discuss with Bob, in the month Wanda would be away. They would talk more when she got back. Patty seemed happy with that. Wanda had already decided that she would be fine either way. If Patty played hard ball, then she would just find another job.

Medwin flew to Zurich a day ahead of Wanda. Everything had been arranged for his group. He would get them onto their coach personally and give them everything they needed. The rest would be down to their own team leader. Medwin would join them again, as a fellow competitor, on their last leg of the triathlon.

A fun little car had been rented, for Medwin and Wanda to drive to Lauterbrunnen the next day. She arrived in Zurich quite early so they could make the most of the visit.

The long and winding road up the Jungfrau was no stranger to Medwin. Quite some drive from his home town in Austria but his KTM motorbike had been lined up several times, with hundreds of others bikers experiencing the Swiss delights of these crazy mountain bends.

Now he wanted the little car to perform just as well. Wanda had to admit, it all made her stomach turn. Quite spectacular scenery though. She just had to keep her eyes focussed outside the car and trust in Medwin's fast and furious attack into the mountain bends. He loved every minute.

It took Wanda back to the days when she was a bit of biker. Not the sort that was hungry for sharp bends and high speeds though. Her little 120cc trail bike served her well, both on and off road. She was 18. Working two jobs so she could save up to travel. One being in a car park trailer, making hamburgers into the early morning. How she looked forward to jumping on that bike, at the end of the night. Fresh air clearing the nostrils from smells of onions, bacon and meat.

The pension Medwin had booked in Lauterbrunnen, looked out onto the area where the runners would line up in the morning. A typical carved wood Swiss chalet, with mountain views to die for. Perfect. What a stunning little village.

As they mingled with the hundreds of participants outside, a local band gave them a flavour of the guggenmusik competitors could expect to hear, as they finally reached the Schilthorn summit the next day. The atmosphere was electric. Beer and gluhwein flowed. The smell of spicy sausages on the barbeque. Just mouthwatering!

Medwin sat Wanda with food and drink, while he ventured off to check-in under his registration and be assigned a special number.

Unbelievable sights as race day finally unfolded. Young and old. Fit and perhaps a little fat. They came in all shapes and sizes and from all over the world. The multitude of colours. The laughter and smiles. People were out to have fun but Wanda could not help but think, some of them really did not look up to it.

Wanda understood only experienced mountain runners took part in this gruelling challenge but some of the people she saw wearing numbers, did not look fit enough to make even the first valley.

This 21km half-marathon run was not called 'Inferno' for nothing.

First eleven kilometres was said to be fairly harmless, with a gentle climb of 800 metres. After that it really got steep. The last couple of kilometres would see them climb 400 metres almost vertically, to the Schilthorn summit. Very often, that rocky part of the run would be covered with snow and ice. Tough stuff!

Bang! The starter's gun went off and so did the runners.

Wanda ventured back to the room, to gather things for her trek up the mountain. A train ride and two cable cars, required to make the long journey up to the almost 3,000 metres high peak. It would take a couple of hours at least for any runners to get there so she had plenty of time. Fresh clothes for Medwin and warm jackets and gloves for them both. Even though the temperature was over 20°C in the village, there was snow on top and it would be cold.

Once on the cable car, Wanda could see the hundreds of ant-like figures below, running like demons. Coming off the second cable car, she read promotional material that reminded her this summit building, with its revolving restaurant and massive terraces, had been the location for a James Bond film. She had seen 'On Her Majesty's Secret Service'. Now she was in the spectacle herself.

The views left her speechless. Not just the Eiger and the Jungfrau peaks. It could not have been a clearer day. Over two hundred mountain peaks were hers to behold, stretching as far as the eye could see, across the stunning Swiss Alps.

Guggenmusik troops started to arrive and began dressing in their colourful and quite odd costumes. Alligators and varying different smiling creatures. What fun!

The first runner came in, just under two hours. A spritely thin little Kiwi, who looked like he could do it all again. Amazing to see them all coming up the final climb, to finish on the terrace. One man must have been at least seventy. As rugged as the mountain itself.

Medwin came in at two and a half hours and was really pleased with that. Runners were still arriving over an hour later. Wanda and Medwin had a bop to the guggenmusik and socialised a little, then they were ready to head back down before the masses.

Medwin was so wired with adrenalin. All he wanted to do was get naked with Wanda and release his excess energy. She was happy to oblige. No sooner were they in the door of their pension room, then the frantic love making was in play. No Hug and Fug required. Just a gruelling mountain run. Medwin was on fire.

Exhaustion took hold on waking the next day. Breakfast was missed and they just managed to get their bags packed and out of the room, before the manager came chasing them. Bags left downstairs and a relaxing visit to some of the nearby waterfalls. Lauterbrunnen did after all mean 'many fountains'. The area had seventy two amazing waterfalls to choose from. So beautiful!

Sitting on their flight from Zurich to Athens, the exhilaration of the preceding days made both Wanda and Medwin tingle. They recounted all the special moments. Listening to Medwin describe things that happened during his run, Wanda could not help but think what an interesting grandfather he would make, if Lou or Jay were ever to have children. All his amazing mountain stories. Such an athlete. Such a beautiful and interesting man. Medwin reminded her that in January he would return to the Schilthorn, for the massive downhill ski race from that summit. Also called the Inferno.

Clara was at Athens airport to greet them. She and Wanda went way back over twenty years, to those fun days living in London. They had not really spent much time together, since that ski week in Crans Montana almost two years earlier. She was thrilled to have Wanda come to visit. Especially with her new handsome 'Yummy' Austrian.

From the airport to pick Franky and Lena up from school. Later on that evening, into the centre to meet Ken at his office and go for dinner, looking up to views of the incredible Acropolis. Medwin was like a kid in a candy store. He had only been to a few countries in his life and now here he was, out in the big wide world. His endearing 'Please?' had everyone melting.

'We have tickets for the Athletics tomorrow. Thought you might like to see those,' informed Ken, after they had ordered dinner.

Wanda thought Medwin's eyes would pop out. He was so excited.

As it happened, there were hundreds of seats left for the Athletics. Who would have thought? Ken was a senior director for an international hospitality company. The family had moved to Athens to live so he could manage the build-up of business coming in for the Olympics. Franky and Lena went to the French school, as they did wherever they had lived. Ken recounted the nightmare of trying to secure hotel beds at sensible rates and the uncertainty of deals he had put in place with the Greeks. They had asked outrageous prices in the build-up and people just decided not to come. That was why there were so many seats still available for major events. The Greeks had cut their nose off, to spite their face.

As much as everyone was happy to be able to attend such important events, they felt sorry for Ken and the pain he had clearly suffered, trying to do business there. A few months post closure of the Paralympics and they would all leave Athens. Moving to Australia then so he could be closer to China, for what would be required in the run up to Beijing 2008 Olympics. They had lived in Sydney before, working on the year 2000 Olympics, so that would be like going home for everyone. No problem there. He would need to travel up to China often but had decided that living there with the family, would just not be an option.

The Athens apartment was enormous. Wanda and Medwin had a huge bedroom, with its own super large bathroom. The massive jacuzzi bath was black and very sexy indeed. So big that it needed a little step, to get down into it safely. Umm. Hot bubbly water, in a super-sized black jacuzzi. Hug and Fug went wild, as soon as they clapped eyes on that. Wanda sitting on the little step, placing her pussy at the perfect height for easy penetration. It was all systems go, for the very first night. They moved quietly and the sensuously smooth waters engulfed their bodies, as they reached orgasm together. It was a quick one but oh so satisfying!

Walking to the main stadium that next morning, Medwin shared ski stories with Ken. A bit of a mountain man himself, having lived in Colorado for a long time and done quite some ski racing also. They got along famously. Another one who would be keen to hit the slopes with Medwin.

'Must be time for you to organise another Crans Montana gathering don't you think Wanda?' asked Ken with a smile. Medwin had heard so many tales of the fun everyone had in Crans Montana. Could be an idea. She would want to do it in a different location though.

They could not believe just how many empty seats there were, in the main Olympic stadium. Athletics had always been one of the most sort after tickets so what could it be like for other events? The Greeks were there in reasonable numbers initially but as soon as the Greek competitors had done their thing, the Greek members of the audience all seemed to go home. Eventually there were so few people left to support the remaining athletes, they all moved closer to the activity. A combined force for cheering was needed. These unbelievably hard working people, had trained endlessly to get their place at this major event. Medwin and Wanda would not be going anywhere, until the very last of them had shown what they could do. Cheering them on, as loudly as they possibly could.

Four days of exploring the sites of Athens and visiting cool bars with Ken and Clara, were interspersed with other Olympic event visits. Wanda had emailed flight details to Ken and he just organised the rest. What an amazing time they had. A little miffed, why they seemed to have free time on the very last day though.

Ken had to be at a work function that last night so a fun dinner at the el cheapo cafe, right near their apartment, had been organised.

Clara and the children raved about the food. The best truly Greek food in town apparently. Franky and Lena had been learning Greek at school and seemed to speak it rather well. They took charge for the ordering. An excellent meal. Loads of laughs with the locals too. Medwin and Wanda thought it had been the perfect way to spend their last night in Athens.

'Can't thank you enough Clara. What an incredible visit we have had,' said Wanda, as Medwin unloaded their bags from Clara's car.

'Really big thank you from me too Clara. Great that you could also bring us to the airport,' followed Medwin.

They stood and waved, as Clara drove off into the distance.

Scanning the departures board, to see what desk they needed to check in at, Medwin observed that Wanda had turned a strange colour. Her hand was grasping her mouth and she just kept staring at the departures board. Her eyes seemed to get wider and wider.

'Our flight is not listed,' she finally said. 'I kept thinking all morning I should phone or try to get on line to check it would be on time but I did not want to spoil things for everyone. Getting here with plenty of time to spare would be enough, I thought.'

Medwin had felt it was best to leave all these travel details to Wanda. He had not given their flight timing a single thought.

Wanda took out their e-tickets and, as she read the details, her eyes widened even further.

'No. It can't be!' she was almost shaking by now.

Medwin did not want to add to her alarm, by asking what was going on. Instead, he suggested they sit at the cafe nearby and have a coffee. A good idea.

By now, Wanda had taken to excessive deep breathing.

'Are you feeling OK my love?' asked a very worried Medwin.

Wanda seemed unable to speak. She drank the coffee and just kept reading the e-tickets over and over.

'Our flight was for yesterday,' she finally said, in a slow and robotic way. 'I truly can't believe it. How could this have happened? Ken even had the flight details and he is always on the ball with these things. That's why we did not have event tickets yesterday. I felt a little strange all day and did not know why. Oh my god. In all the years and with all the flights I have ever taken. Showing up the next day. Who could ever believe it? What the hell do we do now? Flights out of Athens have to be full. I still can't believe it.'

By now she had begun to hyperventilate and Medwin was really concerned.

He took her hand gently and said, 'Just breathe. We can work this out. I will get us another cup of coffee.'

It must have taken at least a half an hour for Wanda to calm down. The tickets they had, could well be null and void for this leg to Sydney now. What then? Airlines would be charging a fortune, if they even had any seats left with all the Olympics traffic.

Never one to tell lies, Wanda was struggling with the fact that she felt they needed to approach the airline with a good story. Medwin agreed, it was the only thing to do. Eventually they had its content.

They had been off exploring Greece with friends. On their way back to Athens, for getting Medwin and Wanda to their flight the previous day, there had been a car accident. The night had been spent in the hospital and they were very shaken. Everyone was OK and their only thought was to just go to the airport and see what could be done for getting them onward to Sydney, bearing in mind they would have missed their flight.

They had not believed their luck. One of the most beautiful airline staff they had ever seen, came to them like an angel. It was an Arab airline and she was dressed impeccably, with a small veil across the top of her face that hung from a tailored hat. Her concern for their wellbeing, made them feel guilty but they were also elated when she confirmed she would make every effort to get them on a flight the next day. Currently it was fully booked. They would be listed on stand-by and just need to be at the airport. She was relieved to hear their friends in Athens would be able to accommodate them for this extra night.

'I know. How could it possibly happen right?' the phone call to Clara was a bit of an embarrassment to Wanda but all Clara could think of was, that it was great to get another night with them. She wanted to return to pick them up but Wanda insisted they would be fine on the train. Already stored bags in the airport facilities.

'So lucky that we have you guys to come back to,' a relieved Wanda concluded with Clara, after getting all the directions finalised. 'See you real soon.'

Ken was beside himself when he heard the news. How could he have missed that one? He looked at the flight details Wanda had sent again. Clear as a bell. That was why he had not arranged tickets, on what they all thought was their last day. Unbelievable! All the thousands of people he had responsibility for getting to flights. A whole day late. Incredible!

A fun bar was suggested for them all to rendezvous, when Ken had finished with some work demands. Wanda and Ken continued to question their sanity. Neither of them could believe the airline had reacted so well. Fingers crossed, they would manage to get them out the next day but Ken had other people he had tried to get flights for, with no success.

Only a couple of weeks scheduled for their stay in Sydney and now that would already be a day shorter. They sent messages to the family. All of whom could of course also not believe what had happened.

Arriving at Athens airport bright and early the following day, Wanda gave a huge sigh as she saw the massive queue waiting to get to their airline desk. It seemed there were loads of people on stand-by.

'Sorry darling. It is not looking good I'm afraid. Oh well. Let's just join the line and see how we go,' said Wanda in an accepting tone.

Before they knew it, the very beautiful airline lady had walked up to them at the end of the queue. She was so concerned for them and happy to see they looked in good shape. Taking them to one side, they were soon presented with boarding passes. Wanda took them humbly and with enormous gratitude. She did not even look at the seat allocation. She was so relieved, she just handed them to Medwin.

'Oh my goodness,' said a very surprised Medwin. 'It seems we will be travelling first class!' He lifted Wanda in the air and hugged hard.

What an incredible flight that turned out to be. Wanda had travelled at the front of the plane before with work but it was a first for Medwin. Their seats were not beside each other so he needed to figure all the different workings out for himself. Staff could not have been more helpful. They had been told about our 'car accident' for sure.

Arriving in Sydney, they should both have been totally rested. Wanda had stretched out and slept but Medwin stayed awake most of the flight, exploring the functions of his seat/bed and everything that came with it. Staff kept offering him food and he kept taking it.

'We are in the car rental and just leaving the airport,' said Medwin shyly for the fourth time. Wanda was driving so she had handed the phone to him, when she saw the call come in from her niece. They would spend one night at her house and several family members were there to greet them. 'Please?' he asked several times, not understanding one word of reply that was coming back.

Wanda had warned Medwin that he might not understand the broad Australian accents spoken at high speed. Her family also had great difficulty understanding Medwin. Did not seem to matter though. Everyone was laughing and enjoying the occasion. He was a big hit.

They were all keen to hear about the travel adventure with Pete and Mary too. Now happily bussing it around Europe.

'Trust you to be heading straight down to the snow Wanda,' her brother Joe had piped in.

She had already told him, they had this great offer from a friend who had two other friends cancel on her at short notice. They had super cheap accommodation, right on the snow at Perisher and would do two days of skiing on discounted lift tickets, then drive back via the hinterland towards Bega and up the coast road back to Sydney. Stay one night at a beach. Away five days in all. A quick little tour for Medwin. Good for him to at least see something. The other eight days, would be busy catching up with people in Sydney and checking everything out there. Medwin could not have been more excited. Kept asking Wanda to pinch him and remind him he was actually in Australia.

'These are the skis I was thinking of buying for next season's races,' said an even more excited Medwin, as the ski rental guy offered up special trial skis for his new Austrian friend. How small could this world be? The guy came from a village in Austria, just 50kms from Medwin's.

They shared a triple room with Wanda's friend so fairly basic on the accommodation. Snow was perfect though. Medwin had been quite surprised, by the extent of runs and facilities. Also a little surprised when a ski patrol officer stopped him for speeding, as he skied into a chair lift area at the top of Blue Cow.

'But it is not possible to go so fast here,' he exclaimed to the officer politely. The officer just smiled and reminded him to go slower next time, then let him go. Provided plenty of laughs for everyone during the après ski.

After a great couple of days in the snow, they were off again. Medwin was pleased they would be alone that night. He took in every sight with great interest. Not confident with driving on the other side of the road, they had agreed Wanda would do all the driving. He loved that this meant he could fondle her. Constantly grabbing her hand to kiss it. Playing with her nipples gently. Occasionally kissing her neck. His hand hugging her pussy softly. Always telling her how much he loved her and how he could not believe what a great life they had together. Australia had always been a dream of his and now he was living that dream, with the most beautiful girl in the world. Singing to her often, from the song that always reminded him of her

'You are so beautiful ..... to me ..... can't you see. You are everything I ever wanted. You are all I ever need......'

As they drove through the tropical forests of the hinterland, Medwin was captivated. Hug & Fug had been playing in his mind for hours.

Suddenly aware of an enormous erection trying to burst from his jeans, Medwin could no longer take in the views. Fixed on Wanda, he took her hand and placed it on his penis. A wide clearing near a waterfall, provided an excellent spot for them to park well off the road. No sooner were they out of the car, than Medwin grabbed Wanda quite sharply and moved her onto the warm car hood.

She wore a skirt over the top of leggings that were easily removed. As he did so, he stopped to kiss and lick her pussy slowly. She came in moments. Seconds later, his enormous penis was inside and thrusting her into the car hood. The warmth underneath, added to the sensation. It felt as though his penis had reached well past her belly button. They both gasped loudly with his final orgasmic push. Holding on to each other with incredible intensity, they were wrapped up as one again.

How quickly the rest of the visit passed. Medwin loved it all. They visited kangaroos and koalas at a wildlife park. Took the ferries around stunning Sydney harbour. Met with a seemingly endless stream of friends and family.

It was the last day at the picnic, that seemed to change things. Quite a cold day but still lovely and sunny. One of the young lads was the same age as Mino and clearly reminded Medwin of him.

During the birthday visit to Mino, he had told his dad that phone calls made him feel strange. He would prefer just to see his dad, whenever he could and understood that could be not so often.

Medwin told his family that the Australians he was staying with in Amsterdam, had invited him to join them on their trip back to Sydney and he had decided to do it. He would come back to visit Mino, as soon as he returned in September. They had all been really excited for Medwin and knew it was a dream of his being realised.

A pub gathering on the last night in Sydney, brightened Medwin up a little. Nephews had challenged him to drink some 'special' ozzie brews and he had been a willing participant. They really had a laugh and he felt he had bonded well. Happy and sad farewells followed. Promises were made to come back and visit again soon. An early flight the next morning so straight to sleep, when they finally got back to the friend's house they were staying at.

'Been a hectic couple of weeks heh my darling?' asked Wanda, as they waited to board their flight back to Athens. The distant nod of confirmation, told her Medwin's mind was not with her.

'Will be nice to just do nothing, when we get to Mykonos,' she continued. 'Quite hot there at present so lots of swimming and just relaxing by the beach or pool will be perfect. Such a beautiful little Greek island. Quaint little lanes for us to explore in the evenings too.'

Medwin smiled and said yes several times, trying to sound interested. Wanda could tell his heart was just not in it but she did not push. There really had been so much for him to take in. A quiet flight was in order. Luckily they had five seats to themselves so they would be able to stretch out.

It was the first time they actually lay on a beach together. Medwin had tried to ride a surfboard in Sydney but that had been as close as they had come so far. He could not relax. The athlete needed to be doing something, on their quiet Mykonos beach. No watersports in sight. He swam but then what? It was only the first day and he already seemed distressed by it all. For the first time, Medwin and Wanda exchanged cross words.

'We only have three days here. Why not just relax my darling?' appealed Wanda to a clearly unsettled Medwin.

'I think it would have been better to go straight back to Amsterdam. I need to find work. I need to visit Mino. It feels stupid to be laying here,' he snapped back.

Wanda was shocked. He had not spoken like this before. He had been keen to have this stopover on the way back too. She reminded him it was too late to change anything so they had better just enjoy themselves. He seemed determined not to. The moody and abrupt Medwin she had seen months earlier, had returned.

How could Wanda turn things around this time?

• CHAPTER SEVENTEEN •

'REALLY GOING WELL AT SCHOOL mum and I have been through loads of the UK University websites. Several options for subjects too. We can go through it all when you get back. Open days are during the last week of September so we will have time to book ourselves in. So exciting mum. Can't wait. Danny's getting a bit sad about it all but that is only to be expected I guess. Can't wait to see you. Hi to Medwin. Hope you guys have had a great trip. Love you lots and lots mumma. mwa mwa. x x x x x x x x'

Wanda had managed to check her emails quickly at Athens airport. Excellent free internet in the transit lounge. She missed Lou too. Not long and they would be reunited. A quick chatty email back. Lou did not need to know, the last couple of days had been hell.

Medwin had perked right up that morning though. He had been on line and booked a flight to Austria, for the day after they arrived back in Holland. As Wanda emailed Lou, Medwin emailed his sister to let her know when he would be arriving.

Sitting back in his seat, Medwin gave an enormous sigh of relief. For the first time, in what seemed an age to Wanda, he actually looked at her lovingly.

'I am so sorry about my behaviour these past days,' he said as he leaned across to give Wanda the softest of kisses.

Wanda felt herself melt. She had been thinking what a waste of time and money it had been, going to Mykonos.

The sullen mood that Medwin had been in the entire time, made her seriously doubt whether they could stand the test of time. The man that was with her on that beautiful Greek island, was not the man she had fallen in love with. After the first day of doing everything she could to try and cheer him up, she had decided it was best to leave him alone. No hugs. No sex. No nothing. They had hardly said a word. He would take a swim with her mid-morning and then go back to their room. She returned later in the day. Wanda tried to just laze on the beach and hope he would come around. One day she suggested renting motorbikes and touring the island. He was not even interested in that.

No mistaking the look of love that was now back in his eyes. The longing kiss and hug. That man Wanda loved deeply had returned.

Wanda decided not to reflect on the negative. Although she had not liked his behaviour one bit, she realised it had been driven by his sadness about not seeing Mino for so long.

How to positively impact things so they did not end up in that horrible place again? It had been heart breaking, to have such distance between them.

'I have been thinking. Maybe it would be better, if you split your time equally between Austria and Holland. Looks like that group out of Vienna for Portugal next year, will be going ahead. Lots of work to be done on that and it seems there could be other possibilities, for groups from Vienna. Really needs you to be there on the case don't you think? Why not plan to split your month in an organised way?

Spend two weeks in Austria and two weeks in Holland. Then you know what you are doing and can schedule things accordingly. Also nice for Mino, to be clear on when you are going to be around. You do not mind the commute up to Vienna so maybe just stay with your parents. Mino knows he has that access to you regularly then. What do you think my darling?' Wanda asked with a smiling beam and eyebrows raised, to express how good an idea she thought it was.

They discussed it all the way back to Amsterdam. Medwin became more and more animated. He would of course miss Wanda terribly. Better than being in such a terrible mood, that he might actually drive her away. It was agreed. They would give it a try. By the time they all moved to the UK the following year, Medwin should have a clearer picture on how and where he would earn money. Mino should also be getting used to the idea of his dad coming and going. They could reassess things then.

Medwin had not stopped telling Wanda how much he loved her. Very watery eyed, saying sorry again and again. How could he ever make up for those bad days? It was not him. He would do everything in his power, to stop those moods taking him over. Making her happy, was his main mission in life and would be forever.

By the time they reached home, all thoughts of Mykonos had been erased. Wanda was so excited to see Lou. Medwin was happy to see her also but more focussed on the next day and heading back to see Mino. Small travel gifts were exchanged and they chatted for hours, about the adventures they had all had.

'Lou. Check this one out.' Wanda had been on the web for hours, looking at all the potential University courses Lou had been considering. 'This one could have been written for Jay.'

BA (Hons) Sound Art & Design, with descriptor and prerequisites pretty much listing what Jay had been doing since he was nine.

'Wow. How did you find that one mum?' Lou chirped, after reading the text. 'Do you think Jay could actually do it? Has he said anything about going to University? Sounded like he did pretty well with that IT course. How cool would it be, if we were going to Uni at the same time? What about those courses for me? Which ones do you think work best?'

Moving right along to focus on Lou's options, they left the topic of possibilities for Jay until later. Wanda did not quite know how Jay would respond anyway. She might just email him the link. The IT course had gone well. Maybe he was ready to commit to some more serious study now. The years working full time since high school, really had given him a different attitude towards learning.

Jay could not believe his eyes. Everything this degree study mentioned had been dear to his heart for such a long time. There were limited places apparently and an audition had to be undertaken to get in. Candidates needed to have a portfolio of music they had created. No problem with any of that.

'I can't believe they actually have a University Degree for everything I love to do. How did you find it mum? Do you really think I could do it?' Jay was over the moon.

Wanda had always told Jay and Lou that, so long as they were in serious studies and working hard, she would always support them for their main costs. They had both had jobs for their spending money, since their early teens, so the work ethic was definitely in place.

As Wanda headed to bed that night, she felt an enormous sense of pride and satisfaction. Her world could not be more perfect. How lucky could one woman be? She had a well-paid and stimulating job. Two wonderful children, who were excited about possibilities for attending University in London next year. An amazing man, who she was about to phone. All her loved ones were healthy and happy. What more could anyone ever possibly want?

Medwin was so happy down the phone. Sharing all his stories and photos of the big travel adventure with his family, had gone really well. They loved the little gifts from Australia. All well with Mino.

After the chit chat, Wanda and Medwin talked about their wild night of love making, that night before he left for Austria.

'Was it really four times in the one night my amazing man?' asked Wanda, with sullen sexy tones. 'How did you manage it my love?'

Hug & Fug were back in play, as they had been that night. This time they were encouraging Wanda and Medwin to repeat what they could, even though they were in different countries.

'I told you I had to make up for those bad days, you beautiful woman.' Medwin had the slower sexy voice happening too.

'Can you feel me playing with your hard nipples?' He knew she would take them in her own small fingers.

They had always been reluctant to be hands free on their phone calls, in case other people could hear them. Lou was staying over at Danny's house that night. Medwin was also alone. His parents had gone to some village event. Agreeing to each have both their hands in play, made things all the more exciting.

They put their phones on loudspeaker, pretending they were together in each other's arms. The voices talking to them, were those sensuous little Hug & Fug characters.

Visions in their heads were as clear as anything. Closing their eyes, they admired and adored each other's bodies, mentioning every crevice. Just as they had done, through most of that last night together.

'I am inside you. Can you feel it?' asked Medwin. They had been anxious to feel fully connected again, after the bad days apart. Wanda had dropped to the bed on all fours and watched Medwin plunge his throbbing penis deep inside, as he stood behind her by the bed. Who were those people in the mirror? They could have been watching a porn movie. Seeing their reflections of passion, made it all that more intense.

Thinking back to it now, Wanda could again see the mirror images clearly. She told Medwin how that couple in the mirror looked, as she entered her own fingers into herself. He too saw the images clearly. Both masturbating, they came almost as quickly as they had that night. Round one complete but three more had followed.

The man in the mirror arched his back, before falling forward to rest on the woman. They were panting and heads were spinning. As they fell to the side, the mirror kept a vision of her shapely form. In minutes he was kissing her back, from head to toe. Not again visible to the mirror, until his head moved gently into the gap he made between her legs.

Her pussy had only just settled from the first encounter. Gently he kissed her buttocks and legs. Downwards to suck her toes, as he hugged into her entire body. His hand had been hugging her breast. She took it and began to suck his middle finger. They lay gently sucking, for what must have been at least half an hour.

'You are laying on your back now my love and I am licking your balls,' the sexy phone voice called out to Medwin softly. 'I want you to sleep now. We can continue with the rest of that evening, another night. The mirror porn stars will be waiting for us.'

They wished each other a good night's sleep, as they shared closing words of love and the peace that comes after sensual satisfaction.

'We arrive Thursday evening around 7pm,' said an excited Wanda to Jay, as they finalised on schedules for Lou's University inspections and Jay's audition. Jay still could not believe he was getting this chance, after having been so painful to get through high school.

Wanda told Jay and Lou about the email she had that day, from Pete and Mary. They were now on their way to Vancouver and could not be happier. Such a cool trip they were doing. A lovely couple. They really did deserve all the happiness they could get. As Wanda told Jay and Lou about the email, she recalled a nightmare she had about them recently. Details were sketchy but she now recalled how bad it had made her feel.

She kept those bad thoughts to herself. No need to spoil all the good vibes they were sharing, about the upcoming London trip. Lou initially had one or two Universities in the Midlands she was considering but now it had come down to just three in the London and Surrey area. Much easier. They had loads of people they could stay with nearby.

That green Italian wagon was ready to rock and roll yet again. PJ had returned to Denise for another visit. They could almost put the car on auto pilot, to get them to the channel ferry. Although this time they had decided to try Dunkirk, instead of Calais. Just for fun. A little longer in crossing time but less distance to drive.

Jay's audition could not have gone more smoothly. The panel also loved his portfolio of music and what he had achieved with music to date. Twice the number of people than they had places for were auditioned but Jay felt sure he would get a place.

Lou's audition for Acting, at the elite drama school, had not been successful. Both Lou and Wanda were pleased. Way too intense.

Her preference was now for the University in Kingston, where she fancied the Digital Media and Performance degree. Excellent facilities and the people seemed nice. All she needed was a high enough score with her International Baccalaureate. Hopefully she was on track for that.

Having breakfast on the morning they were due to leave London, Wanda received a frantic call from her niece Kitty in Melbourne. At first all Wanda could hear was sobbing. Kitty was Pete's sister. Eventually she managed to speak.

Pete and Mary had been in a car accident in Canada. Mary had died on impact. Pete was in hospital in Edmonton unconscious. He did not know about Mary. Someone needed to go. Kitty's first reaction had been to get the first plane from Melbourne but she knew that would take a long time. Her husband and two daughters, also thought she would not be strong enough to handle this. She immediately thought of Aunty Wanda.

'I am on my way,' responded a totally shocked Wanda immediately. 'My bag is here beside me, packed all ready for driving back to Holland. Lou will either fly back and leave the car here or see if Jay wants to drive her back in it. He had been planning to come over for a couple of weeks anyway. Medwin is organising a weekend in the Ardennes, for us all to mountain bike.' Wanda then thought what a stupid thing to be talking about. The tragedy had not quite sunken in yet.

Wanda grabbed her bag and asked Lou to phone Air Canada and get her on the first flight. She would jump in a taxi to Heathrow and Lou could let her have details by the time she got to the airport. Credit card details were written out for Lou. They hugged with tears in their eyes but went into hyper drive, to get things sorted. Lou was just like Wanda in a crisis. Get things organised and get it done quickly.

'They are trying to hold the flight for you mum. I told them what has happened. You just need to give them your credit card quickly, at the airline check in counter. Kitty called back. Edmonton police are going to meet your flight and take you to the hospital. If I do not hear back from you, I will presume you made this flight and let them know. Love you so much mum.' Lou hung up from the call and for the first time since the news, she burst into uncontrollable howling tears.

'What do you mean the flight is closed? I don't think so. Get me your supervisor please. This is an emergency.' Wanda was trying to stay calm and luckily the supervisor walked through at that very moment.

'We were expecting you madam. Your daughter told us everything. Quickly let me scan your credit card. Now. Come with me. Just hand luggage right?'

The supervisor personally took Wanda through all fast lane access points and controls, then to the flight gate. An air hostess was waiting for her. So too the plane load full of informed passengers. Luckily they had not missed their take off time slot so all was well.

They had given Wanda two seats to herself. She sat by the window and cried her way to Calgary. The cabin crew tried their best to get her to eat and drink but all she could say was, 'Just water will be fine. Thank you.'

On landing, they called her name to come forward. A charming policeman was at the aircraft door to meet Wanda and lead her quickly to the connecting flight for Edmonton.

'Such an awful accident ma'am. We are so sorry for your loss.' He could not have been kinder but Wanda had no information at all about the accident so she really did not appreciate his comments. She followed him without saying a word. Wanting to ask if Pete was still alive but not being able to bring herself to even think he could possibly have died too. In any case, she might wake up shortly and find it had all been that horrible nightmare again.

'An officer from the Edmonton force will meet you on arrival there and take you to the hospital,' he concluded as they reached the relevant gate.

'Thank you. So very kind of you,' was all Wanda could manage.

Again she was called to the front of the plane on landing. This time, the police officer looked like he had been crying. Wanda now realised this was for real. This tall, tough policeman could hardly speak.

She thought the worst, 'Mary is dead. Now they are going to tell me Pete is too.'

She stood in front of the policeman unable to move. She was numb. Uncontrollable sobbing and shaking took hold. The young police officer took her in his arms and hugged her. All he could say was, 'We think Pete is going to pull through OK.'

Wanda howled loudly with a strange sense of relief.

'Strong and sturdy as she goes,' she soon forced herself to refocus. 'Keep the mind clear. Listen well. There will be a lot to take care of. Everyone is looking for me to be in charge. Must be strong for Pete.'

Her head was spinning but soon they arrived at the hospital.

'Pete has come round ma'am,' said an officer waiting for them, almost in slow motion. 'He insisted on knowing what happened to Mary. We told him an hour ago and at the same time told him you were coming. He is a tough little cookie. All he said was. I thought she was. Then he paused for a long while before saying. You will like my Aunty Wanda. He is naturally in denial. Great that he has you here now. One of us has stayed with him, ever since the ambulance brought him in. We have wives the same age as Mary. Hate to think how we would be, if this happened to us. Whatever you need ma'am. Anything at all. We are here for you.'

Wanda asked him to tell her everything he knew about the accident.

'Pete was driving a car rental from Vancouver. Mary was in the front passenger seat. They were driving at normal speed, through the Rockies, being tourists. A trailer home RV bus, coming in the opposite direction, lost its brakes. It crossed to the oncoming traffic. Hit the car in front of Pete and Mary, then them and afterwards the car behind. After that, he went off into the ditch. Mary died on impact. Several ambulances attended, as well as the chopper. Mary's body is in Calgary. Everyone else was taken to different hospitals and Pete ended up here. We were not sure he was going to even make it but now he has come round.'

'Thank you. You have all been fantastic. Now I think I am ready to see Pete, if that's OK.' Wanda was not so sure she could stay strong but she would give it her best shot.

Pete sat up in the bed as Wanda walked in. They smiled at each other but with strangely blank faces. The shaking tight hug said it all.

'I should have stayed longer at that last stop. Mary loved the lake there but I was anxious to get going. Why didn't I stay longer? I knew she was gone. She didn't know a thing. Taking photos out the side window. It was so quick. I came round on the road and managed to crawl to her side. Most of the engine was on the road in bits everywhere. She was just looking so peaceful. I knew she was gone. Then I passed out. I don't remember any blood on her. She just looked asleep. It was all so quick. I don't know.' Pete was rambling now and his face quivered with the strain of talking.

'Enough. I want to tell you something,' said Wanda calmly and with an inner sense of deep spiritual contact. 'Mary has been with me on the flight over here.'

'It was not your fault. Mary wants me to tell you, she realises it was just her time. She told me that you were going to be OK.

I got a little worried, when the policeman met me. He looked like he had more bad news he was not saying. You came around just as I landed apparently. Mary told me you would. She needs us to be super strong. Her parents are devastated. I feel her presence all the time. Such a strong amazing energy. I think she wants to help us get through everything we need to, before she lets herself go. She loves you so much and could not have been happier these past years with you.'

Pete allowed the tears to flow. Wanda held his hand, while he cried himself to sleep. It was not long before she had also fallen into a deep sleep, with her head resting on the side of his bed.

'Ma'am. The hospital has given you a room, just along the corridor. Might be good if you both got a proper night sleep, if you can.' The policeman was back and on the case again. 'I will be here with Pete and come get you if we need to. OK?'

Wanda nodded and followed the nurse to her room.

Two days later, Pete was able to be discharged from hospital. He had only superficial exterior wounds. Seemed pretty much everyone from the accident, was OK. Only Mary had gone.

The two young policemen, who had been rotating their shifts keeping watch on Pete, insisted they use their own private time to drive Pete and Wanda to Calgary. They would pass by the wreckers, where the car had been taken, and pick up the personal belongings still in the car.

Pete had been saying he wanted to take a look at the wreck. He wanted to know how Mary had died. Being a mechanic and a bus driver, every little detail rang in his head. He could name the bits of the car he had seen scattered across the road, for those brief moments he was conscious. He had not seen any blood. Why had she died? An autopsy had been carried out in Calgary and we would soon have specifics. Wanda encouraged him not to go looking over the wreck. In the end he agreed. The police officers were quick. Pete confirmed they had retrieved everything. He could see the car in the distance. It was enough.

Calgary police had arranged a hotel for them. Wanda insisted on buying the Edmonton guys dinner before they left to return home. They shared stories of families and adventures. Pete would stay in touch and always be in their debt. His speech had become slow and broken but he had forced himself to summon up the energy, to talk with these amazing men.

Wanda now needed to swing into action big time. People wanted information. Kitty had advised the travel insurance company straight away and they had been in contact with Wanda regularly. Not terribly helpful though. Wanda could not help but think their only real objective, was to make sure they paid for as little as possible.

The Australian Embassy had been contacted, to arrange clearance for the dead body to be returned to Melbourne. Wanda had made it very clear to them that Pete would not board any flight, unless he was certain Mary's body was on that same flight. It was crucial.

He had to make sure he at least delivered her dead body home safely. Her parents were Egyptian and totally devastated. They also had traditions needing to be observed.

It would be a couple of days before Pete and Wanda could view the dead body. That gave Wanda some time to prepare Pete. By then he had accepted Mary would speak to him through Wanda. It helped him massively, to know she was still present in some way.

'Mary wants you to know that is not her,' a nervous Wanda told Pete as they waited outside the viewing room, at the Calgary funeral home. 'She is in your heart and in the endless happy memories. Those beautiful photos we looked through last night. That's her.

So lucky your camera was still OK and we could get those photos off. No question how happy you guys were. The lifeless vessel you are going to see, is not the Mary we love.' Wanda felt faint but knew she had to be strong for Pete.

'We respect this body for carrying Mary's incredible spirit around these 27 years. They have put the fresh clothes on we gave them and tried to make it look like that photo you picked. That's it. You go in alone at first and stay as long as you want. I will be at the door and nobody will come in. Do what you want. Look the body over. Lay with it. Cry. Shout. Whatever. Mary is staying outside with me. She wants you to know again, how much she loves you. OK?' Wanda reassured a shaking Pete, as she held back the tears.

He came out after just five minutes.

'You're right. That's not her. Come in with me.'

Wanda's nerves made her a little flippant. 'Not a good job with trying to match her smile heh? Maybe we can get them to work on that a little. Her parents will wonder who she is. Such a beautiful smile. Yeah. Mary is agreeing with me.'

It took a week for everything to be arranged and the clearance granted. As much as Pete and Wanda had tried to deal with things positively, Wanda knew he would not be able to make the journey back to Melbourne with Mary's dead body alone. Finally she convinced the travel insurance people, she needed to go with him. It had not been easy. She eventually had the head of the company brought into the conversation. He was most sympathetic and smoothed the way from there on in.

Calgary to Los Angeles was the first leg. Wanda had clearance the body had been loaded, before they took their boarding cards.

In LA they had quite a few hours to wait for their connection to Melbourne via Auckland. Wanda decided fresh air would be good. She would take Pete to Santa Monica for lunch. They walked along to Venice Beach and talked about what to expect, when they landed in Melbourne.

Pete had still not spoken with Mary's parents. He could not stop blaming himself, for the loss of their daughter. Wanda had not pushed him. He needed to come around in his own good time.

Wanda kept everyone informed with detailed emails, like a super-efficient clock that was determined to never loose time. She would wait until Pete fell asleep, afraid to leave him alone.

Keeping Pete sane was the hardest task. His heart was broken. So quickly, his whole life shattered. He could see no life ahead.

Wanda kept telling him Mary knew it was not his fault. He had not been speeding and was a great driver. There was nothing he could have done. It had been her time and she was happy with the life she had with him. Some people lived to ripe old ages and still never experienced anything close to the happiness she had with him.

Returning to LA airport to check in for their flight, Wanda was focussed on ensuring the body had been loaded.

'All clear with the body madam but we have a problem with your entry into Australia,' replied the check-in counter staff member.

When Wanda had left Holland, she had no idea she would be going to Australia. All she had with her was her British passport. No visa for Australia in that of course. She would travel on her Australian passport, when normally travelling there. She was Australian by birth. Surely they could see that in the system. This was an extraordinary event. A journey she had not planned on taking.

In the end, they worked out they could call Lou and get Wanda's Australian passport details, then they would phone through to Australia to ask permission for Wanda to board. Luckily Lou was back in Holland. Jay had decided to drive that green Italian wagon and Lou home.

All of this red tape became the straw that broke the camel's back. Wanda broke down finally and the nightmare of everything hit her. She could no longer speak. The tears flooded out as she shook.

All this time, she had been strong and holding everyone together. Now it was her turn.

Pete rose to the occasion and took charge. Final details were sorted with Lou and the airline staff. They were eventually on their way. The airline had given them upgrades to business class and the crew could not have been nicer.

Everyone was horrified to know this pleasant young man had his wife travelling home with him, in a coffin below.

Total exhaustion saw Pete and Wanda sleeping the entire way to Auckland. Departing Auckland, for their connection to Melbourne, the airline initially said the body had not been loaded and would be on the next flight. Wanda insisted, they would also need to take that next flight. Magically, they managed to get the body loaded and the planned arrival into Melbourne could be maintained.

Mary's father came alone to the airport. Wanda requested nobody else was there. She had rehearsed this over and over with Pete. It was going to be very tough but she convinced him he could get through it.

Pete had been really close to Mary's dad. He was the son they never had. Just three beautiful daughters. Now one was gone. Their grief would never end but they wanted Pete to know they did not blame him.

Arrangements had been made to see the coffin in freight but they would have to wait until later that day, to view the body. Pete returned with Mary's family in the early evening. Wanda reminded him, it was not Mary. He would relay those same thoughts to her family, when he could be heard through their howling.

A picnic gathering was organised for the following day, at one of Mary's favourite parks. Wanda was booked on a flight back to Holland, for the day after that.

She would not stay for the funeral but would instead spend time with those who were closest to Mary, at a location where she loved to be.

It was an amazingly sunny day and warm day. Everyone was determined to make this occasion one full of all the happy memories they had of Mary.

It was, after all, the day she would have been celebrating her 28th birthday.

• CHAPTER EIGHTEEN •

ALMOST A MONTH HAD PASSED since Wanda returned to Holland from Melbourne. Regular calls with Pete had helped him stay sane. The funeral had been excruciating. So many of the Egyptian family howling and inconsolable. Pete wished he could have done the same as Wanda. The picnic to celebrate Mary's birth and life, had been so beautiful. If only he could have opted out of the funeral too. Wanda had her work and life demands back in Holland to get back to. Totally acceptable reasons to leave straight after the picnic. Pete felt like he had nothing but emptiness. No excuses for him not to attend.

'OK Pete. I have emailed all that information to the travel insurance company again. Hopefully that will be that. How much more painful can they be? Your solicitor sounds to be on the ball at least so that's good. We need to make sure you get what you are supposed to. These companies get off way too lightly. Mary would have wanted us to squeeze them as tight as we could so let's make sure we do.'

Wanda knew that all the organising was helping Pete. He needed to be kept busy. He told Wanda on that call, that he would return to work in a week. They had agreed for him to just do a couple of days and build up, according to how he felt. Pete had loads of support. He knew he could call Wanda at any time and they had emailed every day. She encouraged him to write down how he was feeling, as a means of release.

The General had been more than understanding, about the sudden extra time Wanda had away from her job. Endless messages of condolence were sent and colleagues tried not to pile work up for Wanda in her absence. Tragedies like this always did tend to bring out the best in people.

That said, now that Wanda was fully operational again and not having to run off to the bathroom in tears so often, she felt it was time to have that conversation, about working from the UK the following year. Patty had kept avoiding the subject. A meeting was finally agreed for the coming week.

'Will take train from airport mum. See you at home,' said Jay via an sms to his mum, just prior to boarding his flight from London. *'Should get there around 7pm. Love you. x'*

Jay had taken the Friday off from his temp job and flown across after work Thursday. During the day Friday, he would catch up with mates in Amsterdam. Medwin had arranged a fantastic weekend for them all in the Ardennes. Keen to teach Wanda and Lou how to ride a mountain bike and use gears properly. They were not so sure but had agreed to at least try. Flat cycling they loved. Anything else was questionable. Danny was joining them. Medwin had given that green Italian wagon the once over and fuelled. Wanda would get home early Friday and they would take the three hour drive to the nearest hills they could find. Belgium's beautiful Ardennes.

'Cool hotel Medwin,' cried Jay and Danny almost simultaneously. They spotted the indoor swimming pool and gaming room straight away. A late arrival so no access that night but they made plans to be up early and in there for a swim before breakfast.

Medwin had been a total rock for Wanda throughout all the trauma. He could not have been more caring. Hugs were even more intense and constant. Love making often began and ended with tears. He knew it might take a while, for Wanda to become herself fully again. The loss of Mary and being there supporting Pete. Wanda had returned home totally exhausted but, in true Wanda style, had been ready to take everything on and outwardly seemed to be in full swing. Medwin knew better and hoped this weekend he arranged, would help to get her laughing again.

The amazing hotel in the Ardennes, included top quality bikes for everyone. Even helmets. Not something they were used to wearing but the hotel's insurance would not be in effect, if they were not worn.

After the morning swim and a hearty breakfast, they had been ready to hit the mountain. The boys were off in a flash.

Wanda and Lou had not been allowed to go, until they showed they could move through the gears. Easy enough to do on the flat around the hotel grounds. Medwin had been quite impressed.

Arrangements were made to meet the boys at the top of the second hill. Everyone figured Wanda and Lou would have mastered the art by then. The first hill was all it took. Just not happening.

They tried their best for what seemed an age. Pedalling to their hearts content and going nowhere. Medwin had patiently tutored them but it was just not working.

'I really do not see the point,' said Wanda eventually. 'My legs go round and round but I might just as well be walking. Would get me up the hill a lot faster.'

By this time Lou was in fits of laughter. She had been thinking the exact same thing as her mum. What on earth was the point? She had not wanted to let that on to Medwin though. He had been so sweet and gone to ever so much trouble. Her mum was laughing too by now.

'Come on mum. We can do it. If we sing and can get our legs working at the same time, we can be up that hill on these bikes in no time.'

Medwin looked so relieved Lou was taking charge. He was also very pleased to hear them singing and laughing.

'You carry on and enjoy yourself with the boys Medwin,' said Lou. 'We will meet you at that café, just after the second hill. That one the hotel dude mentioned. Meanwhile you guys can go tackle some real off road countryside. Mum will be much happier knowing you are having fun.'

Wanda agreed and eventually Medwin relented. They kissed and hugged.

'Have fun my sweet man,' Wanda shouted as he cycled off.

Laugh! Wanda and Lou could take no more. No sooner would they start to feel they could conquer the stupid hill, than they would say something funny and start in fits of laughter again. Quite hysterical.

The Pete and Mary saga had its impact on Lou too. Crying herself to sleep at night. Worrying about her mum. Now the hysterical laughter seemed to be a great release for them both.

Finally walking most of the way, they were still in fits when they arrived at the café. Luckily, ahead of the boys.

'Those hills really are tough heh,' said Lou as the boys sat down. Then she and Wanda laughed until they cried. The boys just looked at each other in awe. Women!

They needed to be back reasonably early on the Sunday, for Jay's flight back to London that evening. Wanda and Lou relaxed around the pool and let the boys go off for a serious bike ride first thing. Lunch in a nearby village and then home. An extremely pleasant weekend had by all. Sunny afternoon providing the perfect light, for enjoying the spectacular scenery. Medwin finally accepting that Wanda and Lou were not meant for bike gears.

'I'm in!' exclaimed Jay down the phone. He arrived back in London to find his response letter from the University. 'Can't believe it mum. The letter says I was the most outstanding candidate and they have great expectations for my success. Wow. How cool is that!'

Fantastic news! Everyone was so excited for Jay. Wanda knew his time had come and this was going to take Jay down an entirely different pathway, for his life journey. So great!

Lou had been offered three places at Universities so her options were still open. It would finally depend on the IB points achieved.

Medwin had two sports groups signed from Amsterdam and could see quite some potential for business out of Holland now. He had decided just to stay one week in Austria and spend the rest of his time in Holland.

As Christmas approached, there were also loads of parties and functions on the calendar. Medwin did not want to miss out on any of the fun and Wanda had certainly wanted to have her very handsome and tall Austrian, on her arm for them all.

'We really need to see what the big global changes mean to the business Wanda. I can't say yes or no to you working from the UK until after we hear those in February,' said Patty finally to Wanda.

Work was busier than ever so Wanda had decided to just get on with it and forget all about chasing for the move. If they were stupid enough not to try and keep her in the role, then so be it. She knew she would have no trouble finding a good role in the UK. Especially now it seemed Lou's first choice had become the Kingston option.

A beautiful place to live by the Thames River. Wanda could perhaps move to a role at the General's corporate offices in London. It might all work out much better in the end. Usually did for Wanda. Stay positive and go with the energy flows. That had always been her motto.

Wanda had spoken with Medwin about all the plans for the UK, on numerous occasions. He had always seemed enthusiastic. Why now did he suddenly seem to be against the idea?

He could have not been more direct or blunt.

'I really do not think I would like to live in England. Even though I have never been there, I always found English people to be difficult,' had been all he could say.

Wanda reminded him that Jay and Lou were born in London. He did not see them as English though. They were Australian.

She then reminded him that Clara and the children they stayed with in Athens, were all English. They were different he said. They had always lived in other countries.

In the end Wanda decided it was best to say nothing. Drop the subject. Wait until the New Year and take him over so he had first-hand experience. He would be sure to love it.

'We have the party on Al's boat Saturday night my love.' Wanda changed the subject. 'What do you think I should wear?'

They had been getting ready for bed. Medwin had just lifted the sheet. He loved to slip between their special silky soft sheets.

'Wear? Umm. Right now you look so stunning. I do not want to think of you wearing anything. Hug & Fug are playing in my head,' replied Medwin, as he grabbed the naked Wanda and wrapped her up in the silky sheet.

Wanda squirmed and slithered, feeling the sheet soft against her body. Medwin cradled her wrapped body in his strong arms, as he sat upright at the top of the bed. As he rocked her back and forth, the silky sheet was soft against his body. Wanda's arms locked up in the sheet. They kissed and played a tongue game with their mouths.

Medwin could see Wanda's hardened nipples, bulging under the sheet. The tips of his fingers aroused them even more. Fingers then moving to Wanda's feet, massaging her body through the silk as they edged slowly downwards. A toe popped out from the sheet. Medwin covered it with his mouth and began to suck.

Wanda needed to suck too.

She slithered towards Medwin's toes.

Connecting with a throbbing hard penis as she slid, her pussy rubbed against it through the silky sheet, with an amazing strength. Her back arched and Medwin was still sucking her toes, as she took herself to a fulfilling orgasm.

Pulling the sheet back, Wanda began to suck Medwin's penis. He groaned with ecstasy and soon lifted her so he could enter her with an almighty thrust. Reaching climax as he held her tightly, they fell back down to the silky sheets below.

Finally giving a deep and contented sigh, they bid each other good night and slid back into the sheets. Weighted heads drifting into their sensuously soft pillows.

Medwin had made sure their special white feather was on the bedside drawers but it had not come into play that night. He would wake Wanda in the morning, with its gentle caressing movements all over her body. One of her favourite ways to start a day.

Her next favourite thing, was to watch Medwin's tight buttocks and strong athletic body, as he performed his shaving ritual at the bathroom sink in their ensuite.

He would often be singing or humming along to a tune, coming from their bedside radio. She just stared at him and wondered how she could ever have been so lucky to win this amazing man's love.

Sometimes they sang along together and would always laugh when they said something silly, not knowing what the actual words were in the song. Constant laughter led to playful pillow fights and wrestling on the bed. They could not be more in love.

Wanda also reflected on how well adjusted Medwin had become, with playing an active role in things to be done around the house. He had even bought a German cook book and become quite a dab hand in the kitchen. His mother had given him all her special tricks, for washing the expensive lycra sports gear and he seemed to even enjoy doing the washing. Wanda and Lou had never been ones to iron anything but now they had the master ironer Medwin, asking them if they had things he could iron for them. So sweet.

Life seemed so perfect.

Al's boat was heaving. 'Hope we are not boarding a potentially sinking ship,' said a hesitant Medwin. 'Looks like way too many people already.'

Partygoers were dressed to impress. All the beautiful people of Amsterdam. So many gorgeous looking young ladies and loads of tall handsome men.

Wanda and Medwin had booked a room in a nearby hotel, anticipating a big night. They were not usually heavy drinkers but tonight they thought, they might just let their hair down.

Al was celebrating not just the festive season but also a huge win for his advertising agency. Caterers had been commissioned to keep the food and booze flowing. He even had a live band, playing on the deck of the boat under a marquee, plus a top DJ doing his thing during the band breaks. Wow!

They danced and laughed. It had been a great night. Then 'she' made her move. No. Not Patty. She had been at the party for a short while but had a man in tow and another engagement to go to.

Al had introduced Medwin to this athlete he had agreed to use, as part of a health drink promotion. She did triathlons and mountain bike competitions. Al thought she might be able to introduce Medwin to some groups, that he could arrange travel for. Quite good looking so Wanda was pleased the conversation stayed very business focussed. She had, however, observed that the woman kept an admiring eye on Medwin, after they moved on to talk to other people.

No sooner had Wanda gone to the bathroom shortly afterwards, than the woman zoomed across to re-engage Medwin.

When Wanda returned, the woman was twirling her long blonde hair and fluttering her big dark eyelashes, as she giggled and stood close to Medwin talking. The conversation was now about the many hot and sweaty achievements she had with her sports. He was looking at her in an entirely different way and Wanda almost felt like she was intruding. Just as well they had already agreed it was time to leave, she thought.

'So. We are off now then my love?' said Wanda to Medwin, as she moved between the two of them.

'I really think those sports groups could have some business for you so make sure you contact me,' said the young woman to Medwin, as she handed him her card.

Back in their hotel room, any concerns Wanda might have had about Medwin being attracted to that woman, were quickly allayed.

'You are so beautiful,' Medwin started to sing. Gently pulling Wanda towards him, to lie on the bed still fully clothed. They kissed and chatted. He sang some more and looked deeply into Wanda's eyes, as he told her how beautiful she was. What an amazing person. How much his life had been made complete, since meeting her. For what must have been almost an hour, they laughed and chatted.

Realising how tired they both were, Medwin finally said, 'we should sleep now don't you think?' But as the words left his mouth, Wanda had already undone the zipper on his trousers.

Just knowing her hand was anywhere near his penis had been enough. Without even removing her underwear, Medwin had manoeuvred his now very large and throbbing penis, to push aside her knickers and plunge into her longing vagina. They stared into each other's eyes and moved sensuously as one.

'So beautiful!' said Medwin again and again, as they came to an earth shattering climax together.

Why did work get so crazy at that time of year? Suddenly everything had to be finished before Christmas. People went insane with excessive workloads and combined it with way too much partying. Wanda and Medwin seemed to be no different.

They were both so totally exhausted by the time they got to bed. Always lots of hugging but it seemed the past week since that night at the hotel, they had not had sex once. Most unusual.

Wanda came into the house quietly that afternoon. She had decided to surprise Medwin and be early. He was on the phone in the living room and had not heard her open the door. The conversation sounded most odd. Wanda could not help but wait to announce herself and listen in. Medwin was giggling and speaking like a teenager about to go on a hot date.

'What the hell was that all about?' demanded Wanda, as an indeed very surprised Medwin finally ended his call.

That woman from Al's party. Chasing Medwin again to meet up. Telling him she had checked up on some of his sporting successes and could not have been more impressed. His ego was flying high. She insisted she might have some travel groups for him. They made arrangements to meet the following week. It had to happen then or he might not be in the running for the business apparently.

Wanda stopped herself from saying it all sounded way too personal. She could see Medwin had been really shocked by her having heard their conversation. Maybe he had flirted a little. Any man would do the same. A gorgeous woman, saying all the right things to make you feel good about yourself. All very natural but Wanda did not like it one bit.

Wanda was always being approached by men but she had no trouble at all making it very clear, very quickly, that she had a partner and did not think the line of conversation was appropriate. A pity Medwin had not done the same. Chasing business or not. Wanda could not help but feel a little disappointed.

'I have to phone Mino before 6pm so I need to do that now my darling,' said an embarrassed Medwin.

As Wanda observed the tone of voice coming from that conversation, she could tell the call had not gone well. She wondered why she had bothered to leave the office early.

Medwin had told Mino he would be with him for Christmas Eve and also two days before. Christmas Day he would fly back to Holland in time to have dinner with Wanda, Jay and Lou. Having made several new appointments in Amsterdam and Vienna, he now realised he would not be able to see Mino until the morning of Christmas Eve and just for that one day and night.

Mino was not happy. He ended the call, saying he did not want his father to come at all. Medwin was shocked. Mino had never spoken to him like this.

'Are you OK my love?' enquired Wanda, when Medwin ventured into the kitchen after the call. Not speaking German, Wanda had not known what they were talking about. Now she had Medwin in front of her in tears.

'He hates me!' cried Medwin as he broke down crying.

'He will be fine,' said Wanda hugging the tearful Medwin. After he explained the contents of the call, she continued. 'An 8yr old, who normally gets things his way. Just a little tantrum. Don't you worry. You will have a great Christmas Eve with Mino and your family. Everything will be fine. Are you training tonight?' Wanda thought a little distraction was called for at that point.

Medwin had the Inferno downhill ski race coming up in a few weeks. Back to the Schilthorn summit, for one of the oldest and longest ski races in the world. Well over a thousand skiers would compete.

Skiers started by launching themselves from the famous restaurant platform and onto the treacherous slope. Just as James Bond did in the film, 'On Her Majesty's Secret Service.'

Medwin finally agreed with Wanda. Mino would be fine. Tonight he would train with the local mountain biking squad, in the specially created terrain nearby. It was getting late. He needed to be leaving. A good workout would clear his head.

'Enjoy my love,' said Wanda, as she helped him gather his things and be on his way. 'Dinner will be ready when you get home. Love you.'

He stopped to say how much he loved her and how much better she always made him feel about things. Later he hoped she would not be too tired for him to ravish her.

'Ummm', thought Wanda. 'I will be looking forward to that.'

The crazy festive season had passed. Jay had stayed in Holland a week and had New Year's Eve with his mates. Oud en Nieuw as it was known in Holland. Seeing out the old year and welcoming in the new. In Austria they called it Silvester. No matter what the name, it had been a joyous time for them all. Except perhaps for Lou.

That night a few weeks earlier, when Wanda and Medwin stayed at the hotel after Al's party, Wanda had returned home the next morning to find money missing from her bedside drawers. She remembered distinctly each of the note values. Unusual for her to do that but she had counted the money, to see if it was enough to take out that night.

Deciding it was not, she simply left it on top of her drawers. They would stop at a cash machine, to get what they needed.

At first she thought she might be going loopy. Medwin had not seen her leave the money there. It was 35 euros. She knew exactly. Not such a lot of money but she knew she had left it there.

Lou had not been in her mum's room. The only other person that had been in the house that night, was Danny. Lou asked him if he maybe used the upstairs bathroom and had seen the money on the drawers. No. Never went upstairs.

Over the couple of days that had followed, Lou noticed Danny had more money than usual. It turned her stomach, to think that Danny might steal from her family. Her mum had been so good to him. Always made him feel welcome and often helped him with different challenges. Lou loved Danny and he loved her. He felt a part of her family. He could not possibly do such a thing. Telling lies about it all, would also not be possible.

'I am so sorry Wanda. It is unbelievable. When I quizzed Danny a few times about where he got the money, he eventually said he earned it doing a job for you. Then I mentioned it to Lou, that it was nice you gave him some work. Lou knew nothing about it. She just told me she had to go and next thing the phone had been hung up.' Danny's mother was beside herself.

Wanda felt invaded, in the worst possible way. A trusted and loved person she cared about. How could he do such a thing? She could not have him in the house again.

Lou decided she could no longer have him as a boyfriend either.

It had been hard but how could she ever trust him again. He lied.

He stole from her mother. Impossible to go on with any sort of relationship after that.

Danny wrote a long apologetic letter to Wanda, with the money returned in full. No doubt provided by his mother. Wanda sent a letter back, saying that she could eventually forgive him but she could not forget. His loss with destroying the beautiful relationship he had with Lou. That would be punishment enough. She hoped he would learn from the experience and wished him success in his life.

It had been a sad time for Lou. Friends had dragged her out for Oud en Nieuw. Her spirit had begun to lift. They convinced her it was all for the best. She would move to London soon and be in a whole new world at University. Just as well she did not have to try and manage a long distance relationship with Danny. Lou could see their point but it still hurt bad.

Wanda had not been able to join Medwin at the Schilthorn. A major corporate presentation had to be put together and presented in Munich, on the same day as the race. Plans had been made for Wanda to drive that green Italian wagon to Munich. Medwin would join her there, the day after the race. He would take the car back to his parents' house and load it with the rest of his things, to move properly up to Holland. She would fly from Munich to Brussels for the second leg of this major meeting, hosting staff from all over the world.

Their one night in Munich, was one of their hottest ever. Medwin had been so animated about the Inferno race. It really brought out the devil in him. Really pleased with his results and excited about finally doing the proper move to Holland, he wanted to play hard. Hug & Fug were driving him crazy.

Not wanting to wait until they got to their hotel room, Medwin had coaxed Wanda into the washroom at the bar they met up at. Very flash. Super large washroom, with extra big cubicles. Marble everywhere.

Medwin locked the door and told Wanda she was not to say a word. He remained totally silent too. Every piece of Wanda's clothing was removed. He had to see her naked and lick every inch of her. Parting her legs, he told her to think he had her tied spread eagle. She was not to move an inch. His head was soon locked into her pussy. Her body soon shaking with an erotic explosion of passion.

She fell back against the wall, as Medwin released his trousers to fall to the floor. He wanted to lick her even more but she could not take it. Holding his head back but still motionless, she suddenly felt his massive penis inside her. Stillness maintained. Medwin pounded into her body frantically, to the point where she thought she might actually go through the wall. He climaxed with an almighty groan. The silence was broken.

'The car is fully loaded. I had to leave one bike and two pairs of skis behind. Just have one snowboard with me too. Great to have the space, with that green Italian wagon. Roof racks help a lot too.'

Medwin wanted to keep chatting but Wanda had to get back into the meeting. Seeing his call on her silenced phone, she had made the excuse of needing to go to the bathroom so she could speak with him.

'So many big wigs in this meeting my love. I really have to get back in. My presentation is up soon and it is one of the main areas for discussion. Will be really hard to take any other calls so I hope all goes well. I will try to reach you when we break for lunch,' replied Wanda. 'Safe journey. Love you.'

'What the ....????!!!' A horrified Medwin exclaimed.

He had been revving that green Italian wagon through the gears, like he was driving his motor bike. Keen to make good time for the 900km drive. Why had he not checked the oil recently?

Breaking the speed limits and zooming past the traffic making their way on from Vienna, he had only driven 110kms so far. Suddenly, out in the passing lane, the engine died.

Narrowly avoiding an accident, he finally made his way across to the emergency stopping lane. Lifting the bonnet, smoke streamed out. Every light on the dashboard was on.

'Shit! This can't be good,' thought Medwin.

• CHAPTER NINETEEN •

TWO HOURS HAD PASSED. Should he call his father to come pick him up? Wanda obviously had her phone off but surely they would break for lunch soon. At least Medwin had managed to get well off the road. Had plenty of clothes so could manage the cold too. Running the few kilometres back to a service station, provided some exercise and the required toilet. His mother had packed plenty of food and drink, to sustain him throughout the journey.

'What do you mean it just blew up?' a distraught Wanda finally said, once she was able to call.

She had not been at all impressed with his attitude. The car was old, Medwin said. Probably best to just leave it there and ask a wrecking yard to pick it up. Maybe he could get his father's car.

What? Did he not know how Wanda felt about that green Italian wagon? The great adventures it had taken them all on. Always totally reliable. One hiccup in France way back. That had been a fairly major repair but ever since, her very special car had run like a dream.

Wanda loved that car. Jay loved it too. It had been the catalyst for him really learning to drive. Lou wanted Wanda to teach her to drive in it too. Plan was, to start her lessons once they moved to the UK. Wanda was already preparing to change the registration over.

Medwin was sounding like that spoilt boy with too many toys again.

'I have Europe wide road cover that includes bringing the car back to Holland on a trailer if necessary. The papers are all in the glove box.

I will report the breakdown and give them your phone number so they can liaise with you directly. Send me a text that everything is OK. My phone will be on silent but I can keep checking it. I will tell them about our emergency. They already started the meeting again so I better get back in there. Take care. Love you. See you later tonight hopefully.'

Medwin had said very little. He could tell Wanda had not been happy with his reaction. How embarrassing to have to sit there waiting for a tow truck, was all he could think.

Wanda arrived home, to see that green Italian wagon parked in the front garden as usual. Medwin had only just finished unpacking it. The tow truck driver had been super-efficient and they had made the journey in excellent time. He had turned straight around, to take the drive back to Austria through the night. A real professional.

'I hope it is OK if this bike also stays in the dining room?' asked Medwin. 'Also worth quite a lot. Much of the rest of my things, have managed to fit in the cellar,' he continued.

'Really?' thought Wanda. 'How would anyone be able to sit at the table?' She did not quite have the nerve to say that though.

After all he had been through that day, she was happy just to see him safely home. She had been worried about him and wondered if she might have been a little short with him on the phone.

There were also six pairs of sports shoes, sitting along the wall.

'Do the shoes all need to stay there?' she enquired smiling.

Medwin went to great lengths to talk about the impact of moisture on expensive sports shoes. They could not go in the cellar and his space in their walk-in robe, had already gained another ten pairs of normal shoes. Best if they did stay there, he concluded.

Wanda felt a little invaded but again, she just smiled.

Even so, she could not help thinking that Medwin seemed different. A new arrogance perhaps? Maybe he was just relieved that they had reached this point of commitment. Could be that he was really tired. Most likely thing was, that Wanda was just over thinking.

Things did not improve, after that night Wanda went to bed questioning everything. Even the hugs seemed to disappear.

Could that erotic love making in Munich, have been such a short while ago?

Medwin told Wanda very little, about what was going on with his sports travel groups. Seemed to be going to loads of meetings though. When she tried to engage him in conversation about it, he would just say he was pleased with how things were going.

'That's great,' was all she said. Not wanting him to feel he had been put on the spot. She felt sure he would tell her, when he had definite successes to share.

One night, when Medwin had seemed totally unreachable, he admitted something to Wanda.

Something Wanda would never have expected in a million years.

As she listened to what he said, she was filled with an incredible fear and sadness.

'Today I was standing at the railway crossing. The usual waiting for ages to let the fast train zoom pass, before they raised the barrier. Those trains must be a good few stations away, when the lights flash and the ringing starts. Stupid cars trying to beat the barriers, before they drop down. Always seems to take so long before they open again.'

He was talking so slowly and with a strange glare in his eyes.

'I had spoken to my father on the phone just before. He had not been well. Neither had my mother. My finally leaving their house, was so difficult for them to take. They said that Mino hardly ever came in to see them now. I told them I would come in two weeks and stay with them five nights. I had not been gone so long. Mino would settle. It did not seem to help. They just cannot understand it,' he continued.

'Then I called Mino. He said he did not want to talk to me ever and hung up the phone,' Medwin finished even more slowly, as he began to cry.

'I honestly considered throwing myself in front of that fast train.'

The tears now increased, as he choked the last words out and began shaking.

Wanda took him in her arms, as she would a child that was lost and afraid. What could she possibly say, that might console him?

She was lost for words. Leading him upstairs, she got him into bed and pulled the cover over, as she stroked his cheeks gently.

'Everything will be OK my love,' being all she could manage to say.

Medwin stayed in bed for two days. Wanda did not recognize him. Where had the positive man, with the spark in his eyes, gone?

She tried to excite him about the planned visit to the UK, to celebrate Jay's birthday in March.

What would he like to see at the theatre? Maybe her friends in the music industry could get them some tickets to a concert as well. She would check who was playing.

'Really Wanda? That would be fantastic!'

Medwin finally came round on the third day, hearing she had secured tickets for Bryan Adams. He jumped out of bed singing

'Back in the summer of '69. Oh yeah!'

Medwin was born that summer. It was one of his favourite songs.

Suddenly it flashed through Wanda's mind that he was 17 years younger. It had never come up in any discussions ever. The age gap was not a problem but she could not help wondering now, if maybe he still had quite some growing up to do.

Unbelievable how bright and perky he became over the following week. Also unbelievable, how quickly things had changed with him and Wanda.

They made love a few times that week but it was so different. Almost mechanical. Definitely no Hug & Fug supporting their sex life anymore.

Mr Energy himself, had become Mr 'I need to sleep'.

Wanda thought back, to her marriage with Larry. She recalled how their love making had become just like that, once the passion died. That had taken ten years and two babies though. How could it possibly happen so quickly with Medwin?

Maybe he just needed time to settle, after the big final move away from his village. It really was a major thing for him. Wanda decided to just let things ride. Soon they would all be in London, having loads of fun. That would bring the spark back again.

Try as Wanda may, to encourage Medwin to sort out a repairer for that green Italian wagon, he just came up with excuse after excuse.

Finally he had blatantly lied to her.

'They all say it is not worth spending the money to fix the car. The piston went right through. Needs a new engine.'

Something about the look on his face telling Wanda, made her question what he was saying. Again she decided not to push. It was important he felt comfortable about moving to London. She wanted their trip the following month to be perfect so did not rock the boat.

'We can always pick up some cheap flights to London,' had been all Wanda said in reply.

'Meanwhile, the office said we can use the old Jaguar that nobody wants to drive. Goes like a demon. I can check if it is OK for you to drive as well. Only allowed to use it locally but everywhere else we need to go, it works better with the train anyway.'

While Medwin was away in Austria the following week, she would get a mechanic she knew to take that green Italian wagon to his garage and do a proper quote for repairs.

'I need to stay a few extra days Wanda,' said a very animated Medwin, on the second day he was back at his parents.

He sounded so happy again, that Wanda was pleased for him to be staying longer. It had been tearing her apart, seeing the man she loved so much, becoming almost suicidal.

Mino slept with Medwin at his parents. They were all so thrilled about that.

Wanda was also relieved that she could manage what she wanted to do with her beloved car with him away.

On the fourth day Medwin had been gone, she asked him.

'Do you remember meeting a guy called Willem, at that function in the rugby club we went to with Denise? No? It was a while back. Anyway, it seems he is a mechanic with a garage close by. Denise happened to mention to him about our car. He called me and said he would be happy to tow it in at no cost and take a good look, to see if it was worth repairing. Might as well heh?'

A very sheepish Medwin, responded that he was fine with that.

She could call Willem and make arrangements.

A day later, she had the answer. Medwin had clearly not had anyone look at the car. It had all been too uninteresting, she guessed. Wanda tried not to think about him actually having lied.

'Quite some work to do on the engine but everything else is great,' said Willem. 'Excellent body work. Interior is like brand new. If we start tomorrow, you can have the car back in two days. Might be two thousand euros but I really think it is worth it,' he confirmed.

Medwin had already sent a text, to say he would be out with his family that night. He would call her the next evening. Had a couple of good meetings lined up in Vienna the next day and would need an early start.

Wanda sent him a text back saying no problem. She also mentioned about the car, asking if he was OK with her telling Willem to go ahead.

'That is fine. Speak to you tomorrow,' was all the return text said.

No call from Medwin that next night either. Wanda tried to call him but his phone had been switched off.

For some strange reason, Wanda almost felt relieved.

'I thought Medwin was going to be back by now mum,' said Lou. Her head had been seriously down with all the studies and assignments to be completed. Not long now and she would be finished with high school forever.

Everything was on track for good IB results so the Kingston University option should be hers for the taking. Yeah!!

Wanda filled Lou in on the new meetings Medwin had in Vienna and said she was not sure when exactly he would be back.

From the look on Wanda's face, Lou knew all was not well. She had also felt a little invaded, when Medwin took over the house with all his things. Not ever wanting her mum to feel uncomfortable though, she just made a joke about his flash sports gear. Quite the topic of conversation, when she had her mates at the house.

The handsome athlete boyfriend of mother's, providing an interesting diversion from school demands and their concerns about going in different directions, once school finished.

Wanda told Lou, that she felt uncertain about where everything was going with Medwin. They were so in love but life was throwing some huge challenges their way. The biggest of all being, how much Medwin missed Mino.

She told Lou about the incident at the railway crossing.

'Oh mum. That is terrible! Is there anything I can do to help?'

Wanda went on to say how relieved she had been these past days, knowing that Medwin was happy with Mino. That meant the world to her. She truly believed, that was where he needed to be. It made her feel ill to think how sad he had been, not seeing Mino enough.

Wanda was being torn apart by it, almost as much as Medwin was.

Medwin called Wanda the following morning. At first all he could keep saying over and over, was that he loved Wanda beyond life itself.

Finally he moved on to say his love for Mino was, however, something completely different.

He brought Mino into the world and would carry that responsibility for all time. Mino needed him so much.

He began to cry. As he recovered a little, he continued.

'The thing is Wanda. What I need more than anything in this world, is you. I am so confused. Finding you and having you in my life. It has been the most amazing thing ever. I love you so much.'

Wanda had also begun to cry. Eventually she managed to say that she would call him back in ten minutes, when they could hopefully speak more calmly. Then came the real cruncher.

'Last night Mino insisted that I go to his house for dinner. His mum needed to speak with me. He did not know what it was about but was so excited, that he would be able to show me his new computer game.' Medwin took a deep breath and paused before continuing.

'Nina prepared a special dinner. When I walked through that front door, something hit me. This incredible sense of responsibility and maybe also it was a sense of belonging. I am not so sure.'

Wanda had put her hand over the phone so Medwin could not hear her tears returning.

'I put Mino to bed and the look on his face was so angelic. He hugged me, with such a desire. Then he just smiled and said how glad he was that I was there.'

Wanda had raised two children herself. She knew that look. She knew that feeling it created. One that only a parent could feel.

'Nina and I then sat talking for hours. I have known her for so many years but we have never talked like that before.

She told me that, since I finally moved out of my parents' house, she had thought very long and hard. If there was any way that we could try again, it would make her so happy.'

Wanda wanted to stop listening but instead just said 'I see.'

'She missed me, almost as much as Mino did. All that time before, when I was so near and she often saw me about, it had not been so bad. Then when she did not see me, it really made her wonder why we had parted years ago. She said she needs me to come back so we can be a real family again. Mino is my only child and he is so precious to me. I do not know what to do Wanda. All I can think about when I am here, is getting back to you.'

Wanda had gone into a sort of daze. Somehow she was outside of herself and looking in on this conversation. As much as she was relieved that Medwin was happy being back in Austria with Mino, she had never contemplated him getting back together with his wife. She became aware of feeling dizzy and her fingers starting to tingle.

'I think we had better speak again tomorrow my darling,' was all she could say. 'Sleep well.'

Wanda had been laying on the bed speaking to Medwin. As she hung up the call, she found herself sinking into the mattress like it was some sort of cloud.

'Maybe it was all a nightmare,' she thought. She would just go to sleep now and would wake to find things were not as they currently seemed.

Not so.

Wanda woke early the next day but decided she could not make it to the office and instead, fell back to sleep. When she woke for the second time, there was a text message on her phone from Medwin.

'Father saw a great job in the newspaper. Called them this morning and they want me to come in this afternoon. You did not answer your phone. Call you again after the interview. Love you. X'

Wanda stared at her phone and read the text over and over.

A great job? What could Medwin be talking about?

Later that day, it was all made clear.

'It is like you always say my love. Fate playing its hand. My father never usually reads that paper. Who knows what made him buy it yesterday? He just happens to see this job advertised. A major international shipping company, looking for someone to become head of Austrian sales. Must have rail experience,' the sound of Medwin's over excited voice, seemed to echo in Wanda's brain.

He continued, 'the interview went so well. They called me when I was on my way back, to say the job was mine.'

'I have to start in two weeks. They know I have my own private thing going, with sports travel groups, and they are OK with me continuing that so long as I manage it well and it does not interfere with what I must deliver for them. It really could not be more perfect.'

Medwin stopped briefly, to give an enormous sigh of happiness.

'I figure we can go back to the first plan and I buy an apartment in Vienna. You can come to stay with me whenever possible. I can see Mino through the week, as well as have him on some weekends. Being able to go to his football games and school things mid-week. He will love that. What do you think?'

Wanda's head was spinning. What about Nina wanting to get back together? Not a word on that.

As much as Wanda loved Medwin deeply, there was no way she would be the one to stand in the way of a possible reuniting of a family unit but he had not even mentioned it. If there was any hope at all that it could work, Medwin needed to give it his best shot. How could he not say anything about that?

'What about Nina?' Wanda finally responded.

Medwin went to great lengths to tell Wanda that he did not love Nina. He had been swayed that evening, being in the house with her and Mino, but he really did not see how it could ever work again. He loved Wanda so very much.

Wanda was at a loss for words. If there was any way at all that Medwin and Nina could work things out, she believed with all of her heart that they should try.

They had brought a son into this world. If there was even the smallest glimmer of hope, for them to be a proper family unit, that was the path Medwin should be taking.

Relaying these thoughts to Medwin was not easy for Wanda.

They talked for two hours.

Wanda also reminded Medwin about the big changes that would soon take place in her life. The move to London. Finding a new job. Really did not look like working in the current role from the UK, was going to happen. A new home had to be found with Lou, Jay and PJ. She was going to be incredibly busy. Supporting Lou and Jay with University needs. She really was going to have a lot on her plate. Highly unlikely that she would have much time to be flying over to Vienna often. She really did not think it would work.

As Wanda spoke her heart was breaking. She needed Medwin to do the right thing by his family and yet she did not want to let him go. Unable to hold back the tears, she continued.

'I love you so much my darling but I would always be thinking I was to blame, for you not being with your family. You really have to try with this reconciliation.'

Medwin sobbed as he spoke. He told Wanda he could not bear the thought of not being with her. Not holding her and making love to her. Not laughing together and sharing all those precious moments together. He did not see any way he could live any sort of life, without her. Mino would be so much better with him living in Vienna. That was all that was needed. He would have this great job so could easily afford to fly to see her in London often and she would come to Vienna, when she could. Their love was so strong, that they would make this work.

Finally stopping his tears, Medwin went on to say he was sorry he had even mentioned what Nina had said. Getting back together with her would be impossible. Wanda really had to get all of those ideas out of her head.

He would be back in Holland in two days and would convince her that they had to stay together, even if not living in the same country. He loved her way too much to ever let her go.

Wanda wanted so much to believe Medwin but somehow her gut feeling told her otherwise. She got Medwin to agree that they should at least think about it, without them speaking again until he got back.

They had a birthday party to go to the evening he was due to fly in. It would be fun to just meet up there, like they were on a hot date.

'OK my love. Let's talk when you get back. Just go straight to the party from the airport. I will go from the office and see you there. That same canal house in Amsterdam we went to before. A short walk from Central so the train will be easiest.'

Wanda hung up the phone, totally exhausted. There would be no sleep for her that night. No matter how much she went over things, it always turned out the same. Excruciating pain at the realisation she would have to say goodbye to her incredible love. It was all too much for her to bear.

Those two days seemed like months.

'Big night?' enquired Damon. 'I promise not to tell Medwin, when I see him tonight.'

He had not wanted to tell her how awful she looked. Maybe he could make her laugh and then just suggest she go get her hair done or something.

Wanda looked at him in the same dazed and confused state she had been in for so many days now.

'Sorry mate. Just got a lot on my mind. Pretty much no sleep at all last night,' she replied as she tried to muster a small grin to throw his way.

Eventually Damon did encourage her to visit the hairdresser. Clothes were fine. Hair and oxygen might help clear the gloom. She had not told him about the conversations with Medwin.

What if he came back and managed to convince her they should stay together?

As they sang happy birthday, Wanda thought she might well scream if one more person asked her where Medwin was. She had not received even one text from him during that day. He was booked on a flight arriving at 7pm she thought. Now it was almost 10pm and no sign of him. She had expected him to arrive at the party, no later than 8pm.

Having checked with the airport, she knew the flight had arrived on time. No answer when she tried Medwin's phone.

Should she call the police? What would she tell them? Could she admit, that he might just have decided never to come back again?

That would be for the best, she would try to convince herself.

Constantly visiting the toilet to stop herself crying and spoiling the party, Wanda went into hyper drive. Chatting at twice her normal speed. Laughing at things that were not particularly funny. Dancing like a crazy woman.

If Medwin showed up, she wanted him to find her having fun.

When it got to 11pm and still no word, she figured she should just try to get herself home. Thank goodness she had the company car and had not drunk much. Could have been a really pathetic sight otherwise. She managed to slip away quietly.

Approaching her house, Wanda found there was a strange car parked at the front. She was most annoyed, she now had to circle the neighbourhood looking for a spot to park in the street. The car probably belonged to someone visiting a neighbour. Such a nightmare trying to park. How rude for someone to think they could just pull up in her garden like that.

As Wanda finally returned to the house on foot, after parking two streets away, she could see in the distance that a man was loading things into the car parked at her house. She would certainly be giving him a piece of her mind.

Reaching the house, her heart sank. It was Medwin.

Wanda and Medwin found their way to the sofa hugging and crying.

'I love you so much and I am so so sorry,' was all Medwin could manage to say. He said it over and over.

Eventually he calmed down a little and began to speak in short strange sentences. He could not call and tell her or even text. Did not know what to say. Did not want to spoil the party and arrive there. Easier to take his things out of the house without her or Lou home. In the dark of night so others did not see him.

The car was his father's. All of his belongings, had now been loaded into it. He would leave early in the morning, to drive back to Austria.

Wanda was stunned. She kept thinking, how fortunate Lou had stayed at a girlfriend's that night. She would not have liked her to see the state they were both in. Nor to witness this very sudden exit by Medwin.

They sobbed and clung to each other for ages, before Medwin could continue.

A day earlier, his father had insisted on a family meeting. Nina had spoken to him about wanting to try again with Medwin. She had taken the day off work, to be at this meeting Medwin's father called. His mother was also there.

None of them knew about Medwin's great love for Wanda. All they understood was that Medwin rented a room with an Australian family in Holland.

Now Medwin had a great job to start in Vienna soon, there was absolutely no point him staying in Holland one minute longer – as far as they were concerned.

No point taking that flight he had booked either. It was cancelled.

Medwin's father had decided it was time he took a firmer stance with his son. Nina was as precious to them as Mino was and such a great person. They were all happy that she could see hope for reuniting with Medwin. He had to work with her on this and accept his responsibilities.

Medwin had to take his father car and pick up all his things from Holland, to come straight home to his family in Austria, where he belonged.

His father had been shaking, as he made his stand. Medwin's mother could only cry and keep begging him to do as his father said. Nina had not said much at all.

'She just kept looking at me with a sad longing,' said Medwin. 'And all I could think about, was what you had said about it being the right thing for me to do. That I should be with my family, if it could work. I knew I had to at least try but I just can't imagine how I am going to live without you,' a sobbing Medwin finished.

'It is the right thing,' reinforced Wanda, in slow motion and shaking.

Not another word was spoken that final night. Once the tears subsided, Wanda and Medwin took each other's hand, to climb the stairs to their bedroom for the very last time.

Hugs were desperate and intense. They could not bear to let one another go. Their tears made the soft silky sheets so wet, that they needed to move their heads to the bottom of the bed.

As their naked bodies moved apart to relocate, they were suddenly at arms-length and looking deeply into each other's eyes.

Medwin gently kissed Wanda's neck on both sides. He kissed her lips longingly. He kissed her breasts with such a yearning.

Wanda felt as if her whole world was falling apart. Looking at this incredible man, she could not bear to think this might be the last time. His kisses made her shiver all over. She wanted him more than anything in the world and yet she knew she must give him up.

As their bodies met, Medwin's erect penis entered Wanda instinctively. Their arms were locked and they were fully connected once more.

Slow and sensuous movements, made them both start to shake. Eyes widened, as they reached orgasm at the same time. Tears welled up in their eyes, as they tightened their hug and fell to sleep, totally spent and exhausted.

A few hours passed. Wanda became aware of Medwin having released his hugging hold.

• CHAPTER TWENTY •

'A VISIT TO THE TOILET,' she thought briefly but she had quickly fallen back to sleep again. Waking early the next morning, Wanda realised Medwin was gone. Her world had stopped.

'I've been home in bed all day Lou,' a still very dazed Wanda said blankly, as Lou entered her bedroom late that afternoon.

Lou did not ask questions. She could see straight away, that all Medwin's things had gone. From everything her mum had told her earlier, she knew it was over.

Hugging her mum, they sobbed together quietly.

Lou then decided she would just start to talk about her day. Distraction was what was called for.

As they lay on the bed, Lou spoke of her art teacher's comments on the painting she finished that day. It was a subject Lou and Wanda often talked about.

Her teacher clearly preferred abstract art. Lou did the most beautiful life art but his tiny brain saw that as way too simple. The topic always made them laugh.

A little chuckle had been all Wanda could muster on this occasion.

Lou hugged her mum again. They both knew how lucky they were, to have such a close and loving relationship.

As Lou talked about her pain at the breakup with Danny, Wanda talked about how right it was for Medwin to go back to his family.

Lou had lost Danny. Wanda had, it seemed, lost Medwin. They both had sad and painful thoughts but mostly great memories to enjoy.

Forever and for always, Wanda and Lou would have each other. Such a precious love to share. They were indeed so very lucky and knew they would continue to lead full and interesting lives.

'We need to eat mum,' said Lou after some time and with authority. 'I will go down and see what I can muster up.'

Wanda's thoughts shifted to how happy Medwin would now be, to have his precious son Mino. She could also envisage how happy Mino would be, that his parents had re-united.

Wanda made up her mind there and then, to just get on with the great life she had. She would email Medwin to tell him how happy she was for his family.

She would not tell him that she was having difficulty breathing.

'I will come downstairs with you,' said Wanda with a renewed strength.

A call came through on Wanda's phone. Lou answered it.

'Mum. It was Willem. He said to tell you that green Italian wagon, was all fixed and running like a dream. How cool is that. We can drive it across to Jay next week and have a blast celebrating Jay's birthday in London.'

Wanda smiled. That was great news. She would be back into life's adventures with Lou and Jay again, in that green Italian wagon.

Her thoughts then turned to whether Medwin had made it back to Austria OK.

Just then an sms arrived.

'Safe drive home. Took it slowly. Lots of stops to dry the eyes and get fresh air. You will always be the love of my life. Will be dreaming of you and

reminding myself to breathe. Email soon. You are so beautiful and I am yours forever. XX'

'He is home safely,' Wanda relayed to Lou after clearing her throat.

'Maybe I will skip dinner if that's OK,' she managed to get out, before the shakes kicked in, and headed back to her bed to let the tears return.

'Whenever you are ready mum. I will be right here.'